VISIBLE LIGHT

VISIBLE LIGHT

Carol Windley

Oolichan Books, Lantzville, BC Canada
1993

Canadian Cataloguing in Publication Data

Windley, Carol, 1947-
  Visible light

ISBN 0-88982-124-0

  I. Title
PS8595.I52V5 1993   C813'.54   C93-091384-1
PR9199.3.W56V5 1993

Publication of this book has been financially assisted by the Canada Council.

Published by
OOLICHAN BOOKS
P.O. Box 10
Lantzville, British Columbia
Canada V0R 2H0

Typeset by Vancouver Desktop Publishing

Printed in Canada by
Hignell Printing Ltd.
Winnipeg, Manitoba

For Robert and Tara

Some of these stories, in slightly different form, were published in the following magazines: "Moths" and "Visible Light" in *Event*; "The Etruscans" in *Descant*; "In the Dead Room" in *Room of One's Own*. "Dreamland" won first prize in CBC Radio's Literary Competition and was broadcast on CBC Radio on "State of the Arts."

The author would like to gratefully acknowledge the financial assistance and encouragement given by the Explorations Program of The Canada Council during the writing of this book. Special thanks to Ursula Vaira at Oolichan Books for her kindness, patience, and insight during the process of editing.

The publisher and author wish to thank Keith Hiscock for permission to reproduce his painting "Daydreams" on the cover.

And thanks to the Weyerhaeuser Company Foundation and to Bumbershoot for choosing this book for their 1993 Publication Award.

Contents

Moths

Joanna, behind the windows of her house, knows what it means to be alone. Nothing moves outside, anywhere, unless she counts the occasional swift wing of a heron or a hawk glancing past in the fog. The fog rises from the lake, morning and evening, and drapes itself everywhere, a cold, tattered, wet shawl.

Not that Joanna finds the fog cold and wet; she is entirely removed from what she sees and can't even imagine what it would be like to touch the fog, or those dark, high branches, or those clouds, or the cold lake water. She touches only glass; it keeps her in, holds her upright in her house. Joanna is only two eyes, taking in the unknowable, giving nothing back.

It isn't what she wanted.

And yet, what a commendable, what a fine individual Joanna is. Even though the hollow sound of her feet on the endless floors follows her, dogs her, haunts her, she is able to walk in the most ordinary paths: to the washer with dirty clothes, to the closets with clean clothes, to the chill ceramic distances of this vast new, extravagant new, kitchen. She walks and walks, stopping only for well-earned breaks; then she perches on the edge of a chair with her mug of coffee cradled in her hands. Staring out the window. Fifteen minutes. Well then, twenty-five minutes. Timed, in careful imitation of what she is used to, what she was used to, not so very long ago.

She is lonely, but she functions well. His dinner is always ready, perfectly ready, well before the appointed time.

And then—he is home, swooping up the drive, his headlights drilling the dusk, machine-gunning the black cedars, ripping holes in the fog, pre-empting the dark.

Slam goes the car door. The garage door. The house door. The hall closet door.

Joanna wants to run and hide, wants to hold her breath, choke back excited, nervous laughter. Nobody home, nobody home. Find me, catch me if you can.

He says hello, drops his suit jacket across a chair back, smiles, is happily redolent of the city, of town and travel; the warmth, the smell, the casual wonder of human sociability is all about him.

Joanna has not spoken aloud since seven o'clock in the morning, when she said goodbye to him. Eleven hours. She tries her tongue against the roof of her mouth. "Hello," she says. It sounds all right; it is not the chirp of a bird, the grunt of an animal. If it isn't quite the warm welcome of a loving wife either, what does it matter. The small frown that appears on his smooth handsome face is quickly gone, quickly gone. He rubs his hands together, as if in satisfaction. Loosens his tie and rolls his sleeves up to the elbow, shedding the skin of the city for the skin of the country and home. Changing skins, changing colours, changing habitat. No trick at all.

Joanna knows that now she is supposed to ask him if he has had a good day, but she doesn't. She is learning to be cruel in small ways, to get even. She watches Elliot wander around with his wine glass in his hand, smiling and nodding at the walls, the terra cotta, the polished oak.

There are five lighted candles in the candelabrum (Elliot prefers to dine by candlelight) and five answering flames in the black sheet of glass behind the dining room table. Joanna has not yet managed to order drapery material for all the windows, although she promises Elliot that she is working on it; it is just a matter of finding the right fabric in the right shade. It is a matter of being absolutely sure, she tells Elliot. The truth is, she is never ready to drive into town with Elliot in the morning. She sleeps restlessly all night, then falls into a heavy sleep just before dawn. Hard to believe that a short time ago she was up at six o'clock, five mornings a week. Oh, she is filled with nostalgia, with love, for that remembered exuberance, that purposefulness. She was another person then, that was a different lifetime. But it wasn't. It was only five months ago.

"Dear God," Joanna says. Her fork clatters onto her plate. Elliot's head snaps up; he follows the direction of her horrified gaze to the window, where the five candle flames are reflected.

"What? What?" he demands, scraping his chair across the floor. He crouches, alarmed.

11

Joanna points. "Oh, God, Elliot. Look."

He looks. "Moths?" he says, and straightens up, hands on his hips.

Moths. What Joanna sees are four or five creatures. Well, they are moths, but they are huge and bug-eyed, with identifiable faces and bristling whiskers and lost, blind, bumping expressions.

"Moths," says Elliot. "Just moths. You scared me for a minute there, Joanna. And all you actually saw was a few moths. Is that all you saw? Joanna?"

"All? They're disgusting. They have eyes, Elliot. They have faces." Joanna shudders, keeps her eyes on her plate, where the steak, in its small pool of blood and grease, is taking on a powdery look, a greyness, the brittle look of something long dead and flightless.

"We're living in the country, Joanna," says Elliot. "This is, after all, the country. You can't expect citified little bugs out here, you know." Elliot sits down and takes up his fork. He gives her a frown that is half censure, half amusement and shakes his head. Joanna can tell that he's decided to think of her as cute and girlish: afraid of bugs.

And so she is. She pushes her steak around on her plate, then hides it under her napkin. Later, she will shovel it into the kitchen garbage can.

The sun is rising slowly, slowly above the giant evergreens. Long rays of light filter through the branches; forest light, oblique, heavy, the kind of light that nurtures all the hidden, moist growing things: ferns, black twinberry, bunchberry, false bugbane. Joanna sits upstairs by her window, like Snow White's mother, stitching, basting ruffling tape to slippery brown curtain material. If the needle should prick Joanna's finger, causing a drop of blood to fall magically through the glass to the shaded forest floor, would she, in nine months' time, produce a daughter with hair like sunshine, eyes green as moss, lips red as blood? That is what Elliot wants: children. He wants children to fill up the big new house. Sturdy sons, slight-boned daughters, golden-haired.

Perhaps that is what Joanna wants as well, and perhaps not. Could she produce all those lovely children on order? The thought saddens her. She imagines her name at the bottom of a list of household appliances: the vacuum cleaner, the food processor, the convection oven, the fertile womb. Elliot's list.

She imagines herself just three years from now, sitting at her window, stitching and stitching. Patches on tiny overall knees, embroidery on a small white sweater, a thin frill of lace along the edge of a sun-bonnet. Below, in a patch of the same peculiar slanted light, Elliot is teaching his small son, his firstborn, to pedal a shiny new tricycle. How intently, how lovingly, Elliot's head is bent over the dimpled child. She imagines Elliot's hunched shoulders, his strained neck muscles, as he tries and tries to impart the necessary strength and skill to his son. And what is this? An English pram, swathed in mosquito netting, moving gently every now and then on its well-sprung wheels as the babe within kicks and chortles. Elliot's daughter.

How easily this scene could become real, and it is not an unpleasing picture, except in its unrelieved perfection, which makes Joanna run her tongue over her teeth as if she has eaten candy too rich, too sweet, too cloying for her own good.

At the bottom of their driveway there is a stretch of road that is visible from this window, and what should Joanna see there but a young woman, walking. Just strolling by, alone. She is Joanna's age, or younger. She has long hair, loose down her back.

Joanna sits up straight and cranes her neck to see. In over five months no one has walked past on this road. It is only once in a great while that a car goes past. At this moment, Joanna wishes herself outside working in the small garden Elliot has started at the end of the drive. If she were down there mulching the new rhododendrons, she could say hello, strike up a conversation. Talk. She could actually talk to someone.

She understands now, what has been wrong all along. She has needed a friend. If she met this girl, she would know someone; someone would know her; she would be real once more.

Friends, Joanna thinks, we could be friends. And stabs her needle energetically into the soft brown folds of cloth.

She folds away her sewing and puts the kettle on to boil. She walks quickly up and down the kitchen. A friend. A beginning. It does cross her mind that she is investing an awful lot of faith in that briefly glimpsed figure, upright and slim though it may be. In those long, even, unhurried steps.

Elliot leaves Joanna with two green-and-white boxes and a new trowel. If she wants to garden, he says, fine. Goodness knows there's enough to be done. If they work hard they can really accomplish something here, he says, even though it is a difficult property. A challenging property, he amends. So here she is, cleverly positioned by the road among the young rhododendrons. Elliot has also planted daffodil bulbs. Green spears appear here and there above the peaty soil, and Joanna will bet this is as much in response to Elliot's commands as to the season's urgings.

Joanna takes a shovelful of bone-meal, a shovelful of blood-meal. The earth is surprisingly cold just beneath the surface. She overturns sleepy earthworms and curled, dormant centipedes. In an undisturbed hollow just beyond their property line, green-skinned skunk cabbages prepare to unfurl their clumsy yellow for spring's indiscriminating sake.

Someone is walking down the road, trotting along in an even, measured way. Joanna hears, and digs more vigorously into the damp soil, showering blood-meal into the air. She straightens up, and turns at what she considers to be exactly the right moment, so that she can say, in surprise, "Why, hello!"

She sees at once what is wrong.

It is the same young woman with the long brown hair, but . . . her eyes are tilted in a strange, flat way; rimless and red; watery-looking. She has no bridge to her nose, and her face is flat, squished flat. When she smiles, a child's shy smile, Joanna sees the peculiar serrated edges of her small white teeth. Joanna thinks that if this girl did not have one chromosome too many, or one too few, she is not sure how it goes, she would have been lovely, with clear, large blue eyes and milky skin. And all that hair.

"Hello," the girl says, so softly Joanna scarcely hears.

"Hello! Hello, there!" Joanna's voice booms out, false and

15

hearty, a voice she has never, before now, used. "Nice and sunny, isn't it. So much warmer," Joanna trills, and the girl nods her head, seriously, consideringly.

"Are you going for a walk?"

"Yes. Now I'm going home." Her voice is level and slow, measured, like her steps; it has a slight, gravelly undertone, like lake water dragging itself over stones.

"My name is Joanna. What's your name?"

"Fay," she says, and Joanna thinks, well, of course. Fay, fey. Nothing is as it seems here; everything is under a spell, enchanted, witched, upside down, inside out. The laws in this land are cold and precise; Joanna thinks she'd do better herself as something wild and green. She tosses her trowel down under a rhododendron and wipes her hands on the back of her jeans.

Fay wears a neat white collar under her coat. Her throat rises from this prim little collar in an exact and hopeful manner. An inch of white cuff shows at each wrist, and she wears a ring: a small amber stone set in gold. When Joanna holds out her hand, it is the hand with the amber ring Fay extends.

"It's nice to meet you, Fay," says Joanna.

"It is nice to meet you," says Fay.

"Listen, would you like to come in? We could have some tea. Milk and cookies?"

Fay looks sideways up at Joanna's tall glass house.

"I have to go home. I have to go right home."

"Is your mother at home? Anyone? We could phone and see if you could stay for a little while."

Fay stares at her feet. Her forehead is bunched up—a white rose.

16

"No, no. Listen, I know what. Let's both walk to your house. I'll meet your mother, and we'll see if you can visit me at my house soon. Okay?"

They walk down the road together, Joanna in her gardening clothes, her hands smudged with damp earth. She is careful to match her steps to Fay's. Every now and then a cool wind stirs the trees along the road's edge, and Joanna turns her head to receive its chill upon her flushed face.

Fay lives, it turns out, close to the lakefront, in a cream-painted house with red window-boxes. There are red clay plant pots on the front steps, and frilly white curtains at the two front windows. Fay's mother welcomes Joanna in with just the right amount of surprise. She is a tall, spare woman with springy grey hair and a gold filling between her large front teeth. She removes a pile of knitting and an old brown teddy bear from a chair so that Joanna can sit down. It is at once obvious to Joanna that this woman sees her interest in Fay as some kind of charitable gesture, a good work. Fay's mother is probably very good at good works. Joanna imagines her rushing from one place to another with washed grapes, old magazines, recycled toys, crocheted potholders. "Of course Fay can visit you, how lovely of you to ask. And how clever of you, Fay, to find this nice lady. We're very isolated here, you know," she says to Joanna, smiling largely with her gold filling.

So, Jocelyn, that is her name, Jocelyn, gives her blessing to Joanna. She does not, however, never would, think of Fay as a friend for Joanna, of Joanna as Fay's friend.

And the next day, Fay does indeed walk up Joanna's steep driveway to knock at the door. Joanna has a plate of freshly baked chocolate-chip cookies waiting. Fay kneels on the carpet, contented, and moves chess pieces across the coffee table. March, march goes the king. Scurry, scurry, the queen in his wake. The bishop falls with a soft plop to the floor. Fay picks him up and fondly wipes him clean, scours his mitre with a fingertip. She is lost in play and does not even bother to watch the television, which Joanna has turned on for her.

Joanna watches, though, with her feet propped up on the edge of the coffee table, watches the coloured flickers moving back and forth. Outside it is raining, the sky is low and dark; comforting. When Joanna was a child she wanted a sister, a baby sister, sweet and malleable. That is Fay. She is like a doll; she smiles and smiles, and sometimes she sits perfectly still.

"Would you like to see the rest of the house, Fay?" Joanna asks suddenly. That is what Elliot always says, very early on, when he has friends to visit. But Fay does not say, as Elliot's friends say, "What a beautiful house." Instead her attention hangs for moments at a time on a deep windowsill, an exposed beam high up against stark whiteness, a cold curve of glass where there should, perhaps, be no glass at all. "Pretty," she says, but with a grave doubt, which Joanna shares. How can any dwelling look so beautiful, and be so cheerless, so comfortless? Joanna and Fay stand with their necks strained back and look up, up, at the high, pure angle of wall and ceiling, and Joanna thinks how easily she and Fay could simply disappear, their molecules unlinking, thinning, drifting into those odd, impossible spaces.

Fay shrugs, and wanders off. She picks up a framed picture of Elliot and butts her finger against the glass. "Your Daddy?"

"No, no, that's Elliot. My husband."

The picture was taken the summer before, on the balcony of their apartment in the city. Elliot is fond of this picture because the camera gives a foreign look, an air of holiday excitement, to the bland local sky. The place might be Spain or the south of France or Italy—destinations to which Elliot aspires. Or did aspire, the old Elliot, before he mortgaged his wings.

"Elliot," Fay repeats, and giggles behind her fingers.

"Oh, now, what's so funny?" says Joanna, taking the photograph from Fay. "Elliot isn't so bad."

"He looks like a man on TV."

Joanna wipes the glass in the frame with an edge of her shirt. "He looks like an actor?"

Fay is on her way back to the chess pieces. "No, just like a man on TV," she says.

When Elliot comes home that night, he closes the door very quietly behind him. "Do we have any aspirin?" he says. "I have an awful headache. I never get headaches, do I Joanna?"

"You aren't the first person I've spoken to all day, for a change," Joanna says, although it couldn't possibly be what she meant to say.

Elliot holds onto his head and looks at her as if she is a light that hurts his eyes.

"I met someone yesterday. She came over today. Her name is Fay."

"Good. We need to get to know some local people." He kneads the back of his neck, rubs his eyes with his knuckles. "What does her husband do?"

"She's not married," says Joanna. She slams a casserole dish down on the counter, hard. She stares at Elliot, who

19

stands there, bleak and cranky, the corners of his mouth pulled down. Old, dissatisfied, remote, involved entirely with his own selfish pain. That is how Elliot looks to Joanna.

"I'm going to lie down for a while. You go ahead and eat without me." He pauses in the hall by the living room and calls back, aggrieved, "Joanna, why in God's name is the chess game all over the floor?"

He limps off, head in hands. Joanna sits on the kitchen stool. It is dusk, and soon after, it is dark. Joanna does not bother to turn on the lights. The chicken breasts in mushroom sauce grow cold.

At last she slides off the stool and goes to look at Elliot, who lies with his knees drawn up under the comforter. His face is moonlit, white; his breathing is a soft sigh. This is Elliot's healing sleep, deep as the ocean. He will have forgotten his headache by morning. He will say, I never get headaches, I never get sick. He will be as full of energy as a child, and he will undoubtedly find Joanna, with her vague unhappiness, her demands, pleas, sudden movements, quite incomprehensible. He will begin to wonder if they speak different languages, so difficult is it for him to understand just what she wants.

She lies on the edge of the bed, not disturbing Elliot at all. She lies with her eyes open, staring up at the distant light of the moon caught in the trapezoid of glass high on the bedroom wall.

"Elliot, I'll tell you what. I don't think it's working out. Our living here," she says to him first thing next morning. She spreads marmalade on toast and passes it to him. "I'm alone here every day. All day long. I didn't realize it would be like this, but it is, it's awful."

"Joanna, please. Let's talk this over later. When we've got more time. Damn. I missed the news." He fiddles with the dial on the radio, bites into his toast.

"I want you to listen now, Elliot. I can't help it. I don't like it here. I can't live here, Elliot."

"Joanna, give it a chance."

"I have. I have given it a chance." Joanna's voice trembles; she wipes at her nose with the back of her hand.

"Five months?" Elliot pats her hand. "You'll adjust. Personally, I love it here. Perhaps we should get another car. Then you can get out more. Is that what we should do, Joanna?"

She shrugs away from him and pours herself another cup of coffee. After he has left, after he has dropped a careless kiss on the top of her head, after he has dismissed her and left, the words come. Everything she wanted to say. This is what I miss, Elliot, she tells him in her mind: sidewalks, warmed by the sun. Little bits of chocolate-bar wrapper rolling past in the breeze; faces, smiling, not smiling; all the variety, all the humanity. Dusty awnings above the greengrocers; bunches of cut flowers, eighty-nine cents each, in dented metal buckets. Flocks of schoolchildren in blue serge uniforms playing hopscotch in front of the red-brick Catholic school. Flocks of pigeons. The city, Elliot. The city.

Elliot, her imaginary Elliot, leans forward, clearly intrigued. She has caught his attention. But wait. Elliot is not, will not be convinced. He is amused by all the obvious things she has left out of her pretty picture, some of which he lists off for her, counting on his fingers: street muggings, pollution, high rent, pigeon mites, noise, drunks sleeping in gutters and on park benches, graft in City Hall. Now there

21

are bars in front of Elliot's smug face. Thin, looped iron, a priest's confessional. In a minute he will draw a thick, short curtain over the bars. He will vanish. First: "Joanna, you are not consistent. And as for logic! Why, you present the city as a fairy-tale world, all sunshine. Then you expect me to believe that you're afraid and unhappy in our beautiful new house. Joanna! Be reasonable! You're not giving yourself time. You need time, Joanna."

Elliot is not a priest; he is a crow, holding his black crow wings tight against his sleek body. He is a crow, and he speaks a language different indeed from Joanna's.

Joanna throws the breakfast dishes into the sink and wipes toast crumbs off the table onto the floor. She goes to the telephone and calls Jocelyn, who chirps and sings like a finch at the idea of Fay having dinner with Joanna and Elliot. "How extremely kind of you, dear," she tells Joanna. "Fay has led a very protected life, I'm afraid. Very protected, and rather isolated. This will be just lovely for her."

Fay is dressed for a party, dressed for a celebration, dressed in taffeta, stiff and rustling, the colour of unpolished brass. Her mother's best dress, thirty years old, with the folds shaken out, Joanna suspects, but still Fay looks young and doll-like; her neck and shoulders rise tenderly out of the exotic foliage; she is not at all spoilt by such tawdry coverings.

Joanna brushes Fay's long hair, sprays perfume on her neck. Fay shivers and laughs noisily, moistly, through her small bridgeless nose; laughs and points at the mirror;

curtsies clownishly. Joanna stands beside her; together, they bow at the mirror.

The kitchen is hot and steamy. Joanna has overdone things a little. Fat splatters against the oven walls; water from a pot sizzles on the stove-top.

Soon Elliot will come home; he will walk into the kitchen; he will see that someone is here. He will see Fay.

What exactly is Joanna trying to prove? That is what Elliot will want to know. Oh, he'll go right to the heart of the matter and accuse her. He'll say she is using Fay. He'll say she wants him to think that the only friend she has is a retarded girl. But Fay really is her friend. And what harm, in any case? What harm?

"Here, you slice the tomatoes for the salad, Fay." Joanna gives her the knife. "You must be careful though. Be careful not to cut yourself."

Fay bends over her task. Her hands move slowly, slowly. The tomato bleeds into the cutting-board.

"And candles," says Joanna brightly. "Let's have lots of candles for a pretty light." The candelabrum, and five crystal candle holders. Joanna strikes a match. Outside, the garage door slams shut.

∽

She knows Elliot; she should know Elliot by now. But she doesn't. He is always one step ahead of her. There is no change of expression, nothing to watch, nothing different from what she sees when he meets anyone for the first time.

"Ah, you're Joanna's friend. Fay. How do you do! Well,

this is quite a party. Joanna, my love, you should have told me."

Fay is overcome: the man on TV in real life. She smiles shyly up at Elliot and bites at the side of her finger; her amber ring sparkles in the candlelight.

"My, it smells good in here," says Elliot. "We must be having my favourite, roast moose."

Fay chuckles. She stands with the knife in one hand, a tomato in the other. "Not roast moose."

"Well then, roast hippopotamus?"

"No!"

"Roast dinosaur?"

Fay is scarlet with laughter. "No, no, no," she says, and drops the knife to the floor.

"Stop it, Elliot," Joanna says. She picks the knife up and smiles. "Stop it."

"It's roast beef then, I suppose. Well, you should have told me, Joanna. I would have been prepared. If you'd told me I was having roast beef for supper, I would have been prepared for roast beef. I wouldn't have expected something quite different. I wonder why Joanna always leaves me guessing, don't you wonder, Fay? I think I'll give up trying to second-guess old Joanna. Well, shall I carve the roast beef, Joanna? Does it matter to you how I slice it?"

"Not a bit," says Joanna. She undoes Fay's apron and shows her to the table.

Three for dinner. Mummy and Daddy, and baby makes three. Joanna spears a roast potato, brings it slowly to her lips. The flames from the candles, ten flames, leave blue and green after-images on the retinas of her eyes. "Would you like some more water, Fay? Or a glass of milk?"

"Milk, please," says Fay quietly. She has gone very quiet, aware, probably, that something is askew in the room, that something is wrong between Joanna and the man. She smooths at her taffeta skirt under the table.

"You grew up around here?" Elliot moves a candle half an inch, so that he can talk to Fay. "You live close to us?"

"Yes. My house is by the lake. It has a red roof."

"By the lake. You go swimming there?"

"In the summer. When it's hot." Fay grins. "My dog swims in the winter, too, though."

"He doesn't mind the cold water?"

"He doesn't care. He's just a dog."

"You like living by the lake? Yes, it must be nice. Joanna wouldn't like it, but then Joanna doesn't like anything very much. Do you, Joanna love?"

"I think I'll get dessert, if you'll excuse me," says Joanna.

In the kitchen, Joanna leans her forehead against the refrigerator door. Hot and cool. Everything is going wrong. She has to find the little gold dessert forks; Fay will think they are pretty. They were a wedding present, never used. They are in a box somewhere, a box with white satin lining. Not where she thought they were, not in the next three places she looks, but on the top shelf of a cupboard over the stove. Joanna wipes them carefully with a soft cloth, sets them down on a tray beside the dessert plates, beside the wedges of lemon meringue pie. Then she goes back into the dining room, which is not as it was when she left. Candlelight is going wild; shadows bend and swoop across the dark walls. Joanna sees why at once and hurries to put the tray down on the table.

"No, Fay. No," she cries. Then she says, in a voice meant

to sound reasonable, reasonable and calm: "Please don't open that window, Fay," but Fay has already pushed the window wide, one foot out behind her for balance, like a dancer.

"It is hot in here," says Elliot, conversationally. He reaches across the table for his coffee. "Hot and muggy."

The moths appear as if they had emerged from Elliot's mouth, as if he had blown them softly from his mouth, like bubbles. They fly to the candlelight, of course, dusty brown bombers, trekking across the room, fixed, blind, lusting terribly for Joanna's pretty candle flames.

They seem big as bats to Joanna, big and willful, especially those that brush against her arms, that flap dry wings against her skin, against her hair.

Elliot grabs her by the wrists.

"Stop that, Joanna," he says, as if he is upset by the way she is trying to hit out. "They're only moths. Only moths." He nods his head toward a corner of the room, the corner where the window meets the wall. Fay is there, with her knuckles in her mouth, her eyes huge.

"You're frightening her," Elliot says.

Fay removes her fists from her mouth. "I am not frightened," she says. Her eyes move quickly, searching out the room; they shimmer. And, unaccountably, she smiles.

Joanna almost misses the movement, it is so quick, but suddenly Fay is in front of her. She is radiant, lit from within. She holds her cupped hands up. "I have one," she says, simply.

Joanna shakes her head: No. But it is difficult for her to protest, to say anything at all. She is confronted with this young saint in taffeta. An image, a likeness—of what? For a moment Joanna is drawn irresistibly to her and even lifts her own hands to place them over Fay's, but Fay's hands are slowly opening. Joanna pulls back to avoid the dreadful revelation.

The moth does not fly as soon as the hands open—perhaps it is under the same spell Joanna feels. It shuffles to the top of Fay's finger and perches there, a particularly fine and vigorous specimen, tentatively passing its hooked feet in front of its shuttered eyes.

"See," says Fay, with a small, tight laugh. "You don't have to be frightened. It can't hurt you." She moves her hand forward, to give Joanna a better look.

"I don't want to see it, Fay. Stop that."

"It's pretty. It tickles," Fay says softly. The moth flutters its wings, only inches from Joanna's face.

"I was scared at first," Fay offers.

"You're too stupid to be scared," Joanna says, and after the first shock her words cause, she goes on: "You're an idiot, Fay. Stupid, stupid. You are. To open the window. That was so stupid."

"Joanna, stop," Elliot hisses into her ear. "What is it you want here, Joanna?" He places the palm of his hand on her back and gives her a little shove. "Go into the bedroom. Lie down. I'll take care of this."

She does as she is told, making her way down the hall to the bedroom door, where she pauses, supporting herself against the wall. The air in this part of the house is cooler, less dense, easier to breathe. Still, she doesn't want to be here. She wants to be with Fay; she owes an apology to Fay. My dear little friend, she wants to say. She would like to offer cookies and milk, a more sensible and sustaining meal than all that beef and starch served on the best china, which, she now realizes, she hates. But Elliot is comforting Fay; his voice, soft, low, soothing, goes on and on. There is another sound—perhaps Fay is crying. Or laughing. Perhaps Elliot is telling her little jokes and making her laugh.

In a while, Joanna hears footsteps, doors closing. She goes into the bedroom and closes the door tightly. Are the moths still in the house? And does it matter? How irrational she has become. And how frightened! It seems to her there is a trace of greyish powder on the back of her hand, a trace of something like pollen, left behind as one of the moths grazed her. She wipes her hand quickly across her skirt, and then again on the quilt folded at the foot of the bed. The car moves down the long drive to the road. She hears tires bite into gravel, sees briefly two oblongs of reflected light, pale and swift as wings, cross the walls and ceiling of her room, and then she is alone.

Everyone
is
Dancing

Not entirely at peace but nevertheless polite, uncomplaining, the Duke and Mrs. Beatty, awash in sunlight and sea air, wait for their evening meal. Almost always the only guests at The Cottage on Saturdays, they sit on the patio looking out over a clipped boxwood hedge at the flawless blue waters of the Strait of Georgia. Boats sail past. Gulls swoop. Mrs. Beatty keeps on her dark glasses. The Duke begins, spontaneously, eloquently, to speak of Princess Margaret, that most beautiful of princesses, whom he once saw in person at an orchid show on the Isle of Man.

"She had a complexion to rival any highly bred specimen of orchid you might care to mention," he says. Although they were related to one another through a Scottish connection on the Queen Mother's side, the princess had, regrettably, passed him by without a glance.

"What terrible lies you tell," Mrs. Beatty says. With what seems the most severe reluctance she removes her attention from the guileless blue of sky and sea and looks reprovingly at the Duke.

"Not such lies," says the Duke. "If it wasn't the Isle of Man it was some other place, some other kind of show—horses maybe. Come here, lovey," he then says, drawing France toward him, getting her to stand between his fat knees, so that he can rearrange her curls. She bends her head to one side to make it easier for him to undo the butterfly barrettes her mother, Micheline, pinned in her hair this morning. Keeping the Duke happy and entertained, especially when dinner is late, is France's job, assigned to her by her mother. "Easy money," Micheline always says at the end of the weekend as she hands over the two dollars and fifty cents she owes France.

"Little girls should never hide their pretty curls," the Duke tells her sternly. This, he says, is a more flattering style, it emphasizes her eyes, her lovely blue eyes. "Now, give Mrs. Beatty a smile." He takes France by the shoulders and turns her toward Mrs. Beatty. "Charming?" he asks of Mrs. Beatty, who chooses not to reply.

France, charming and completely charmed, leans against the Duke, who is warm and doughy as freshly baked bread, and who smells, it occurs to her, exactly like the undisturbed dust in the closets up on the second floor, not that the Duke has ever made it up to the second floor. He stays down here, counting the pleasure boats as they sail by and conversing with Mrs. Beatty, who allows only the briefest comments to pass her pursed burgundy lips. She rarely acknowledges France with a glance or a word.

In the kitchen Lee embarks on another tantrum. His style is broad and unhindered. He grabs Micheline's wrist and drags her across the blue tiled floor. "I can take only so much," he shouts at her. "I get fed up, believe it or not, with cooking dinner for phoney dukes. Am I some kind of indentured servant? Is that what I am?" He scowls into Micheline's face. She doesn't protest; instead she seems intent on searching out the real Lee beneath this maniac's mask. Her expression is resigned, removed, almost hopeful: this will pass, she seems to be telling herself.

France has closed the kitchen door firmly behind her, to keep the noise from reaching the Duke and Mrs. Beatty on the patio. As usual, as soon as Lee catches sight of her he abruptly releases Micheline's wrist. He wipes the back of his hand across his mouth as if to erase a scowl so angry and mean it is almost funny. France doesn't feel like laughing, though. Lee says, "Someone's here," as if Micheline hasn't already noticed, and then he slouches over to the stove and begins stirring the cream of salmon soup. His aspect remains carefully benign until hot soup splashes his hand, then he shouts, "Goddamn it to hell." France doesn't pay attention. These storms, she has learned, erupt and fade. Lee is wearing an apron and a chef's hat, but, as Micheline is always pleased to point out, he isn't a real chef, just someone she picked up off the street and trained in the art of slicing onions and deboning chicken breasts. Micheline absently rubs her wrist, where the pressure of Lee's hand has left ugly purplish red marks.

"Did he scare you, my darling girl, that stupid man, that demon?" she asks, gathering France into her arms. At first France thinks she means the Duke. Did the Duke scare her? She shakes her head: The Duke, that funny man; of course not. She

31

has been sent by the Duke to ask for some little thing to tide him over, a biscuit, a cracker, a piece of cheese, anything. *"S'il vous plaît,"* the Duke told her to say. *"S'il vous plaît."*

"Oh, Lord," Micheline says, at once arranging biscuits, green grapes, cheese, on a plate. "Tell them dinner will be just a teeny, tiny minute more," she says. "Smile nicely and tell them just another minute." She is wearing a rose-coloured dress that swirls like mist around her skinny ankles as she dashes from the sink to the stove, from the pantry to the cutting board—the perfect chef, the real expert in the family. France, entranced, cannot take her eyes off her mother, her beautiful mother, who was born in a faraway wonderful village in the south of France and then had her own daughter baptized with this astonishing gift: the country of France, forever and ever, the length and breadth and actual geography of an entire lifetime.

Every Saturday, Lee picks the Duke and Mrs. Beatty up at 4:35 in the afternoon, which is when the passenger ferry docks. He drives the 1958 Cadillac limousine that once transported Princess Margaret up and down Vancouver Island in royal style. France loves this car. It is black and sleek, immense, with bars and ribbons of chrome that catch the light and gleam splendidly. Inside, the seats are as soft and deep as dreams, especially in that mysterious shadowy region where the princess had (once upon a time) reclined, her gloved hands and elegantly shod feet quiet, non-functional, her own, so to speak, the adoring crowds having been, for the moment at least, outdistanced. France thinks of herself as a princess, as the daughter of a princess. She imagines a ball-room, a party, the Duke greeting her eagerly across a room filled with white and purple orchids, the air scented with perfume.

Lee isn't a fast driver; he is competent and fastidious, and so the ecstasy of the journey lasts for exactly as long as can sensibly be managed. France sits up front with him, her toes dangling above the richly carpeted floor, her chin raised so that she can see, although just barely, out the window. "Get your fingers off the glass," Lee commands. "Get your feet off the seats." She isn't allowed to eat in the car. She isn't allowed to chew gum in the car. She does as she is told. On the return journey, she manages to catch glimpses of the Duke and Mrs. Beatty floating behind her like mysterious deep-sea creatures. The Duke points out scenery to Mrs. Beatty—leafy forests growing right down to the roadsides. Forests full of sunlight and mischievous elves and nymphs and giants even, France knows. Micheline believes that France, like all children, should know of such things, because they might be true; they seemed true to her, when she was a child. Micheline once lived in a farmhouse with white chickens outside the front door and a fat, lazy pig asleep in the backyard and beyond that, she said, the enchanted forest, where no one with any sense would set so much as a big toe once night had fallen.

"See the size of that tree?" the Duke says. "This whole coast used to be trees that size. That's first growth. The primeval forest, untouched by the woodsman's ax. Look at the sun on the branches. That's better than an oil painting,"

Mrs. Beatty looks where the Duke tells her to look. At the same time, she rummages through her purse for hankies, peppermints, sunglasses. Lee follows the broad, gleaming hood of the Cadillac around the next corner and the next one after that. Lee is a tall man and the Cadillac suits him perfectly. His hands rest comfortably on the steering wheel. Once or twice he sounds the horn, pretending he has spotted a deer on the road, and the blast, not melodious at all, causes a shiver of disquiet to run down France's back. She composes herself. She sits with her hands in her lap. She is wearing a denim mini-skirt, a blue-and-white flowered top, white patent leather shoes, and a touch, just the faintest touch, of Micheline's red lip gloss on her lips. When the Duke and Mrs. Beatty visit, Micheline likes to dress France up so that she can play hostess. Not play so much, she corrects herself—The Cottage is a business that belongs to them all. Her and France and Lee. It's something they're in together, she says to France, loud enough and often enough that Lee has to hear, too. They will all share in the success, when it comes, Micheline says. They will all share.

Lee brings the Cadillac to a stop in the drive beside The Cottage. He gets out and opens the doors for the Duke and Mrs. Beatty. They exit the car as if to cheering crowds, self-conscious smiles on their faces. So this is what it is like, they seem to say. Almost, the Duke lifts a hand to wave. Then they proceed along the walk to the patio, where Micheline has just finished setting out, in their honour, potted pink and red geraniums in front of the boxwood hedge. "Welcome, welcome," she says. She says hello first in English and then in French. "It's so very good to see you again," she tells them, placing her hand at the same time on the top of France's head, the hand warm, solid, proprietary, as if it has just been removed from a bowl of soapy, hot water here, in the kitchen of this house, which she owns, adjacent to this garden, which she owns, beside this beach, which she owns and so on, unendingly.

Later, when dinner is ready, Micheline appears at the French doors leading to the patio and recites for the Duke and Mrs. Beatty the evening's menu: cream of salmon soup with peppercorns, *poulet quarante gousses d'Ail* served with *petits pois à la Paysanne,* and for dessert, orange cream tart.

The Duke wipes at his round blue eyes in joy, in anticipation—he and Micheline share the belief that he is a true gourmet, the only guest capable of fully appreciating Micheline's skills—and hoists himself up, offering his arm to Mrs. Beatty. Micheline seats Mrs. Beatty at one end of the dining-room table, where, splendidly isolated and withdrawn, she immediately begins twisting and untwisting her necklaces of amber glass beads. The Duke, opposite her, his broad back to the Welsh dresser on which are displayed Micheline's collection of dried purple starfish and sea urchins, wastes no time in shaking out his snowy white napkin and spreading it across his lap. Through the window the sea is clearly visible—the sail boats, the motor boats, the soaring gulls.

The Duke and Mrs. Beatty have, always, the best wine, the finest linen, the fanciest silverware. Micheline begins preparations for them at least one day in advance, and by the time dinner is ready to be served, she is, according to Lee, living on her nerves, a complete mess. "Only because of you," she retorts, pushing the kitchen door open with her hips, a silver tray balanced in her hands, steam from the soup bowls obscuring her path, so that she has to hum softly under her breath to keep herself steady.

When the Duke and Mrs. Beatty have begun their meal, France wanders into the kitchen, where Lee has decided to throw the last tomato, over-ripe in any case and of no culinary interest to Micheline, against the side of the refrigerator. The storm clouds have rolled in, France sees. It is the pain, according to Lee; he should be lying down, he says, pressing his hands to the small of his back. He suffers with muscle spasms in his back. Once he fell to his hands and knees on the kitchen floor and stayed there for half a day, a blanket supplied by Micheline wrapped around his shoulders. Now he takes a bottle of pain pills out of the cupboard and swallows two pills without water. Micheline, hurrying around the kitchen between serving the soup course and the entrée, walks around Lee, just as she did when he spent the day lying in pain on the floor; she talks over and through him. "Come and eat, my darling," she says to France, placing miniature portions of chicken and peas in front of her at the kitchen table. Enjoy your dinner, she says, as if France also is a paying guest. She refuses, however, to clean up the tomato. "Let it rot," she says. "Let it stay there, a testimony."

Lee, his hands clamped to his back, says she can clean it up or look at it for the rest of her life, he doesn't care which.

All he honestly longs for, Lee says, is a solid, open highway and access to high-octane fuel. When, if, they move off this stinking island, he will have to hire a barge for the Cadillac. It is a complete mystery to him how the Cadillac got here to begin with. Obviously someone brought it here. Obviously it didn't fly over the water like a duck. Lee came across it in a barn on the north side of the island. Cats were sleeping on the hood; hay was jammed up in the wheel wells. Halt or I'll blow your head off, the owner of the barn is supposed to have said, when he found Lee there. He had a rifle. The way Lee tells the story, he ignored the rifle and wiped the dust off the Cadillac's windows with the sleeve of his sweater. The cats, scrawny and wild-looking as they were, rubbed around his ankles, purring. The farmer, if that was what he was, rested his rifle against the barn wall and brought his hands down slowly, heavily, on the roof of the car. No one had driven this car in the past five years, he said. The battery was dead. He kept the anti-freeze topped up in the radiator and that was about it. The spark plugs needed changing, the generator was going, the carburetor was bunged up. "How much do you want?" Lee asked. "This is a famous automobile," the farmer said. "A historic automobile. An automobile like this doesn't lose value; it gets more and more valuable as time goes by. At least, that's how it's supposed to work," He was an older man, with a grease-stained baseball cap pulled low on his forehead and cowboy boots on his feet. "You'll have to tow it off my property," he said, according to Lee. "You'll have to bear the expense yourself. You aren't going to work on the damned thing in my barn."

What this car is, Lee later tells Micheline and France, is just the most amazing find. "Look at it: not a speck of rust, not a scratch." Also, he truly believes that for him it constitutes a form of direct and miraculous recompense for all he has given up, for his miserable servitude in Micheline's chamber of horrors, her "Cottage." Well, now there is a coach, a gold coach, a princess riding up to the door: The fairy tale is complete. "Hop in," he says. "Hop in and see what it feels like."

At first Micheline refuses even to sit in the Cadillac. It looks like a hearse, she says, or a gangster's car. She doesn't believe Princess Margaret ever rode in it. Says who? she wants to know. Lee intends to search for photographic evidence in newspaper archives. In time, he will provide her with all the proof she needs. Princess Margaret definitely rode in this car in 1958. It was summer; it was a royal tour. British Columbia was celebrating its centenary. He has read about the giant birthday cakes and the fireworks. He has read about it and he has heard about it; it's all on file, in the correct places.

Once a week, Lee washes and waxes the Cadillac. He has just finished vacuum-cleaning the interior, and now he has a bucket of soapy water and a pile of soft, clean cloths ready. Micheline says he is a fool to waste well water on a car in the middle of a dry summer. She circles the car warily, watching her footing on the loose gravel. Then, as if on a dare, she runs past Lee and throws herself onto the back seat, full-length, her hands folded on her chest. "*Je suis morte*," she says. Then she sits up and tosses her honey-coloured hair over her shoulder. "Do I look like a princess?" she asks France.

"Yes, yes," France cries in delight. Lee says, sharply, "You look like a scullery maid," and Micheline, scrambling out of the car, replies, "I am a scullery maid, idiot." She smooths her skirt and stands a distance away from the car. The scorched summer grass stretches between the rose beds down to the black rocks of the shore. The sea glistens, pure blue and gold as far as the dark line of the horizon, where the world transforms itself all at once into endless blue atmosphere. Micheline, her lips parted, inhales this ether deeply, then says, "The kings and queens of England ride to their coronations in a golden coach, but the kings and queens of France have their heads lopped off like Peter Rabbit, and then they sleep in the cold ground for a million years."

"Peter Rabbit didn't die," says France loudly. "In the book, he only got a tummyache."

"In the book, they lied," Micheline says. "They lied."

"Your mother is implying," says Lee, "that only the English are addicted to the artifacts of majesty. Which is, of course, yet another lie."

Personally, France cannot imagine living anywhere but here, although Micheline sometimes speaks of moving across the country, to *La Belle Province*, where she will feel at home. Micheline believes she remembers an aunt settling in Quebec City, years ago. She says she could phone the telephone company and find out her aunt's phone number. But then she says, No, no, she can't go anywhere, she would miss the Pacific Ocean too much, she can't survive without the sea at her front door. Besides, she has invested all of her money in The Cottage, and she knows she would never get it back if she sold now. She is a realist, she says proudly, in the same tone she uses for: I am French.

One night, France awakens from a strange dream in which a man as tall and thin and stooped as Lee, a man who may in fact have been Lee, full of menace and cunning, was slowly mounting the stairs to the second floor of The Cottage, half-singing and half-whistling a song Micheline once taught France. It went: *Sur le pont d'Avignon, on y danse, on y danse.*

Sur le pont d'Avignon, on y danse, tous en ronde. Everyone is dancing. Who, in the dream, was dancing? No one, no one. The wind is battering the house; it is the wind, not the dream, that has woken France. Her room is icy cold. The sea is crashing into the rocks on the beach. The rooms of the upper floor are all empty; Micheline's and Lee's bed is empty, the covers smooth, unslept in. The moon shines in coldly. If Micheline is to be believed, the danger on such nights is that the giants and elves of the forest will take to the road, searching for children like France. France believes in this only a very little. She is a practical girl, part-owner in a business. Downstairs, she finds her mother in the kitchen with Lee, both of them squashed up against the counter, Micheline's bare feet side by side on the floor like two pale fillets of codfish waiting to go in the oven.

There is just enough moonlight coming in the window for France to see a row of freshly baked pies on the kitchen table. Micheline has been baking pies in the middle of the night, which is why it is warm, much too warm, in the kitchen. In contrast to this warmth, there is the coldness of Lee's actions; he takes hold of Micheline's hair and pulls her head back, exposing her long white throat. When he lets go, suddenly, Micheline's head flops forward as if her neck has been broken. Again he yanks on her hair, a little harder, with less care, the white throat gleaming, unguarded, slim as a stalk of celery on a cutting board. This is repeated. Lee wraps his hand in the long, honey-coloured hair, now a hazy, indeterminate shade, the same colour as the night air. Micheline doesn't make a sound, although France imagines her whispering, sadly, *Je suis morte.* It can't be very nice, to have your neck pulled back like that. France hates all of this, the hot kitchen, the darkness, the silence, the stupid row of pies. She knows that no matter how long she stands there, her mother will never notice her.

On her way back upstairs, France imagines herself climbing and climbing the steep arch of a stone bridge, wearing herself out, half-asleep, nearly back in her bad dream, the dark man close behind her. To keep from stumbling on the stairs, she hums to herself: *Sur le pont d'Avignon, on y danse, tous en ronde. On y danse, sur le pont.*

∽

The first time the Duke sees the Cadillac, he smacks the whitewalls with his cane and says, "I know this car. I've ridden in this car before now. In a minute, I'll remember exactly where and when."

"I've never seen this car before," Mrs. Beatty says, "and neither have you."

"Imagine this particular car turning up here," he says. Leaning on his cane, he tells France that his sisters, each with an ostrich feather in her hair, were presented to the King and Queen of England as soon as they turned eighteen years of age. Did France know that? One sister wore pink satin, the other wore blue lace. He has the pictures somewhere. George V, he says. And Queen Mary. She was a tartar, he says. She made people mind their manners. One of his sisters fainted during the occasion, he can't recall which one exactly. Still, it was a more gracious era altogether.

Mrs. Beatty snorts incredulously. "Your sisters," she says. "How old do you think you are? Do you think you're a museum piece?"

41

The Duke wears a blue blazer and a yachting cap with a gold anchor on it. France, lost in admiration, thinks, The precious cargo, the precious cargo. She pictures the Duke flat on his back, his stomach in the air, being barged across the water, arriving in the same sort of style the Cadillac originally arrived in. She pictures a more gracious era, the water still as soup, the gulls lined up along the beach.

"What would we do without the Duke and Mrs. Beatty?" Micheline says to France, busily making inky marks in neat columns in a ledger. This is at night, at Micheline's desk in the kitchen. "Bless the Duke," she says, "bless his money and his funny old ways." She bounces France on her knee as if France were two again, which is exactly what France wants to be, most of the time. She sticks her thumb in her mouth and pretends she is a baby, even though she knows that having reached the age of nine years there is no hope for her.

Other guests come to The Cottage in the course of a summer, and stay a day, two days, and depart. Finicky honeymooners who prefer their morning coffee made with hot milk; sadly garrulous German tourists who become nostalgic, always, for other places, other similar, but unquestionably superior, bed-and-breakfast establishments in Switzerland, in New South Wales, in Maine; university students clumping along the hall in hiking boots. They sign their unimportant names in the guest book in the front hall, along with, "Had a great time, glorious scenery, delicious meals!" And then on Saturday, peace, silence, and at last the Duke and Mrs. Beatty arrive.

The Duke, that fine gourmet, as Micheline refers to him,

that great *bon vivant*, tucks his napkin into his collar and takes up his knife and fork. France is sitting nearby. "Don't leave me alone, my poppet," he says to her. "Don't leave me alone with Mrs. Beatty. She's giving me such looks, she's putting me off my food." He winks at France; Mrs. Beatty stares with great determination out the window at the black sky, the white-flecked ocean. The weather has changed. When the summer ends, the Duke and Mrs. Beatty will no longer come here. Time is passing; France cannot bear it. She wants everything to remain always the same, this room, the Duke, the hot dishes steaming into the charged air. But things will change; things will change and change again, France knows it. In just a little while, for example, she will excuse herself to the Duke and sneak quietly out so that she can eat by herself in the kitchen. She can't help it; she is nearly as hungry as the Duke; her stomach is growling. She will have what the Duke and Mrs. Beatty are having: poached cod, new potatoes and white sauce, without the dinner wine but with a glass of ice-cold milk. For a moment all she can think about is her dinner, and that is how she comes to miss the exact moment when the Duke, who has been happily devouring his poached cod, begins to gasp and spit. He looks horribly surprised. His eyes pop open. His jaw stretches wide. Choking to death, she thinks, immobile in her chair. The Duke is choking to death on a fish bone. Why does she have to witness these events? She feels like an invisible person, a ghost, with two huge, lidless eyes. A memory comes to her, of picking up a rock, an ordinary smooth, dark rock, from the beach. The rock was so smooth and so cold she had touched it with her tongue, out of curiosity. Then, without thinking, she placed it in her mouth, where, cold and tasting of salt, it refused to dissolve.

She was younger then; she didn't know any better. When she tried to spit the rock out, it had nearly slipped down her throat. If she had choked to death alone on the beach, no one would have known; she would have rolled into the cold sea and been carried away by the tides.

Micheline, hearing the commotion (apart from the anguished gasps being emitted by the Duke, Mrs. Beatty is wailing, Oh no, oh no, and knocking spoons and dishes onto the floor), dashes in from the kitchen and throws her arms around the Duke's broad chest, half lifting him, heavy as he is, out of his chair. France covers her face with her trembling hands. Peter Rabbit certainly did not die, as her mother said; he got sick and was put to bed by the mother rabbit, where he at length recovered.

The Duke once took France for a long walk down the beach. He told her that when he was a young man he had gone duck hunting on a regular basis with King George VI. The king had relied on the Duke's instinct when it came to weather, wind velocity, the flight paths wild ducks were likely to take. It had all been very complicated and outrageously enjoyable. Before hunting they dined on lavish breakfasts consisting of fish, fowl, and good roast beef. France informed the Duke that she had been born in France in a tall white castle with flowering vines growing over the windows. Outside the castle was a bridge, and on the bridge children played and danced. When France saw these children, she had smiled for the very first time in her life, at the surprising age of two weeks. In spite of having been so young, it seemed to her she remembered the moment clearly—the children waving their arms and pulling silly faces simply to elicit a smile from her. They called her by name, and the name they used, soft and sweet as the summer wind, was also the name of the country they would never leave, never. "I was a baby and they danced and laughed for me," she said.

"Yes, I can see it all, just as you describe. You are a poet," the Duke told France solemnly.

The truth is, she considers it unfair that she was named for a country she has never seen, and probably won't ever get to see. When she thinks of France, she thinks of rooms, villages, mountains far beneath the ocean, all deeply green and vastly silent, lost, while sleeping kings, their faces affable and innocent as the Duke's, and queens, as fair and lively as Micheline, tumble slowly past. Her throat tightens; she is afraid she is going to cry, and then Micheline would be ashamed of her, Micheline would say, Be a big girl, grow up, mind your manners.

Something shatters on the floor; a shard of glass hits France in the leg, possibly drawing blood. She does not look. She hears Mrs. Beatty moaning. She hears loud footsteps as Lee comes into the dining room. "Bloody hell, what now?" he demands. "Not a word from you," Micheline warns, panting. France knows that the Duke is dead, the poor Duke. But he isn't; he coughs and pulls raspy-sounding breaths down into his throat and thumps his chest, and Micheline thumps his back between the shoulder-blades; the stone, or rather the fish bone, is dislodged. Micheline holds it up between her thumb and forefinger, and says, "The culprit!" The Duke is removed to a guest room on the first floor and given feather pillows for his damp, perspiring head. He smiles weakly, gratefully, and falls asleep, or at least seems to sleep, his large stomach rising and falling in a reassuring way, his fat sausage fingers spread out over the white sheet. He is,

France thinks fondly, her best friend. He looks handsome and very real to her, substantial, exactly as someone related to royalty, on the Scottish side, through the Queen Mother, ought to look. France has already checked the spot on her leg where the flying glass (it was a water glass, the Duke's, as it happened, dropped from Mrs. Beatty's flustered fingers) hit her, and she is relieved to find no sign of injury.

Mrs. Beatty is taken upstairs, where Micheline runs her a hot bath. A glorious calm seems to have overtaken Micheline, now that she knows the Duke is alive and breathing. "The Duke and I are not married," confesses Mrs. Beatty, sitting on the edge of the tub. She blows her nose into a clean facecloth. "We've never been married. We have no children, no family, no one to call our own." France, who is trying to emulate her mother's calmness, is waiting at the door with more towels and a bar of scented soap. Micheline takes Mrs. Beatty's hand in hers and pats it tenderly. Mrs. Beatty pulls her hand away and says, "I am not looking for sympathy."

"Of course not," Micheline says. "Who ever gets sympathy in this life? Well, I was married once, but it didn't work out. It lasted four months and ten days. That was a very brief marriage. Still, nothing is wasted, is it? I mean, a good cook doesn't throw much in the garbage, does she?" Micheline takes the towels from France and hangs them on a rail near the bath. Then she says to Mrs. Beatty, "Never mind, all you need is a nice hot bath and a good night's sleep," which is exactly what she tells France, every night, night after night, immediately after all those stories of dark forests and white chickens and the fat, pink pig that was Micheline's favourite pet for years and years, until, a grown woman, she left her home, her motherland, and came here to live beside the sea.

The Spirits
of
Many
Small Fish

A summer house," said Erica, "is delightful when your children are young, of course. Like when David was young."

"I agree," said Gerald. "Or when you're retired and have the time and inclination to get away from it all."

"And it must be worth a fortune by now," said Erica. She was referring to her summer property, on Carmel Island. She played with the gold bracelets on her arm. "It must be worth hundreds of thousands." She paused, seemingly to give herself time in which to consider the immensity of this amount.

"One hundred thousand, anyway," said Gerald. "Anyone for dessert? David?"

"No, no thanks," said David. He was, he said, going to have to be horribly rude and leave. But what a lovely evening it had been. He pushed his chair back and stood up. He kissed the air beside Erica's apricot-tinted cheek. She patted his hand, and then caught it tightly and held on.

"Oh, David, don't go," she said. "We have to talk. We have to talk about this business of selling the summer place. I think we should put our heads together and come to a decision as a family, don't you?" She smiled up at him brightly. She had her hair in a pale lacquered swirl on top of her head. Her dress was like gold cloth, medieval; the high neckline was fastened with a gold pin in the shape of a rose. Beautiful, beautiful Erica, he thought, meaning it. Traitor, he also thought.

"Well, you already know what I'd say."

Erica smiled radiantly and said nothing. Gerald appeared engrossed in the approaching dessert cart. He rubbed his hands together and moistened his lips. He urged David to sit down and try the Black Russian cheesecake. "How often do we get together, for God's sake?" he said, extending his scrubbed pink hands to embrace the raspberry flan, the Black Forest cake, the key lime pie. Gerald was a dentist. He was a dentist verging on retirement but always pulling back. He was making new discoveries in his profession, he had told David. He was exploring hypnotism and music, especially music from the Baroque period, as effective adjuncts, or even, in some exceptional cases, alternatives, to drugs such as novocaine. He believed, and this belief, he assured David, was new to him, new and fresh, that inside everyone's psyche resided a fist-shaped space, much like a dental caries, that had to be filled with serenity and a hard-packed base of good self-esteem, otherwise the organism tended to decay from the inside out. He had smiled in pleasure at the brilliance of his metaphor, just as, now, he smiled at the dessert cart. "Definitely, the Black Russian cheesecake," he told the waiter.

"He's angry with us, aren't you David?" said Erica. She kept her hand tightly over his. "If you're mad, stay and be mad. Call us names. We don't care, do we, Gerald?"

He pulled his hand away. He thanked them, again and

again, profusely, and then he left them, his father and his stepmother, two people who had been married and then had separated and were, they maintained, now the best of friends, anxiously regarding him across the remains of their meal— the half-empty wineglasses, the coffee cups, the crumpled napkins.

Outside the sky was a pale violet; stars were beginning to appear. He got into his car and sat for awhile. Imagine Erica suddenly announcing that she wanted to sell the summer house. She hadn't even warned him, she had just said, "This is what I want to do." He couldn't let it happen; he would stop her. Technically, the property did belong to Erica, and therefore he supposed she could do what she wanted with it. Yet she must be persuaded to consider the larger picture, in which his memories of all the summer vacations he and his father and Erica had spent there as a family, not necessarily a happy or ideal family, but a family nevertheless, took precedence over everything else.

He started his car and pulled away from the curb. He had been parked under a flowering Japanese plum, and the hood of his car was littered with pale, very delicate petals which blew one by one onto his windshield. A plan that seemed to have been formulating itself in his head for a long time came to him. He already did a certain amount of work at home, and with a little arranging he was sure he could do almost everything at home, and his home—this was the important part of the plan—could be on Carmel Island. All he needed was his computer and a modem and a fax machine. Wasn't that the way the world was going, in any case? Everything now was a cottage industry. He had solved the problem; Erica didn't need to part with her property on Carmel Island after

49

all. He arrived home feeling elated. He sat near an open window reading a book by a celebrated psychologist, a book suggested to him by Gerald. David would read a page or two, and then his mind would begin to wander. He couldn't understand what Gerald wanted him to discover in the book. Gerald gave the impression of a man counting doggedly backwards from one hundred; he had gone from a fixed point of view, conservative, unemotional, rigid, to this new sort of psychologically attuned liberalism. Would it last? Things tended not to last with Gerald, in spite of his doggedness.

David thought of Erica in her gold dress with her pale gold hair. Because she was fair and slightly built and pretty, she looked much younger than she really was; in fact, she didn't look much different than she had when he first saw her. Then, he had thought she was a figure from a fairy tale living in an enchanted cottage. A wonderful cottage at the edge of the sea, possibly even at the edge of the earth, a witch's cottage with a wisp of smoke rising from the crooked chimney and a scent of gingerbread baking in the kitchen. A child could creep through the forest and through the house and come out unscathed on a wide, shaded verandah that faced the deep and frequently difficult currents of the narrow channel between Carmel Island and the next island over. Life was everywhere: seagulls and mink and occasionally sea otters; seals and clams and oysters and cormorants and even great, soaring eagles. One could live there for quite some time on very little money and very little company. When he was a little boy, he wanted to live on Carmel Island all year and take the ferry to school along with the other children who lived on the island. His father had said, Be sensible. He said

David knew perfectly well he, Gerald, couldn't leave his practice in the city and, in any case, in the winter it rained all the time and David wouldn't be able to play on the beach, so what would be the point?

David was six years old when Gerald first took him to the summer house to meet his new mother. Perhaps not even quite six. His first mother had died when he was two years old. This mother was not to be his stepmother, not a replacement mother, his father said, but his real, true mother. She was here, not in heaven with the angels, and she would take care of him; she wanted to take care of him. There had been a wedding and a honeymoon, but David was kept away from both. He stayed with his grandparents. Then one day, Gerald came for him and brought him to Carmel Island, where the wind smelled of the sea and the sea was everywhere. Gerald lifted him out of the car and set him on the ground. The woman who was to be his mother took him by the hand and made him walk with her down a path that went past a fish-pond. On the far side of the fishpond sat an immense stone figure with a round stomach and round cheeks and a round, bald head. The stone figure seemed to be laughing at him.

"This is the Smiling Buddha," Erica said, bending down to speak into David's ear. "He's smiling because he likes you."

"You have algae in this pond," said Gerald, removing his sunglasses and bending down for a better look. "It needs to be drained and cleaned, Erica. It's a perfect breeding ground for mosquitoes, if nothing else."

The Buddha laughed at Gerald who was down on his hands and knees with his nose in the water. "This is your new mother," said the Buddha to David. "Her name is Erica."

From that moment David and Erica were never apart. Erica gave him cups of tea with milk and sugar and entertained him with stories that were true. She told him that the summer house was a birthday present from her first husband, whose name had been Thomas. He had been a very important, brilliant man and he had died in a terrible plane crash in Europe. He had died and Erica had sifted his ashes into the sand on the beach. "In those days, the beach was more sand and less rock. Even the beach changes with time," she said.

"His *ashes*?" David said, astonished. Ash, crash, he thought. He looked out at the beach in solemn, slightly hysterical, shock. He began then to develop an unnerving sense of a presence, a strange, bright, restless presence, in everything: the beach, the sea, the creatures that came up out of the sea and stranded themselves on the shore.

Gerald phoned David with a request. Would David go with Erica to the Carmel Island property? If the place were to be put on the market, then it should be straightened up, made ready. Personal or valuable property should be removed, put somewhere safe, said Gerald, with some of his pre-enlightenment asperity. Some of the furnishings would be sold; some could be junked. "You and Erica can decide what's what," he said. David replied, more or less honestly, that he wasn't sure if he had the time.

"Well, you know," said Gerald, "I would be more than willing to go, but I'm completely stuck here."

"Is this such a good time to sell anything?" David asked. He mentioned depressed prices, high taxes. He mentioned the current recession.

"There's always a recession," Gerald said impatiently. David could hear water running in the background, metal clinking against metal as instruments were readied. Gerald was calling from his office, where his next patient, no doubt supine and draped, mind flooded with the pure, high notes of a Brandenburg concerto, awaited the promise of painlessness.

"Well, I suppose I could go," David heard himself say. A picture of the summer house, serene, sleeping, the verandah in shade, came to him. He thought of long, peaceful June evenings on Carmel Island, the clear, fresh mornings.

"It'll be lovely there this time of year," Gerald said, reading his thoughts. His tone was coercive, as in, Open wide, this won't hurt a bit.

Erica and David arrived at the summer house at about ten o'clock at night, and Erica immediately plugged in the telephone and made a lengthy call to Gerald. She described the journey in detail: They had a sandwich at a café near the ferry terminal; she thought she was getting a migraine from the bright sun, but it went away, thank God. While she talked, David lit a fire in the fireplace and made coffee. Erica hung up the phone and said, "This has become quite a ritual, hasn't it?" She was referring either to the coffee or the telephone call, he wasn't sure which. He was tired from the long drive but also exhilarated at being there. He could hear the sea, the rhythm of the sea, which seemed also to be the rhythm of his mind, slow, expansive, timeless. Later, he and Erica made up the beds with clean sheets Erica had brought from her apartment. The sheets in the linen cupboard here at the summer house always felt damp at the beginning of the summer, Erica said; they needed to be laundered and aired. Then she said her headache had returned in full force. She went to look for some Tylenol. David said, "Go to bed, Erica. You'll feel better in the morning."

"Yes, I think I will," she said. She reached up and undid her hair, letting it fall down almost to her waist. This was Erica as David had first known her: her hair loose over her shoulders, her feet bare. He had thought: A witch. But she did not look exactly as she had then. She looked tired and, in fact, ill. "If I could only warm up a little," she said, hugging herself. He found an electric space heater and set it up in her bedroom. She flopped down on the bed and yawned until her eyes watered; then she wiped at her eyes with her hands. He was alarmed. "I'll be fine," she murmured, "in the morning." She lay back on the bed with her eyes closed.

"Can I get you anything else?" he asked.

"I'll be fine," she repeated.

He went outside after a moment and knelt on the grass in front of the Buddha, a figure which, taken along with the setting, the cottage, the sea, constituted what the psychologist David had been reading might have called the centre of David's own personal mythology. The Buddha was changed, yet unchanged; his power, it seemed to David, was in no way lessened by time. Ivy now grew rampant over his vast stone torso. His pudge of a nose was chipped. The goldfish pond, a circle of rock slabs set deep into the ground, had been drained and filled in years ago, but David imagined he could still feel its rim with his fingers, sense the spirits of small goldfish clustering at his hand as if feeding. He heard tree-frogs, cicadas, waves along the shore.

He thought of his first night here at this house, when Erica had taken him on her lap and read to him from Edward Lear: "Though the sky be dark, and the voyage be long, / Yet we never can think we were rash or wrong." That, he had at once understood, had to do with the sea, with voyages by sea, such as the one he and his father had undertaken on the car ferry to get to Carmel Island, to the summer house.

The latter-day history of the summer house, which David had never tired of hearing from Erica, was this: In 1959, which happened to be also the year of David's birth, Erica's first husband gave her the summer house as a gift. He was a wealthy man, and he liked to give things to Erica. He gave her cars, holidays, jewellery, fur coats (in those days everyone wore fur coats, Erica said; no one thought about the poor little fur-bearing animals). They had discovered Carmel Island by chance while bumming around the Gulf Islands, looking, they imagined, for the most serene, most beautiful, spot on earth. Their lives were very busy, frantic, and they wanted a place where they could rest and do nothing and be at peace. And when they found it, it was, happily, up for sale. At that time, the summer house was the year-round residence of an elderly couple who had once served as Methodist missionaries in China. The house, Erica told David, was exotically decorated with lacquered screens, ornate carved tables, silk wall-hangings, rice-paper paintings of bamboo and delicate flower petals: all booty from Chiang Kai-shek's beleaguered China. And beyond this, visible through the windows, was the special booty of place: the sea, the shore, the arbutus trees, the distant mountains. "Thomas and I looked at each other in disbelief. We had found exactly what we wanted," said Erica.

The missionaries were old and physically diminished, but they had evidently learned a thing or two from all those years of persistent piety in the midst of turbulence. They held out for their price, which was, Erica said, much too high, ridiculously high. Thomas offered what he considered a more reasonable price, but was forced again and again to increase the amount until finally he arrived, breathless and disbelieving, at the very figure the old couple had been after all along. He pulled his pockets inside out to demonstrate: I have nothing left. Of course, he was overstating his case. The missionaries had been overstating their case, as well. Everyone had been dramatic, bold, instinctively canny.

The fact was, Thomas told Erica, the missionaries had never lost sight of the simple fact that God was negotiating on their behalf. Some people did believe the elect were rewarded in just this manner: with cash. He tended to believe it himself. In the end, the missionaries were happy. They packed up and vacated their property within a month. Then Thomas and Erica rushed back to the island and used their newly acquired keys to let themselves into their summer house. And how shocked they were. The house was stripped of its Chinese screens and its silk wall-hangings, its rice-paper paintings and its lacquered screens and pots. All that was left was a hollowed-out shell, smelling of damp, and a half-used, stained box of rodent repellent in a cupboard under the sink. And the weather turned bad; outside, a small, restless, unhappy, grey sea struggled down the channel through a thick fog.

According to Thomas, the missionaries had taken the spirit of the house away with them. And that was his fault. He should have had it written into the sales contract, that the spirit of the house was to stay behind. He said these things, Erica told David, to make her laugh, so that she would forget the sad state of her new house.

"My fault entirely," Erica would say, in a gruff joking voice, imitating Thomas, when she told the story. David would stare at her in fascination, hoping to catch further revelations of Thomas in Erica: the true Thomas, alive and real, rich and powerful and laughing at his own mistakes.

Erica told David that Thomas had not minded being cheated on the price of the summer house. He took it all very philosophically. What he did do, was hire painters and carpenters and electricians. And then, rather surprisingly, he went to a considerable amount of expense and trouble to have the stone Buddha shipped over. It arrived, sealed in cardboard, on a flatbed truck—a mystery. Cars had followed along behind; children on bikes had raced after the truck. And when the cardboard was stripped away and the Buddha lowered into place, a cheer went up from the crowd. Or so Thomas, who had personally directed these proceedings, told Erica. Soon after, Thomas had the pond made and stocked with goldfish, so that the Buddha would have something to gaze upon as he waited for time to pass and for various events to circle around on each other like great winged birds.

ᘁ

In the morning, David and Erica had breakfast out on the verandah. David had carried the wicker chairs and table out from the storage room, which was, of course, the opposite of packing away. The sun was warm, the sea blue, and he realized with relief that of course Erica would never part with this property. In fact, she had begun to talk about removing the verandah to let more light into the cottage. She would have a patio, open to the sky, and a table with a yellow umbrella to provide shade. It would be more modern and a little Mediterranean in tone. What did David think?

"Good idea," he said, looking up, estimating the ease with which the roof of the verandah could be removed from the roof of the house. He could do some of the work himself, he said. He had been waiting for the right moment to tell Erica about his plan to set up an office here, to live here. He had already realized he would have to do some rewiring; in fact, he would have to ask Erica if he could do a number of repairs, make a few changes.

Before he could say anything, however, Erica said, "A good idea for someone else, perhaps." She wasn't really going to keep the summer house, she said; she was going to travel. "Bermuda, Brazil, Mexico—anywhere the sun shines from dawn to dusk. My travel agent has it all written down, and she's working on a schedule. This time next year I will be sunbathing, reading, listening to music. Admiring a much warmer, more congenial sea altogether." She folded her hands behind her head and regarded the cold sea in front of her.

"I thought you hated the idea of travel."

"I do hate the *idea*. But I'm not going to let that bother me. Not anymore."

"You're going to go to all these strange places and live in hotels and eat strange food and listen to people you don't know speaking in a language you don't understand?"

Erica laughed. "Yes, that's right."

"You'll hate it. Are you going to fly? You hate travelling by air."

"I'll learn to like it. I'll take pills. I'll sleep. I'm too old to have phobias."

She was giving him phobias, David thought. He drank his coffee and tried not to show his agitation. He couldn't talk to Erica; she wasn't making sense. First she wanted the verandah ripped down; then she wanted to sell the house. Everything would remain exactly as it was, he decided, with the exception of the wiring, which would have to be up-graded for his home office. He imagined how he would feel waking up here, alone. He imagined the silence, the nearness of nature, without human contact of any kind as a distrac-tion. He noticed that the sea began very blue farther out and then gradually became green as it entered the passage be-tween this island and the next one over. In the summer, he remembered, when the tide was especially low, pleasure boats not infrequently got hung up on sandbars at low tide in the narrow channel. Gerald would then march down to the water and shout, "You'll have to wait for the tide. The tide will refloat you. Sit tight." The people in the boat either waved and called back that yes, they would sit tight, or else they shouted abuse. "Why do they navigate with road maps? Why do they do the same stupid thing over and over?" Gerald would fume. He wore white slacks and a straw hat and took the business of owning, or at least of being married to someone who owned, summer property very seriously. He was furious when tourists wandered onto his lawn or helped themselves to shells from above the high tide line. "You may not be aware that this is private property," he would say. In full view there was a sign: Private, Keep Out. "Watch out, he's defending his territory again," Erica would say, as she and David observed from a window.

One year Erica gave Gerald a metal detector, and he went along the beach finding items dropped by these same trespassers, or so he believed. He found coins, bottle caps, cigarette lighters, the occasional watch or gold ring, once even a rosary with pale amber beads and a gold crucifix. When he came across something of value, he made a point of taking it to the village store in case someone was looking for it. The coins he saved up in a glass jar, to spend on something frivolous for himself. Erica and David laughed at the glass jar and at the canvas satchel Gerald acquired to hold his treasures and at his straw hat. Gerald, under these circumstances, compared less than favourably with images of Thomas in the photographs Erica was secretly showing David. In these photographs Thomas was a distant yet decisive figure on the beach, a red sweater slung carelessly over his shoulder. Or he was sitting on the steps to the verandah, bearded, fair, smoking a pipe. He was grinning. He was tanned, windburned. He was striding along the beach. He was in a rowboat, hands on the oars, a few feet from shore. The boat was called *The Pelican*; it was still here, stowed in a shed behind the house. The man in the boat, in the photograph, was powerful, strong. The sea was rough, the sky overcast, but Thomas obviously didn't care. He was laughing at the camera; he was waving.

At the time, David had perhaps mistakenly believed that Erica was inviting him to make the obvious comparison: Gerald, Thomas. Which would you choose? she seemed to be asking David. The truth was, David had actually begun to pretend not only that Erica was his real mother, but that Thomas had in fact been his real father. He felt quite wicked when he did this, and he knew better than to tell Erica. It was just that Thomas was so obviously all these things—heroic, swashbuckling, better at rowing and enjoying life. On the beach, Gerald scowled and found fault; Thomas, in the photographs, had fun and strode around. In a strange way, also, Thomas seemed merely another aspect of Erica, who, it seemed to David, always knew how to have a good time. Erica made a fuss over David, she called him "Davey" and took him for long walks around the island, picking wild berries and seeing how many different species of birds they could spot. She ran footraces with him and let him, occasionally, win. She knew many of the people who lived, who had lived for years, on the island, and when she met them she introduced him to them as her son. These meetings were infrequent and brief, however; for the most part they were alone on the dusty roads beside the fragrant green forests. Whenever he was asked, as an adult, if he had been happy as a child, he responded eagerly, brightly. "Yes, yes. Very happy. I was incredibly lucky when I was a child."

Observing the closeness of the mother to the child, Gerald would attempt remedial action. "He's monopolizing you. He thinks he owns you. You can't allow it," he would say, pulling David away from her side. He insisted that David accompany him on fishing trips in *The Pelican*, to get him away from Erica. To give Erica time on her own, which he said she must need. David had to sit up straight and keep quiet while Gerald rowed slowly and deliberately on a straight course. Because you had to have respect for the sea, Gerald said. And if you lived near the sea, even for part of the year, you had to know how to swim. Gerald gave David swimming lessons when the tide was high and the shallow curve of the beach made a waist-high pool. He was taught to float face down and on his back; he learned to open his eyes underwater and to do a crawl. Gerald was a methodical teacher. He taught one skill and then moved on to another. David insisted that he knew how to swim; he was a good swimmer. He resented being made to wear a life-jacket when he played on the beach. He decided he would swim without the encumbrance of the life-jacket out to a large rock, which he could then climb on to. From this rock, he would be able to wave to Erica and Gerald, who were sitting out on the verandah. However, the water was colder than he had expected, and of course he wasn't really a swimmer yet; he got into trouble immediately. He went under, his eyes open on an amazing grainy greenness. A translucent saucer with long tentacles drifted past. A poisonous jellyfish, he at once thought, like the ones Gerald had described, capable of inflicting deadly stings. Hundreds of lively silver bubbles erupted from his throat and rose toward the distant surface. Then he was rescued by Gerald, who pulled him roughly out of the water. He was carried up to the verandah and deposited on Erica's lap. "Oh, my God," she shrieked. "He's soaking wet and cold as ice."

"Brat," Gerald said. He was also wet and shivering. Erica laughed and dumped David off her lap. She made them both hot chocolate, and Gerald lit a fire in the fireplace, and they sat around it, and no one said anything to David about what he had done.

Now, when he asked Erica if she remembered the time he had nearly drowned, she said that such a thing was impossible: He had been too well watched-over. He said, "Come on, you must remember," but she said, No, no, she didn't remember, he had never been in danger of drowning.

Erica said that she did not want to be sentimental about a building, a place. She wanted to be free of that kind of attachment. Gerald, in fact, had told her that it was not healthy for the "whole person" to be overly concerned with the past.

"How about the future then?" David wanted to know. "If you sell this place, I'll have nowhere to bring my children on holidays. They'll never to get to know what it's like here."

"But David, you don't have any children," Erica said. They had made a start on cleaning out the back porch. All the old fishing tackle, the hip-waders, the life-jackets, could go to the Salvation Army, she said.

"That doesn't mean I won't have children, some day," Then he said diffidently, "This place means a lot to me, you know."

"Yes, I know. I do know that." She pulled a spoon-shaped fishing lure out of a tackle box. "This could be some kind of primitive jewellery, couldn't it? It's quite beautiful." He noticed she had cut her finger while searching through the box, but she wouldn't let him look at it. "Don't fuss," she said. "It's fine."

∽

"A bacterial soup," Gerald said, all those years ago, his face inches from the surface of the pond. He dabbled his fingers in the water, which had a skin to it, an oily appearance. "No circulation, utterly stagnant," he said in disapproval. His tone was cool, clinical: Who would know more about such matters than a medical person? He wanted the pond emptied; he wanted the fish gone. "It seems to me that this pond is a health threat the way it is. Of course, it is a shame . . . ."

A man in a truck came and drained the water out of the pond. The fish, reprieved for the moment, had been put in a glass tank. Gerald bought an aerator for the tank, a book about caring for tropical fish, and a small blue castle with turrets the colour of coral. But in a short while the fish sickened and died one at a time, slowly, their fins eaten away by some unseen and seemingly unstoppable micro-organism. They died and bobbed around on the surface, animated by the bubbles from the aerator. The tank was in David's bedroom. He couldn't sleep; he felt, in his dreams, the soft mutilated fins brushing against his face. He awoke, calling for Erica.

"I told you he was too young to look after pets," Erica said.

"Fish aren't pets," Gerald said. "Anyway, they were diseased to start with, from that filthy environment. It isn't your fault," he said to David. "They're only fish."

"They were perfectly healthy in that filthy environment,"

Erica said. "Fifty generations of fish have been fine in that pond. The pond was a natural environment, not like that tank."

"It was not natural," Gerald said. "It was an artificial pond, and the water was never renewed. It was stagnant. It was a breeding ground for bacteria and mosquitoes."

"Oh, mosquitoes," she said. "I think you're paranoid about mosquitoes, I really do."

This argument continued long after the pond had disappeared and left the mystified face of the Buddha with nothing to gaze on but weeds. His eyes were like coins; his mouth was dimpled, fat, mute. David put his lips to the Buddha's cool face, a quick kiss, then ran away. In his mind, the absent pond began to have less to do with the unfortunate goldfish than it had to do with Thomas, who had, like a god, fallen through the sky onto a mountaintop and could no longer protect what had been his. He existed only on Kodak paper and in the empty rooms of the summer house, from which Gerald seemed determined to evict him. "If you were so happy with him, why did you get married again?" he demanded of Erica. "Why didn't you go on keeping his memory sacred? Why didn't you preserve yourself to his memory?" "I have no idea," she replied distantly; "I must not have been thinking properly." "We have nothing in common whatsoever," Gerald had once shouted, and Erica had said, "Oh, what a stunning insight." David had seen Gerald carry Erica down to the beach at night and threaten to throw her into the water. The next day, things were the same as ever. No one talked to him about any of this. Everything was secret, secret, like the photographs of Thomas. He remembered lying awake at night convinced that the moonlight on his bedroom wall was in fact a rarer light emanating from the unadmitted presence of Thomas. "Father," he had whispered, and then, terrified at what he had said, at what ghosts he might have called up, he had pulled the blankets tight over his face.

Sometimes he wondered if Erica had ever considered the effect her stories of Thomas had on him, not to mention the effect of her admonitions to repeat these stories to no one, especially not to Gerald. Perhaps she had believed she was talking to herself, her voice merely a ripple of sound, like the sea. Or, he now wondered, were these Thomas-stories designed to increase her own sense of importance in David's eyes? Worse still, they may have been intended to let David and Gerald know that they weren't part of her real life, which had been happily in progress years ago, long before either one of them turned up.

"Thomas and I had only five summers here, but every one was perfect," she had told David. "We were always having people to stay—Thomas's business acquaintances, friends he had made on his travels. We had an old cabin cruiser for awhile, and once we went out fishing, about eight of us in all, and the boat developed a slow leak. We had to stay close to shore. We fished over the side and bailed water and sang campfire songs. You would have liked it, David. I know you would have."

How did she know that? he had wondered. There weren't any children on board the boat, from the sound of it. Nobody would have wanted him along. And yet sometimes he almost believed he had been on that boat, with Thomas at his side demonstrating the best technique for reeling in his fishing line. Thomas shouting over the cacophony of voices, all singing and laughing and exclaiming at the amount of sea water rushing up through the planking on the deck.

ᴏ

Erica phoned Gerald and told him that they had managed to fill three boxes with junk to dispose of. The rest of the house, she said, laughing, resisted all their efforts. They had to give up, for now anyway. After Erica had completed the call, David went with her down to the beach. It was early evening; the sea was flat and dull, the sky was drained of light. Erica said, "Once this place has been sold, Gerald and I are going to take a little vacation. We're going to Maui for a month."

David stopped. "I must have missed something," he said. "I thought you and Gerald weren't living together anymore."

"We're not married anymore, that's true."

"But you're going to Maui?"

"We're good friends. Good friends go on vacation together, don't they?"

"Well, yes. But that's not the point." He paused. He suddenly thought: She's going after Thomas. She'll search for him, in the sky, on the routes that tourists take, crossing and recrossing the same paths, walking in and out of the same airports. Even with Gerald at her side, carrying the luggage, selecting the best seats on the planes, still she will be searching for Thomas. This struck him as a tragic and misleading action on her part, much worse than simply vacationing with an estranged husband. She had never realized the implications of her obsession with Thomas, he thought.

Impulsively he bent down at the water's edge and filled his hands with cold sea water, which he threw at Erica. She laughed uncertainly, brushing drops of water off her hair and the sleeve of her blouse. He threw another handful of water. She tried to run away from him down the beach. He ran after her. When he caught up with her, she began wiping her face with the hem of her skirt. "What's the matter with you?" she cried.

"Nothing," he said. "I'm sorry." He found he was shaking with anger, or remorse. He also felt exhilarated. How would she like to be thrown into the sea? he wondered. He said, "I'm sorry, I'm sorry," and finally Erica looked at him and laughed and said, "Oh, David, you're such a jerk sometimes."

The next day Erica washed windows and David rolled up the rug in the living room and got out the vacuum cleaner. "This time," Erica said, "we're going to get the job done properly." She wanted to finish cleaning up so that she could go home. She wanted to be able to tell Gerald the job was all finished. Oh well, let's not disappoint Gerald, David thought. Let me tell you something, he wanted to say to Erica, I'm going to be living here this time next year, and the year after, and the year after that. He pictured himself a recluse, a lonely figure rarely glimpsed, never leaving the island. Self-sufficient; lonely but prosperous. He would have the verandah replaced with a Mediterranean-style patio; he would add on rooms and re-do the kitchen.

Thomas's painters and builders had done little, all those years ago, to alter the original structure of the summer house, which had been built, the story went, almost entirely out of local materials. David remembered being told that the fir flooring had been cut by a sawmill that had operated years ago on the island and the stones for the fireplace had been quarried here as well. Where the summer house now stood, there had been a hundred-foot tall cedar tree from which the shingles had been hand-split.

The amount of grit on the uncovered floor seemed authentic and ancient as well, he noticed. In with the grit was a glint of colour, which, when he picked it up, turned out to be a small jade heart on a gold chain. He wiped it clean on his shirt and showed it to Erica. The jade was pale, translucent, full of light, like the sea.

"How beautiful," Erica said. "It's not mine. If I'd seen it before, I'm sure I'd remember it." She pulled off the rubber gloves she was wearing to wash the windows and sat down with the jade heart in her hands. Perhaps it was one of Gerald's finds, she said. But that was impossible, he would have shown it to her.

"The missionaries," she said at last. This must be the one thing they didn't manage to take away with them."

"I don't think it could be Chinese, though," David said. "A heart is a western symbol, isn't it?"

"I'm not sure," she said. Then she said, "Think how old it must be. The missionaries might have been walking over it for years without knowing."

Then she said, "They gave us tea. After we had seen the house, and had said that we would like very much to buy it, they served us tea and biscuits. We sat in this room, but of course it didn't look like this room because of all the junk crammed into it, the chairs and the carved chests. The missionaries sat side by side on a large dark-red sofa. They looked the same. That is, they resembled each other. They were both thin, almost emaciated in fact, with white hair and long thin faces. They made a point of taking their tea black, passing each other a plate of lemon slices for flavouring.

Everything they did, even the simplest movements, seemed carefully acquired, foreign. They said, 'We hope you shall be happy in this house.' Then the husband said that in China red was a good colour for happiness, so they liked to have a lot of red. The rug was red, and the teapot, and of course the sofa. Even though the husband had been retired for years, he wore a clerical collar and a black suit."

Erica paused. Then she began to tell him that when she had heard about the air crash, she immediately flew to Switzerland, to Bern, which was the nearest city to the crash site. She was told an investigation had been started, and she kept thinking, as she waited for news, that a mistake had been made. She waited for a telephone call from Thomas to say that he hadn't taken that flight after all. "I was lucky; I had a premonition," he would tell her. After all, he had always flown, and nothing had ever gone wrong. Then, while walking on a street outside her hotel, she had a vision of the missionaries, the Methodists. She saw them clearly, the wife with her hand on the husband's arm as they walked with carefully averted faces past the wreckage of the downed plane. And then she knew; she had been prepared.

"I've never told anyone that story before," she said.

David saw from the way Erica curled her fingers around the jade heart that she intended to transfer all her prior emotions to this trinket. The jade heart was from the past, but it was not quite part of her revealed past. He took it from her and fastened it around her neck.

"How does it look?" she asked.

"It suits you."

"It's cold."

"Jade feels cold at first. It warms up as you wear it."

The room had a slipshod look, like a rough charcoal sketch in which the artist had vented his feelings as quickly as possible. But that was because the curtains were down and the rug was rolled up. David understood two things: One was that the jade heart had not been the property of the missionaries. It had belonged to Erica, and had been given to her not by Thomas, but by Gerald. The other thing he understood was that he didn't care if the summer house was sold. The effort of keeping it, of keeping it for himself, was clearly beyond him. He wasn't like the missionaries, or like Thomas. He wasn't a person of spirit, of spirited determination. He was someone who tried to swim daringly, flamboyantly, and ended up in need of rescue. No wonder Gerald kept pressing psychology books on him.

He went outside and stood directly in front of the Buddha. The Buddha returned his look with an appropriate degree of serenity and fortitude from within his nest of ivy and wild grasses. David tried to evoke the mood of a certain day in 1959, when this benign giant had been uncrated and settled into place. He imagined Thomas energetically overseeing the operation, shouting directions. He tried to catch the sense of hope from that time, the expectation of something wildly different, something sly and funny and also transcendent, a cross between a moral lesson and a great joke. The ground beneath his feet was warm and solid, as yet unexcavated, and the small, bright fish swam elsewhere, unborn, uncorrupted and gloriously unaware of the murky future that awaited them.

The
Etruscans

Over lunch in a small Greek restaurant near the sea, Teddy told Leah about an incident that had occurred at a meeting of his support group. The group was made up of people who were incurably ill. Everyone sat on a cushion on the floor, he said, in a tight circle, practically nose to nose. The cushions were dark green, orange, red. The room was much too warm. The talk was about mothers and fathers who had not, the people in the group felt, loved them in the right way at all. One woman said: "But it is ourselves we have not loved, and now it is too late." For some reason this had struck Teddy as funny; he had laughed, and the woman's feelings had been hurt. "But it was funny," Teddy said to Leah, "wasn't it? 'And now it is too late,'" he repeated, holding his hands up helplessly. "Too late," he said. "Oh, dear."

Leah got up and went to the counter for more coffee and for some baklava, because she had a craving, suddenly, for something sweet. She sensed Teddy watching her, and she imagined how she must appear to him. She was wearing black knit pants, pink warm-up socks, a loose pink shirt. Her hair was cut short and wispy, almost shaved on one side and long on the other. She was nineteen. She had never been aware of her youth before, particularly, or her health, but now, being with Teddy, she was aware of it all the time. When she got back to the table, Teddy was wrestling with the open pages of a newspaper he had finished reading. Leah put down the tray and quickly folded the newspaper and set it aside. That was the only way with Teddy, just do whatever he couldn't do, fast, without comment. "Imagine a lack of self-love as the entire basis of all disease," Teddy was saying. "Is that credible?"

"Here," Leah said. "Have your coffee. Have some baklava. It's delicious."

"No, thank you." He pushed his plate away impatiently; as usual, he had no appetite, and she ended up eating both pieces, licking the syrup slowly off her fingers when she'd finished.

"This is really good," she said. "You should have had some."

"It's bad for you, that kind of stuff," he said. He was smiling. Then he stared out the window at the sea. They sat for awhile longer like that, not talking; then they began the task of getting Teddy into his jacket and out of the restaurant. Leah handed him his cane. A man came out from behind the counter and held the door open for them. "Thanks," Leah said. She held onto Teddy's right arm, and he held onto the rail with his left as they went down the stairs. Everything was grey, a different shade of the same cold grey: the sea, the sky, the gulls. There were whitecaps on the water and way off, near the horizon, a red sail—an astonishing spark of colour, like a flame.

Teddy paused to rest for a moment when they got to the

car. His eyes, Leah noticed, were as grey as the day, and cold, as were his hands when she helped him into the car. The car was Teddy's, a nearly new German model with a tape deck and a sun-roof—the first new car, Teddy had told her, that he had ever owned. Leah drove and Teddy fumbled around with a tape, dropping it and slowly retrieving it from the floor between his feet before finally getting it into the tape deck. Vivaldi. Bach. The hits of 1750. Tea-kettle music, Leah called it, being smart. Music to boil water by. She made these remarks primarily to amuse Teddy. To keep his spirits up, on the boil, so to speak.

When they got back to the house, Teddy fell asleep in an armchair in front of the fireplace. Leah thought about lighting a fire (it was almost summer, but it was cool), but she decided she would only disturb Teddy, so she covered him with a quilt that had been left on the sofa. She tiptoed into the kitchen and sat down with a pile of cookbooks to see what she could come up with for dinner. Until a few months ago, she hadn't been at all interested in cooking, but now it seemed to be all she thought about, as if by producing a steady diet of wholesome foods she could cure Teddy, or at least keep him from getting worse.

Teddy had told her that he had a disease that was causing his muscles to waste away. Eventually, he said, he would be paralyzed. The course of the disease was unpredictable, but it was always fatal. He was forty-six years old. He would, he said, try to resist lamenting the unattainable future. But then, he added, in lots of ways the only age worth being was the age Leah was now.

"Oh, no," Leah had said, "I hate the age I am now."

"Nonsense," he had replied. He wanted to hear about her

74

friends, her interests, the kind of music she liked, what her politics were.

"I have no politics whatsoever," she said.

Then he touched her hair lightly. "Is that what they call punk?"

"I guess so," she said, putting up her hands to cover her head. "I don't know. I'm not sure. I'm kind of away from all that stuff right now."

"And what kind of music do punks listen to?"

"I told you," she said, "I really don't know. It used to be groups like The Sex Pistols. Only they're kind of out of date, I think. I don't know, I get mixed up between punk and heavy metal, I don't know which is which."

Teddy nodded. "And do you and your friends do drugs, Leah?"

"Of course not," she said, shocked.

"Oh, well. Drugs were not completely unknown to my generation, you know. At the odd party. Back in the sixties."

"The sixties," Leah had said, delighted. "I love the sixties. That's my favourite time. I was born in the sixties."

"Don't tell me," he said. "Please."

ᴑ

Before she began working for Teddy, Leah was in her second year at the university. Her home town was miles away, up the coast, so she was renting a housekeeping room on the third floor of an old house on a bus route to the campus. The other tenants were all old people, and they seemed, to Leah, to be composed of some ectoplasmic substance that caused them to appear and disappear against their wills on the stairs

and in the long, dark halls. At night Leah heard them coughing and shuffling past her door on their way to use the shared
bathroom. Leah ate sardines on toast while she sat cross-
legged on her bed studying. She had absolutely no idea what
she wanted to do with her life. Alice, an old lady in the room
across the hall, made cushions to pass the time, and one day
she gave Leah a smocked pink velvet cushion. Leah kept it on
her bed, a constant reminder: Philosophy, art history, psychology, and English literature had no significance whatsoever beside the fact that in fifty years she might be Alice, living
alone on the top floor of an old rooming house.

At the beginning of the second semester, Leah came down
with the flu, which turned into bronchitis; at the same time
she broke up with her boyfriend, Tim, who was practically
the only person her age she ever saw outside of her classes.
In truth, she didn't break up with him; he broke up with her.
He was a commerce student, as was almost everyone else she
knew. She often wished she'd gone to university in the
sixties, when students had been into peace and love. Sit-ins.
Students for a Democratic Society, hippies and yippies,
flower children. Tim belonged to the Young Conservatives,
and at one of their meetings, he had met a girl he evidently
liked better than he liked Leah. "Basically, she's more my
type," he told her.

"I understand," she said, coughing. She was taking antibi-
otics and coughing all night, just like the spooky ectoplasmic
forms on the third floor.

Then she had a dream in which she quit all her classes,
and she felt so good when she woke up, that she went
immediately to the university and withdrew. It was early
enough in the semester to get part of her tuition refunded,

and she took the refund and bought herself a red leather jacket, very supple and light, with a yoke and cuffed sleeves. The jacket made her feel thin and powerful. She walked around her room wearing it and thinking how small her needs were, how easily satisfied. All she really needed out of life, she thought, was a job, even a part-time job, enough money to live on. She sat on her bed crushing the smocked velvet cushion in her arms and listening to her Sony Walkman late into the night. She seemed to be balanced on a fine point in space and time, from which she could fall into either peace or disaster. Disaster would be going home, or going back to school. She hoped for peace, serenity, maturity.

Teddy would choose a book, and then Leah would read aloud while he lay under a quilt on the couch. The current book was a thick, weighty volume that laboriously traced the rise of western civilization from what one reviewer referred to, on the jacket, as "the mists of antiquity." The book began with the cave-dwellers, who had evidently kept dogs and fished for trout from the banks of quiet, reedy rivers. They were followed by the Sumerians, who were favourites of Teddy's because of their light-hearted, boisterous approach to life. At least, that was what he said. He evidently preferred to believe that all Sumerians were perpetually nineteen years of age, especially Gilgamesh, who was Teddy's favourite mythological hero. "I see him as exuberant and kind of dumb," he said. "What about you?"

"Yeah, me too," Leah said. She balanced the spine of the book on her knees. The book was so heavy it was making her arms ache. They were now long past the Sumerians. "The Etruscans," she read, "were an aristocratic, pleasure-loving people." She continued reading on about how the Etruscan nobles dressed themselves in purple-and-white togas and sat in chairs carved out of ivory. Wherever the nobles went, they were accompanied by stout guards who carried axes to signify their power over life and death.

Leah paused. She read silently ahead in the book. It was three-thirty in the afternoon, the time when she usually stopped whatever else she was doing to make tea. Teddy loved a cup of Earl Grey at this time; he said it carried him through. She was trying to edit as she read. She skipped several paragraphs on how the Etruscans built cities in which to house their dead, cities where they worshipped and made sacrifices and danced on the graves. Instead she read about how the Etruscans believed they could foretell the future by studying the flight patterns of birds. She pictured thin, white, sharp-beaked birds with fringed wings gliding above an intensely blue and placid sea. She said, "I wonder if any birds would do, or if they had to be a specific kind. I mean, you'd get a different future from watching crows, say, than from watching eagles or peregrine falcons, wouldn't you?" She found her place on the page and read, "The Etruscans were an exceedingly handsome and vibrant people. They loved to surround themselves with beautiful wall paintings and finely crafted vases and bowls."

Teddy, who was familiar with the book, said, "You've skipped the part about the cult of the dead, haven't you?"

Leah closed the book. "If I read every single word, it would take a hundred years."

"Hardly, Leah. I particularly like the Etruscan cult of the

dead. I like to think of a people who believed so firmly in their own immortality that they were not afraid to dance on the graves of their dead. I like to think of myself sharing in that mood of sublimely deluded optimism. Just think: It is night in Etruria, and the law courts and the marketplace are shut, and there am I, dancing on top of a dear departed relative, my purple-and-white toga flying. Makes a damn nice picture, doesn't it?" Teddy closed his eyes. He was wearing a blue sweater, and he had the quilt drawn up over him; an old-fashioned quilt stitched to resemble stars on a dark blue night sky. His hands were folded on top of the quilt, the fingers of his right hand drawn up, as a result of the disease, like the claws of a bird.

Leah put the book down on the coffee table. "I'm going to make tea," she said and went into the kitchen, where she filled the kettle at the sink in a sort of numbed trance. Sometimes just being around Teddy, just talking to him, wore her out. While she waited for the kettle to boil, she examined her reflection in the oven's black glass door. She teased the ends of her hair with her fingers. She wondered if she should change her style, try something more subtle, more well-groomed in appearance. Possibly she was beyond the age for punk; possibly punk was right out of style anyway. She didn't even know what was in style and what wasn't, she was so out of touch.

Once, Teddy had asked her, "What do you do when you're not here? Do you go out with young men? Is there anyone special? Do you go to, say, dances? Nightclubs? Do you go walking in the park with your beaux?"

"My beaux?" Leah said, rinsing a plate under the tap. "Are you kidding?" She was thinking of Tim, her Conservative defector, and a cold January night driving around in his sports car, an old TR7, with the top down. That, she now realized, was probably how she caught the flu. Tim had parked on the side of a mountain, at a scenic viewpoint overlooking the lights of the city, and had kissed her several times before telling her he believed the magic was missing from their relationship. When she got back to her place, frozen, she encountered Alice, the cushion-lady, in a corner of the third floor hall. Alice's watery dark eyes had shone, her skin had phosphoresced white and sickly green in the instant before she melted into the gloom of the bathroom doorway. Minutes later, Leah, getting into her pyjamas, heard the toilet flush, the floorboards rippling and crackling under Alice's slippered feet.

What she had said, finally, in answer to Teddy's questions was: "Oh, I do some of those things I guess." She then turned on the dishwasher in the quick, competent manner she had lately developed.

Teddy didn't always want to be read to; sometimes he wanted Leah to drive him around, so that they could look at houses, trees, gardens, the sea, anything. They lived in a city renowned for its beauty; the scenic routes were mapped out for motorists by means of painted dots on the road surface. One day Leah followed these dots out to the university campus. "Oh, God, I hated it here," Leah said. By this time, she had told Teddy about Tim and how she had suddenly decided to quit school. "Over a boy, you quit school?" he had said, horrified, and Leah had said, "No, it wasn't like that." "You'll go back some day," Teddy kept telling her. "Never," Leah said.

Teddy had once been a student at this same university; he had a degree in science; he was a biologist and an artist, and had worked, up until recently, as a medical illustrator. He was on a leave-of-absence, as if he fully expected, in spite of what he knew about his health, to return to work someday. Leah found it strange to think that when Teddy had been a student here, she hadn't even been born yet. She wished she had been young when Teddy was young; she was sure she would have enjoyed life more. If she'd had friends like Teddy when she was in school, there wouldn't have been a problem, she wouldn't have quit.

Teddy was still friends with someone from his university days, a woman named Nancy, who came to see him regularly. Nancy always talked about the old days at school with Teddy. Do you remember Mike and Dorothy? she would say. Do you know what I heard about so and so? Leah could hear Nancy's voice clearly as she worked in the kitchen, getting dinner ready.

The thing about Nancy was, she kept turning up unannounced, usually at dinner time, with food from a deli. She would march into the kitchen, where she would glance at the salad, or soup, or casserole, or whatever Leah happened to be preparing, and she would say, "Well, that can go in the fridge for tomorrow, can't it?" And Leah would immediately be furious; she would think, Oh, she's treating me like a servant, like an idiot, just to put me in my place. She always felt like dumping the food she was preparing into the garbage can and saying, If that's what you want, Nancy, fine, fine.

She constantly had to remind herself that Nancy was a friend of Teddy's, because she and Nancy had a way of circling each other like territorial beasts contemplating a

81

good fight. The territory they wished to fight over was, of course, Teddy. Which one of them did he like best? Which one of them was the most help to him? Who provided the best care? Who, for that matter, cared the most? These questions were never voiced, and in any case they had no answers, but still Leah thought, I'm the best one to be around Teddy, I'm young, I cheer him up, he likes me. Even though she had known Teddy for only a short time, she had developed the most amazing sense of loyalty—she would do anything for him; she was absolutely dedicated. She believed this to be true.

Nancy had short glossy brown hair, a wide mouth, blue eyes—an optimistic face, always on the lookout for nice things, nice people, the best in everyone. She wore the kind of clothes Leah could not, personally, tolerate: neat white collars, angora sweaters, plaid skirts, even, sometimes, to Leah's dismay, woolly knee socks. Nancy had been married but was now on her own. Perhaps there had been a divorce. Leah suspected that a romance had been developing between Nancy and Teddy and that now Nancy was not sure how to proceed. The situation had changed, obviously. When Nancy arrived she would say, "Oh, Leah, you go on home, I can manage here." She would unpack the stuff from the deli, then start opening drawers and cupboards, searching for serving spoons and napkins, and all the time she would look distracted and anxious. Even though she had told Leah to go, she seemed to want something from her, some kind of direction. But what could Leah possibly give Nancy, what kind of information or advice? She had nothing to give Nancy. She would just leave, as Nancy had told her to, and go home and take her yoghurt and an apple out of the communal fridge in the third-floor hall, or else boil an egg on the hotplate in her room. Sometimes, she wouldn't even bother eating; she would read, or listen to a rock station on her Sony Walkman, something mindless to pass the time.

✎

After leaving the university campus, Leah drove Teddy out to a small municipal park that separated a new housing development from an old farming community. She parked in the shade of a tree, and she and Teddy got out of the car. They walked a short distance along a footpath, then sat on a bench in the shade of a weeping willow. It was getting to be late summer, and the air had a heavy, golden quality, like the state of rest just before sleep. The summer had been unusually hot and dry; the leaves were already turning, and a large number of conifers were going brown from the top down— actually dying from lack of moisture. Teddy told her that at first, observing this phenomenon, he had been afraid that he had somehow externalized and objectified his own inward state of decay, thus inadvertently causing the deaths of all these trees. "What an absurd way to think," he said, and yet, he had been taken over by the thought; it had occupied his mind for days. Now, he said, it was a relief to talk about it.

Leah was upset by this; she couldn't believe he would allow himself to have such macabre thoughts. That's a terrible thing to do, to blame yourself, she wanted to say. But all she did say, finally, was, "Nah, it isn't you. It's just a drought."

And then a woman appeared, on the footpath in front of them, with a dog on a leash. She bent down and took the dog off its leash, then instructed it to sit while she walked a few steps away and turned back to face it. The woman had a blunt, angry-looking face and a blue rose tattooed on the solid flesh of her upper arm. She didn't look like anyone Leah would want to know, but Leah liked the dog, which was small and brown with white patches, and had a mild, hopeful expression. It whined softly and the woman said, "Shut up. Stay. Move and I'll smack you." She shook her fist as she spoke and snapped the leash in the air like a whip. The dog flinched. "Stupid," she shrieked. All the time she was shouting at her dog, she didn't glance once at Leah and Teddy who were at most three feet away. Then she went back to the dog, clipped the leash onto its collar, and tugged him roughly after her down the footpath.

Leah was outraged. She wanted to run after the woman and take the dog away from her, by force if necessary. She wanted to offer to buy the dog. Teddy said, "No, you can't do that. You've just discovered a painful truth—the world is full of pain, and there isn't a thing you can do about it. That's how it is. It's absurd, but life is absurd." He kept lecturing her, breathlessly, on the absurdity of life until she began to think he was enjoying himself, that he liked making her feel depressed. She started to walk back to the car alone. Let Teddy help himself for once, she thought angrily. Everything looked awful to her: the park, the sky, the willow tree, even the farms in the distance, the fields, the weathered barns, the overgrown blackberry hedges. She waited beside the car for him; then, when he finally made it, she gave him a hand to get in and slammed his door shut, hard. Even though she had parked in the shade, the heat in the car was stifling. As soon as she got in, she rolled down the windows.

"Let's have some music," Teddy said. "Something by the

Sex Pistols would be appropriate, wouldn't it?" For a moment, Leah didn't know what he meant; then she thought, Oh yeah, nihilism, anarchy, absurdity. Teddy's new creed. She wanted to tell him he was bitter and he was wrong, but she kept her mouth shut; she kept her thoughts to herself. All the way home, she drove very carefully, paying unusual attention to the exact amount of pressure her foot applied to the gas and the brake pedals, slowing down well before intersections. She was negotiating a safe passage, she believed, between high walls piled with dangers of all kinds. She thought Teddy would probably fire her now for being bad-tempered and rude. But when they got home, he didn't say a word. He was exhausted and went to lie down in his room, with the blind down and the curtains closed.

Leah went into the kitchen and took a cookbook down from a shelf above the stove. Sometimes she had a hard time thinking of something to make for dinner, especially on a day like this, hot and sticky, and with Teddy probably too tired to eat. She came upon a slip of paper in the cookbook, on which someone had printed out by hand a recipe for cauliflower with yoghurt and spices: mustard seeds, cumin, chili powder and turmeric. As she read the recipe, she became convinced it belonged to Nancy, who claimed to enjoy trying different and slightly exotic recipes, although so far all Leah had seen was the prepared food from the delicatessen. She tried to imagine Nancy walking into the kitchen hot and dishevelled, with a bag of greasy, warm potato salad. Leah would show her the ethereally pale cauliflower floating in its spiced, chilled sauce, and Nancy, overcome, would say: Ah, Leah, you are good to Teddy; you are the best thing that could ever have happened to him. In such dreams, Leah thought, absurdity was vanquished and the world was made over.

∽

Teddy's support group had been encouraged to visualize disease, to locate its position in their bodies, and then to draw or paint what they saw. The drawing and painting part was easy, even enjoyable, for Teddy after twenty years spent drawing cross-sections of the pancreas, as he put it. He had given up his work completely some months ago, but he could still draw, using his left hand most of the time because it was stronger than the right and less unsteady. Marginally so, but it made a difference. His lines wobbled, he said, but sometimes that made for an interesting effect. He showed Leah three paintings he had done for the group: fantastical, delicate images of the central nervous system branching out from the stem of an iridescent, violet-coloured brain and from a spine constructed of small, knobbly skulls. Leah said, "Oh, they're beautiful paintings," but she wasn't sure—the skull-like vertebrae made her feel slightly sick. She believed she could see disease in these paintings; she could almost touch it; she had to look away.

In his group, Teddy said, they were told to get angry at their illnesses; they were told to yell and rage and shout abuse, because this was thought to be highly therapeutic: It was a way of taking charge. But so far, he hadn't been able to manage it—he felt foolish even thinking about it. He was not the kind of person who got angry, or, if he did get angry, he certainly didn't show it. In fact, he had more often been accused of being far too reticent, emotionally. Leah, hearing this, knew at once that this accusation had come from Nancy. She could hear Nancy saying it in her quiet, determined way, in the same voice she used to send Leah home early so she could have Teddy to herself.

Now, Leah said to him, "You have to get angry." She wanted to shake him. She wanted to say, You're stupid not to do what they tell you. They were standing in the middle of one of the spare bedrooms, where Teddy had a drafting table set up, with desk lamps and coloured pencils and paints neatly at hand. The room was very clean, swept-out; unused. Virginia creeper had made its way along the outside wall of the house and over the window. In the fall, it had burned a brilliant red, like fire, but only briefly, and now all the leaves had fallen off. It was November, and it had started to rain again, and the rain and wind had stripped the dying conifers of their dry, dead needles. But there was hope in the rain, Leah thought; she preferred autumn to summer, partly because the summer had been too hard on Teddy. In the summer, people were all over the place being visibly active and healthy, but now, thank goodness, they had all gone indoors and the world was a quieter, slower place. "You have to get angry," she said to Teddy again, "if that's what they tell you to do. You should try everything, you shouldn't give in." As soon as she said this, she believed it passionately.

"Leah, my dear," he said. "There are no cures. There is no recovery possible, in my case. Why should I waste my time being angry?" He went over to the window and tapped at a tendril of the Virginia creeper though the glass. The vine, caught by a slight wind, tapped back. He began to talk about the group, how he didn't fully understand his reason for continuing to attend the sessions. It wasn't really his kind of thing, he said; in a way, you had to believe in miracles to belong. You had to believe in the miraculous power of love, and he didn't; he never had. The group was pointless, and what was more, it sometimes bordered on the offensive. Well, consider this: The group leader, who referred to herself as the facilitator, which was in itself a term he objected to, quite strenuously as a matter of fact, talked the most dreadful jargon and read endless passages from books that were drippy and sentimental in the extreme. Love yourself, the books said. Be good to yourself; you are a special person. Well, so what, really? However, in spite of all this extraneous non-sense, something attracted him; something kept him going back for more; there was a certain amount of warmth, of shared warmth—owing, no doubt, to the fact that all the people there were in the same predicament—that he would miss if he quit going.

"Oh, I'm glad you're not quitting," Leah said. "Good for you. I mean, I do think it's good for you to go."

"Oh, you do, do you?"

She did think it was good for Teddy. She also enjoyed driving him to his group, which met on Thursday afternoons at one-thirty in an annex to the hospital. The annex was on a side street, in an area of specialty shops: antique stores and tea shops and bookstores, all with fake half-timbering and small leaded-glass windows. Leah liked to walk around win-dow-shopping, while she waited for Teddy.

One day, she came across a store that sold old records from the fifties and sixties, and she went in and bought a copy of *Sgt. Pepper's Lonely Hearts Club Band*. She wanted to study the album cover because she had heard that its designer had cleverly incorporated clues which revealed that one of the

Beatles, Paul, she thought, had died. He had not died, of course, but the album seemed to Leah evidence of a great lightness of spirit which had characterized the times but which had since disappeared. It was, she thought, like the Etruscans, who had merrily hitched up their togas and danced on the graves of their dead. These moments came and went, she imagined, and then were forgotten, covered over with decades of seriousness and an absorption with mundane matters like finance and politics; no one really sang, no one really danced. The dead slept, quiet and alone among their cold white bones, listening to the wind strip the leaves from the trees.

In October, Nancy had come to see Teddy with what she called an absolutely marvellous plan, which was that she would take him with her on a two-week vacation to Barbados. She had been to a travel agency, and she had picked up a handful of brochures. She dumped them in Teddy's lap, where they instantly displaced the starry night sky of the hand-stitched quilt. Leah, watching this, felt despair. How could Nancy even consider taking Teddy to Barbados? He was weaker than ever. He could scarcely walk across the room, even with the cane. Nancy was practising self-delusion, obviously, for reasons of her own. And Leah was powerless; all she could do from the doorway was silently urge, Don't go, don't go. She felt completely at a loss, as if a decision had already been made, as if she had already said goodbye to Teddy and Nancy at the airport. She felt desolate, worse even than when Tim had broken up with her, worse than in her first days alone with the ectoplasmic forms in her rooming house.

In this state, she had gone back to the store where she'd bought her jacket, and she bought an expensive skirt of the same wonderful, soft red leather. The skirt had its own leather belt and came to about mid-thigh. She loved it; it was absolutely unlike anything else she owned. She had worn it with the jacket and a black sweater and black stockings to work the next day, and when she walked in, Teddy took one look and said, "Good Lord."

"Don't you like it?"

"It barely exists."

"It cost enough to exist," she said, but of course, she realized at once that she was supposed to be the person who read aloud from books of ancient history. She got paid for being here. The skirt was provocative and completely unsuitable. She hung her jacket in the hall closet and went into the kitchen. She could always go back to her place and change, she thought, embarrassed and upset. Didn't she have any sense whatsoever? But then, when she took Teddy his breakfast, a poached egg on toast with tea, he said that since she was all dressed up, they might as well go out for a drive.

By this time, Teddy was having a lot of trouble with things like doing up his shoelaces, and so when they were getting ready to go out, she had to bend down to tie up his shoes. But her new skirt wasn't designed for bending. "It's all right," Teddy said impatiently as she tugged and pulled, trying to remain decent. "I'll close my eyes," he said. She knew he hated having his shoelaces done up for him, and everything she was doing was making it worse. "I'm sorry," she kept saying. "I'm sorry." I can't cope with this, she thought, close to tears. Then she told herself it was all right, she didn't care, she just didn't care: It was her skirt, it was her money, it was her taste in fashion. She had to be tougher, she told herself. Teddy was tough. Even though he was ill, he was tough. He couldn't be touched; he was inviolate. No doubt Nancy knew this about him—it was probably why they hadn't got married, Leah now believed.

Once again they drove the scenic route towards the university, past gracious old houses and golf courses and the sea. The sight made her think again of Nancy; of Nancy and her great enthusiasms, her travel brochures, her ability to possess and take over things as removed and as distant as mountain ranges or exotic island countries with palm trees and white sand beaches.

Teddy, reclining in the passenger seat beside her, had turned his head slightly to look out the window. How could she have thought, even for a moment, that he was tough? This was how he would be on the plane travelling to Barbados with Nancy: utterly listless, apathetic, barely registering events outside himself. The plane, like this car, would simply function as a carapace containing and protecting his weakened body and will.

When he had hired her, Teddy had said, "Now, I want you to understand that this is, so to speak, a limited assignment." This phrase, "a limited assignment," had seemed to Leah unbearably sophisticated. She imagined herself running into Tim, meeting him accidently on the street and telling him she had a job, an incredibly easy job, reading aloud, driving a new car. Then she would say coolly, enigmatically, It's a limited assignment.

What Teddy had meant, he later made clear, was that at some point his condition would worsen, and he would need a nurse, or he would have to go into a hospital. When either one of these things happened, Leah would of course not be needed everyday. If she had the time, she could come once or twice a week and read to him. For which he would pay her, of course. But by then he hoped she would have other things to do. By then, he said, she would no doubt be getting on with her life. He said this very heartily, like a parent encouraging a backward child.

One damp October evening, Leah came back to her room to find Alice waiting for her at the top of the stairs. Alice, who was so tiny she barely came to Leah's shoulder, pointed to the open door of her room. "Go on in. Go on," she said, shooing Leah along in front of her. As soon as they were inside, Alice shut the door firmly behind them. Alice's room was only slightly larger than Leah's, and it was crammed with furniture: a bed, armchairs, shelves, coffee tables. There were at least five cushions on every surface, each one different; embroidered, smocked or quilted; velvet, cotton, satin. Alice smoothed a cloth over a gate-legged table near the window. She had a pot of her own home-made soup simmering on her hotplate. "Now sit down," she said. "This soup is for you, especially for you." Obviously Leah needed feeding up, she was far too thin, a bonerack. Leah was wearing her red leather skirt, and Alice said, "Well, you need to be thin to wear a skirt like that, don't you?" But there was no point in starving. Where had Leah got the skirt? she wanted to know. She had been infatuated with clothes at one time herself, she said. Now she didn't bother so much.

Alice had emphysema, she said. She didn't get out of the house anymore. Of course, the worst place in the world for her to live was up here on the third floor. All those stairs; she nearly died every time she came up them. The doctors told her, get exercise, but how could she get exercise when she couldn't even breathe? She stopped talking in order to cough, pressing her hand to her mouth, rolling her eyes at Leah until she had caught her breath. Then she ladled out a bowl of soup and set it down in front of Leah. Bits of chicken, barley, carrot and onion, she said; everything good for you, and fresh. She sat down across from Leah, her legs crossed, her skinny arms draped like ribbons across the front of her purple satin housecoat. Her hair was dyed a frail strawberry blonde, and her eyebrows were white. She took a pack of cigarettes out of her housecoat pocket and tapped one out into her hand. She lit up slowly, waving the match in the air like a wand. She inhaled, coughed, rubbed her eyes and began again to talk.

She had been a dancer and a teacher of dance; she had nearly married a man who became an ambassador to some very nice places, countries it would have been a sheer joy to live in. The greatest pleasure in her life now was reading murder mysteries from the public library. Believe it or not, she had written a murder mystery, published years ago, under a pseudonym that she invented from a combination of the names of her great-grandmothers. "Women are tougher than men," she said to Leah. "Isn't that the truth?" Leah was trying to eat the soup, but it was barely warm and tasted odd, as if Alice had thrown in a leaf or two from a house-plant, or half a bottle of cheap perfume. "Eat up," Alice kept saying, grinning and nodding her head and blowing smoke through her nostrils. "It's good for you, it's full of nutrition."

After that, Alice always seemed to be waiting for Leah at the top of the stairs when she came home. Leah would hide on the second-floor landing, hoping that Alice would give up and go back into her own room. The thought of seeing Alice, of having to talk to her, made Leah feel horribly depressed. She wanted to get into her room so that she could lie down on her bed and stare at the ceiling and think about how awful her day had been. Teddy was getting worse, as far as she could see. A nurse and a physiotherapist came to the house twice a week. While they were with Teddy, Leah would sit at the kitchen table going through cookbooks, staring unseeingly at pictures of leaf lettuce and red cabbage and loaves of bread in wicker baskets, and wondering how much more she could take. Sometimes Nancy was there, and they sat together, in silence, on edge, listening and at the same time trying not to listen to the cheerful professional voices down the hall. The last thing Leah needed after a day like this was Alice's company. What she needed was the company of healthy people her own age, but there didn't seem to be any left in the world, at least not in the part of the world she now inhabited. She thought longingly, even tenderly, of Tim. She thought of his youth, his nice clothes, his sports car, his uncritical acceptance of everything conservative and, in his opinion, safe, secure, tested. What was wrong with that? she now wondered. You had to get through life somehow. Even Nancy seemed young to her now, or at least healthy, amazingly, wonderfully healthy, all shining eyes and glossy hair and strong, sure movements, someone in whom the illusion, at least, of reality was firmly and reassuringly fixed.

∽

Leah sat in Teddy's living room, the history book open on her lap. Teddy was lying on the couch, staring out the window at a flock of small black-capped birds eating cedar berries in a tree near the house. The sky was flat and slate-grey. It was November; it was cold enough to snow. They had reached the early Middle Ages in the history book: the Visigoths, the Ostrogoths, the Jutes, Angles, Burgundians. Migrations all over the place. The maps in this section, indicating retreats of the Huns and advances of the Khazars and Bulgars, reminded her of Teddy's drawings of his afflicted nervous system—curved lines swooping down across Europe from the Steppes, incursions and displacements. They struck her as awful anyway, the Middle Ages. It must always have been cold November in the Middle Ages. She pictured fields of snow and black-robed monks staggering up hillsides, taking manuscripts and art treasures off for safekeeping in the monasteries. The monks had preserved knowledge; they had preserved civilization, the history book said. And what had they preserved it from? From absurdity, Teddy said. From the awful truth about life. And who was going to keep knowledge and civilization safe in the present age? On the whole, Teddy said, he was getting tired of history. He would have to give some thought to what he would like Leah to read next. Geology, perhaps. The true hideous facts behind earthquakes, volcanos, subsidences deep under the earth's crust. "Wouldn't that be fun?"

"Whatever you say," Leah said, closing the book and getting up to put the kettle on for tea. She had that strange sensation again, of being balanced on a fine point, of being about to topple from a high place. This time, she felt, she would be sure to fall into disaster, not peace. She had no choice: It was the way things were going. That night, when she was alone in her room, she took a pair of scissors to her hair and made it even on both sides, and very short. Now she had a new look, definitely not punk. She looked like a skinned rabbit, a head with no hair. She lifted the ragged ends gently with her fingers. It'll grow back, she told herself. All it takes is time.

The next morning small, dry flakes of snow were drifting out of a flat, grey sky. The snow, cold and silent, felt strangely personal to her, something that had sprung up in nature directly out of her own emotional state, like Teddy's dying conifer trees. By the time she got to Teddy's, her face felt frozen. The house looked deserted; the curtains were still drawn and none of the lights had been turned on. She unlocked the door, went in and turned up the furnace and put the coffee pot on. Only then did she go down the hall and knock on Teddy's bedroom door. "Ready for breakfast?" she asked through the door.

"I'm dying," she heard him say.

"What do you mean?" Her mouth had gone dry; she could hardly speak.

"My arms and legs have fallen off. I'm a limbless torso, a mind without a body."

96

She was so relieved by his tone that she had to lean against the wall for support. "Ah," she said. "You just need a cup of coffee. Did you know it's snowing? Little fine powdery flakes."

"Oh, Christ," he said. "I don't want to know."

She went into the kitchen and began breaking eggs into a bowl for an omelette. She put two slices of bread into the toaster. Outside, the day appeared to have been swallowed by a bank of blue-black clouds, out of which snow was issuing faster and faster. The leafless Virginia creeper was outlined in white; the yew trees wore white hats. Later, after Teddy had finished his breakfast, the little he ate of it, and she had cleaned up, she took some breadcrumbs out for the birds. They were the same small black-capped birds that had been hopping around in the cedar tree yesterday. Teddy called them snowbirds; he said they always arrived with the first cold weather. She threw the crumbs into the air, letting them fall all over. She held her face up, her eyes closed, feeling the snow on her eyelids, her lips. When she opened her eyes, she saw Nancy coming down the driveway with an open umbrella held over her head. Only Nancy would use an umbrella in the snow, Leah thought. "Look what I've got," Nancy said. She put her hand into her shoulder bag and pulled out a cardboard folder. "The tickets," she said, beaming. "Air tickets. To Barbados." She waved the gold folder in Leah's face.

"Oh," Leah said.

"Now," Nancy said, putting the gold folder back in her bag, "we're going to have to be really positive about this. We're going to have to say, Teddy, you can do this. Otherwise, he'll think he can't go. He'll give up on the idea. You'll help, won't you, Leah?"

97

"Yeah," Leah said, scattering breadcrumbs on the surface of the snow. The black-capped birds had flown away, and only two crows up on a hydro line showed any interest in the crumbs. When Nancy started to go up the back steps to the kitchen door, Leah called after her. "Wait a minute," she said. She had to brush her hand across her face, to remove flakes of snow from her eyelashes, so that she could see properly.

"What is it?" Nancy said impatiently, her hand on the doorknob. She wanted to go in and see Teddy and then eat her lunch; she was on her lunch break, and she had gone to the travel agency to pick up the tickets. Nancy worked in the library at the university, which, she liked to say, was in absolute chaos, everyone studying for finals and doing their term papers. Last year at this time, Leah had also been in the library studying for her finals, but this was a whole year later and now she was here, a security guard deciding who could and who couldn't go inside Teddy's house. Not that she really had that power; she didn't; she had no power.

"It's all right, it's nothing," Leah said, and Nancy opened the door and went into the house.

Once, while Leah was reading to Teddy from a thin, worn copy of Lawrence's *Etruscan Places*, Teddy had said, "It is dangerous to think too much of the Etruscans." Not dangerous for him, but dangerous for Leah; she should put the Etruscans out of her mind.

"What do you mean?" she asked, but even before he spoke she knew what he meant: D. H. Lawrence was a very sick man when he wrote *Etruscan Places*, he knew he was soon going to die. Teddy pointed this out, but needlessly—she had already felt the knowledge rampant in the pages, in Lawrence's exasperation with the present and with the people and places he had encountered in his stay in Italy. Only the Etruscans, the distant but still vibrant memory of the Etruscans, had given him any kind of comfort at all. According to Teddy, the Etruscans exerted a sort of pull, a fascination for people who, like him, did not expect to reach old age.

"You see," said Teddy, "the Etruscans did not make such a distinction between the living and the dead. Some sort of commerce continued to exist between those who were alive and those who were not. There was no fear, only the knowledge of this strange and vital commerce," he said. And that was the reason for those cities, those wonderful cities where the living danced for joy and the dead were not excluded or left out.

Leah barely resisted a desire to throw the book on the floor, to get it out of her hands; its thin, dry pages abraded her skin; she couldn't stand it. Then Teddy said, "Well, that's enough reading for one day, don't you think?"

The snowbirds returned; they settled on the ground and began pecking furiously at the breadcrumbs. Then they rose all at once into the air, then settled again, then flew away. The Etruscans were taking note; they were preparing their predictions based on careful observations of these birds and countless others. The birds flew south; they soared above the blue Mediterranean. They sang in olive trees; in fig trees. What had they learned, the Etruscans? Only that like the birds they were free to come and go as they pleased, for a time. Not forever, but for a time. "Are we not as beautiful as the Etruscans?" Teddy had asked. "Are we not as fine, and as fair?"

"Yes," Leah had said, laughing. "Yes, we are. Of course we are."

∽

When Leah went into the house, Nancy was taking the gold folder out of her bag. She put it down on the table. She had put the kettle on already, and it was just coming to a boil. Leah unplugged it and filled the teapot. "Haven't you told Teddy you're here yet?" Leah said. "He didn't get up this morning, because of the snow. He'll be glad to see you."

"Oh, you tell him," said Nancy, suddenly very offhand. She got up and took the milk out of the fridge. "I'll finish making the tea, shall I?" Then she looked more closely at Leah and said, "You got your hair cut. It looks nice."

"No," said Leah. "It looks awful. I cut it too short."

"No, no," said Nancy. "It suits you." She put the kettle down and took a deep breath. The snow fell faster, in a fury, as if determined to obliterate both the earth and the light of the day as quickly as possible. Leah realized that she and Nancy were both staring at the folder on the table. It was so bright, the brightest object in the room, and also, of course, the most foolish. Nancy let her breath out and placed her hands on the side of the teapot, as if to warm them. "What shall I do?" she said. "What shall I do?" She was speaking more to herself than to Leah, it seemed. Outside, the snow was falling and the light was even fainter, and this time it seemed that the little snowbirds had flown away for good.

Visible
Light

I

One summer a young woman living near a small town in the southwest corner of Saskatchewan made this claim: that she had been lifted bodily from her bed by an unseen force and carried feet-first through her open bedroom window. She then floated, as if she were still asleep and dreaming, across her backyard and her vegetable garden, where already, due to the heat and drought, lettuce, radishes, and Swiss chard were going to seed, and was lifted, her heels actually brushing the topmost leaves on the apple trees, into a spinning circle of light. Her arms and legs tingled as if the light carried with it an electric charge, and in the back of her throat she tasted something metallic, like zinc. Her muscles seemed to be paralyzed; she had no power of her own. A wind tore at her hair and nightgown. All she could think of was that her three children were alone in the house far below her. Then an opening appeared inside the light, and she heard the powerful throbbing of a motor. This kind of thing does not happen to people like me, she thought. This is nothing I would ever dream. Ever.

Later, making a formal statement to the authorities, the woman said: "My name is Loretta Hanes. That night, I really do believe I was in the control of an alien power. I mean, I could still think, my mind was still my own, but I couldn't move or speak. I went inside this huge spaceship and found myself alone in a circular room that reminded me, in a way, of a room in a hospital. Everything was so white. I was lying on a sort of table, or bed, I don't quite know how to describe it, and I kept telling myself, Wake up, Loretta. If I could only get hold of myself, I thought. Then two men came in and stood over me. They wore white; their heads and faces were covered in helmet-like things. They began pressing instruments to my forehead, my throat, my chest. Now the taste of zinc was stronger than ever in my throat, as if I had been given some kind of drug or anesthetic. I felt panicky. The more I thought about it, the more certain I was that I really had been drugged. Then I thought, What difference does it make? I'm not going anywhere.

"These two men—I thought of them as men, although they could have been women, they could have been anything—averted their faces and seemed to consult with each other, although I heard no sounds. I could not see their eyes or even tell if they had eyes. They wore close-fitting helmets, with silver windows where the eyes were supposed to be, and gloves which felt cold and dry on my skin. I felt like saying, This is not Hallowe'en."

Loretta Hanes, in her report, went on to describe how a small amount of blood was painlessly removed from a vein in her left arm. Clippings were taken of her hair, her finger-nails, and even, as if they assumed it was part of her flesh, from the hem of her nightgown. It was a new nightgown, a present from her husband, and she became quite agitated, describing how they had cut into it, ripping the delicate fabric, holding it up so she could see what they had taken, and how much. Then photographs (she suspected they were X-ray photographs, or some other kind of advanced technology) were taken of her head. As this happened, she saw sudden, clear images from her life, one after another, like a slide show: the row of potted geraniums on the ledge in her back porch, her white kitten Snowball rolling over and over in a patch of sunlight on the kitchen linoleum, the scuffed, tiled floor in the post office where she went to pick up her mail twice a week. And more: her husband waving goodbye from the truck as he drove off down the road. The faces of her children: Betsy, seven, Kyle, five, and Cheryl, the baby. The sight of her children made her feel sad; she wanted to gather them to her and hold onto them so tightly that nothing bad could ever happen to them. She wanted to go home. Her children were all alone in the house; her husband was away, buying feed and supplies in town. He would be gone only this one night. How had they known? How had these space creatures known that she would be alone on this particular night?

All of this took place, or was alleged to have taken place, shortly after midnight on July 21, 1985. At least, Loretta Hanes thought it had been shortly after midnight, but it might have been later. She felt that she was in the spaceship a long time—hours and hours, days, even. She woke in her own bed at seven o'clock the next morning, with a bad taste in her mouth and a square of fabric missing from her new nightgown. Otherwise, she appeared to be unharmed.

Every word she spoke was true, she swore to God. She put her signature to the statement after it had been typed up, then slowly put down the pen and rubbed her wrist. "I still think about it a lot," she said. "I still can't sleep properly at night. I keep hearing small whispery noises outside my window in the dark. I try to put it out of my mind, but I can't; it's as if they've kept a video recording of my memories, my most intimate thoughts and dreams, and there's nothing I can do to get it back."

II

In August, 1986, in a small vacation town on the west coast of British Columbia, a poet and teacher by the name of Willis Byrne, aged forty-five, stepped outside his ground-floor motel room and walked over to the swimming pool. It was nearly two o'clock in the morning and the pool was deserted. Willis detested this pool and usually swam in the ocean, but he couldn't be bothered walking to the beach at this time of night. Later, when he finally got around to reporting his experiences to the authorities, he mentioned repeatedly how uncongenial he found the motel, how the bedding in his room smelled of pine antiseptic and the air-conditioning unit in the window rattled nonstop. "The pool was the worst, though," he said. It was located on a rise of ground behind the parking lot. A maple tree grew beside it, above a park bench that was carved all over in obscenities. "You would think the owners of the motel would clean stuff like that up," he said, "but obviously they couldn't be bothered." The pool was small and square with stained ceramic tiles around its perimeter. Four overhead lights imparted a pinkish sheen to the water. *Four separate moons*, Willis thought, and immediately discarded this phrase—it was impossibly narrow and trite. He had not written a word of real poetry for four, five years now, and no wonder, no wonder, when he could allow *four separate moons* into his head. He had once published a book of poetry, called *Now We Are Back Where We Started*; now he wished that he were back where he had started. His muse seemed dead, drowned, floating beneath the surface of this oily, pink water in which no one with any sense, any decency, any humanity, would ever swim.

He didn't care for swimming pools in any case. Nothing else, surely, captured more perfectly the sadness and ennui, the meaninglessness of ordinary life, than a neglected swimming pool. Possibly this had something to do with the hard containment of the fluid element, the confinement of a natural substance within an unnatural form. Oh, God, how he hated the present age. He was so tired, so full of ennui. He could go back to his room, but he knew that he would, once there, feel even sadder and more lonely. And if he walked down to the beach, hoping to be consoled by the sight of the moon reflected in the waves, he would only trip over discarded beer cans, or, even worse, encounter someone like him: unhappy, desolate, itchy with despair. For a moment he allowed himself to imagine that he would, instead, meet a fine, handsome young woman rising up from the ocean waves, her long hair dripping wet and wound in shining ropes around her neck and shoulders. He would at first assume she was a mermaid, a vision of his lonely mind, but after a series of impossibly comic and heroic actions on his part, she would reveal herself as being wholly human and completely his for the rest of his life.

He was a poet; he had in him still a residue of poetic power. Twelve or so years ago, he had acquired something of a reputation as a poet and had been invited to give readings in the side aisles of book stores towards closing time; he had signed his name in his book with pride, with flourishes. He needed poetry, his own poetry, to populate the solitary days of his vacation, to fill the emptiness of his soul, to recover some kind of self-worth, even in the sight of this blighted pool. It occurred to him that this, indeed, was the impossible and heroic task that faced him—he must recover his muse from the unhallowed depths of the motel pool. Later, Willis would attempt to explain, to the authorities, to friends, to anyone who professed the slightest interest, that this had seemed reasonable if not in fact foreordained at two o'clock in the morning and that his emotional state and subsequent actions were quite inseparable. His wife had left him some time ago and lived now in the southern United States with a house builder she planned on marrying. Willis had no children. He was vacationing alone, driving wherever he pleased in his Audi Fox. He was not old; he could still write poetry; it would come back to him.

He sat down on the edge of the pool and dangled his legs in the water. He was wearing shorts and a T-shirt. A brown maple leaf moved gently up and down on the water, then floated away. The slimy coating on the side of the pool came off on his hands, but he paid no attention, his resolve being now fixed. He lowered himself into the unheated water and dove, once, twice, three times, searching in a grid pattern for the form, the substance, of his muse. There were things he was obviously capable of believing at this time of night. Actions he was prepared to take.

When he came up for air after a long, slow dive, night had changed to day, or so it seemed. He could not open his eyes fully on the astonishing brightness he now encountered. Light, light. Where was it coming from? He was dazzled, blinded. It was not the sun; it was certainly not the moon, and in such a radiance as this the sick pink arc lights were entirely eclipsed. Willis was overwhelmed, also, with the sound of powerful engines bearing down on him. The soles of his feet throbbed, his heart vibrated against his ribs. Surely others would come running to see what was going on. But no one appeared; no one shouted out. Willis looked up and saw, beyond the light, a profound and immense darkness: a void, as it were. He thought: I, I, am responsible for this. He believed, at that moment, and for a long time afterwards, that his sacrificial descent had in some way expiated his sins, whatever they might be (he knew he had committed many, he was undoubtedly full of sin, hence his loneliness, his isolation, his doomed wandering) and had resulted in this glorious radiant vehicle of salvation (these terms came to him out of nowhere, he was suddenly Elijah, this was the whirlwind, here were the horses of fire) appearing to him and to him alone.

The waters of the pool were gold, pure gold, molten. Was it possible that this, such a small, poor thing, was in fact the river Jordan?

In the underside of the void that hovered above Willis, an opening appeared, and he felt himself hoisted aloft, felt himself drawn upward as if he were lighter than air, a feather, a speck of dust, ash drifting skyward from some quiet autumnal fire.

This is creation, he thought. This is the beginning. Then he thought:

> Four moons
> seasonal and spare, rise
> one by one
> into the desert
> of my heart

As these tentative lines came to Willis, he lost consciousness, so that he had no real idea of how he came to enter the spacecraft, if such it were, or of how he came, finally, to be inside it. He presumed he simply went in through some kind of hatch in the same way that any casual guest might enter the front door of a house that, while unfamiliar to him, nevertheless awaited his arrival.

III

When the spacemen took Loretta Hanes up into their ship, they treated her as if she were a fine and valuable object, a treasure fragile and transparent as glass. Her body, stretched out beneath their cold, thin hands, was attenuated and virginal. The spacemen placed a screen above her face, and gazing upwards, she saw with astonishing clarity scenes from her life illuminated there. She saw herself on her wedding day, walking up the aisle at St. Joseph's Church, her arm linked with her father's arm. Her father was no longer alive, and yet, on this screen, he looked absolutely as he had looked in real life, sturdy, vigorous, his face flushed and beaming. It seemed to Loretta that she could smell, quite distinctly, the small red rosebuds in her bridal bouquet, feel the baby's breath tickling the back of her hand. Then, abruptly, the scene changed, and Loretta saw the parking lot at the Food Palace store where she shopped every week. She saw herself loading groceries into the back of her Pontiac station wagon. She was wearing her blue jogging suit and her hair was in a ponytail. She was struck by how pretty she looked and how wholesome: She looked like a real person, right inside real life, right in there. Betsy and Kyle were with her, but not the baby. It was October; Loretta was placing an enormous orange pumpkin into the station wagon. Her children's eyes were round and wide with delight; their hands reached out to touch the pumpkin, to feel its solid jack o'lantern shape. Oh, this scene, the sense of it, the feel of it: a smell of wood smoke in the air, the cold weather closing down like a lid on the landscape. A witch's cat arching its back before a witch's hearth. Dreams and delusions.

Enough of this. Enough of tricks and witches and smoke. She wanted to get back, to get back to her children, her husband, her home. She sighed, and a half-cry caught in her throat, in her nearly paralyzed throat, reeking of zinc. At that moment, one of the spacemen put his gloved hand on her wrist. Her arm turned to ice, then, surprisingly, warmed. She felt peace, almost a sense of gratitude. Thank you for saving my life, she wanted to say. Then the gloved hand moved, and as the spaceman cupped her face, she turned her head slightly, only slightly, and bit deeply into the smooth, resilient glove, the tender flesh—if flesh it was—beneath.

It was what she wanted to do: to injure, wound, make some kind of radical connection. To bite, to tear, to taste. Even her horrible, induced paralysis couldn't stop her from doing that much.

IV

. . . a new myth seems to be erupting inside the collective unconscious, thinks Gary Bliss. This is the idea he is increasingly preoccupied with, and it is what he thinks of as he walks heavily down Seventh Avenue on his way to his office at the Arbutus Centre (immunization and well-baby clinic on the first floor, mental health on the second, Alzheimer's and schizophrenia support groups on the third) ten blocks away. He is a psychologist. He wears Reebok Walkers with his charcoal-grey, three-piece suit. For years he's been burdened with an excess one hundred pounds, but this year he's planned to lose at least seventy-five pounds by Christmas. It's a promise he's made himself, a promise he's mind-mapped and pinned to his bedroom wall—a huge mandala-like drawing, concentric circles filled in with female breasts and anorexic-looking schoolboys strapped to their desks and being force-fed by thin, cruel young women wearing high-heeled red sandals. Where, he asks himself, do these images come from? What is going on inside his head? It's truly a miracle he's made it as far as he has, a functioning, adult human being.

Gary Bliss is buoyant (he feels buoyant today, in spite of his size) with the excitement that comes from true intellectual discovery. From evidence he's recently gathered and studied of individual encounters with so-called extraterrestrials, he believes that a fundamental broadening and restructuring of human symbolism is underway. The whole mythology is changing. He finds this enormously exciting.

He's following in the footsteps of Jung, of course. Following? Is that the word? He's beginning to suspect, as he formulates his theory, as his thoughts cohere, as they *gather power,* so to speak, that he will eventually go further than Jung. He doesn't mean any disrespect. Things change. Dreams, for example. The human mind moves forward. Even when it appears not to be moving at all, it moves forward. Truth may first be apprehended in the most unlikely corners: supermarket tabloids, dubious television shows. (He has himself a barely acknowledged but irrepressible taste for these forms of mass entertainment; he can't keep his eyes from the improbable headlines as he waits to pay for his meagre supplies of yoghurt and calorie-reduced frozen dinners.) Why are these reports of intergalactic visitations and occasional miscegenetic alliances so compelling, if there isn't something in them of truth?

What if the symbols residing in man's deepest historical shared unconscious do in fact undergo a form of natural selection, an ascent from the past into the future? He thinks for a moment of the durable figure of the man-god, born miraculously of a virgin at the winter solstice, the darkest, most drear time of the year, then sacrificed just as the ground begins to warm and new shoots push through to the surface. Resurrection, rebirth; everything made new. Hope arrives; the heart is shriven.

Now, it seems, there are new gods, completely new, freshly hatched gods, separate entirely from the soil of the earth, from the revolving wheels of the seasons. In place of the earth, in place of the soil, there are these monolithic, aerodynamic, antiseptic space laboratories, hovering above but never quite touching the warm breast of mother earth. Inside these spaceships, superior beings, archetypal men of science, being neither male nor female, spirit nor creature. Clothed in white; radiant; pulsing with light; emitting rays, radio signals, sound waves; they arrive and yet are not detected, depart and yet are not mourned.

Why don't they come for him? Why don't they? At night he leaves his apartment and walks to a nearby park, a small unkempt area, enclosed in chain-link fencing, with two or three maple trees and a lot of litter on the ground—a dismal, but a clear space, the best he can find. It is a sequestered place, in terms of the city. He wishes the only light in all the world were the light of stars. He stands with his face turned to the night sky, his eyes wide, his mouth hanging open, utterly receptive to the first sign, the first sound. He whispers: "Come to me, come to me."

He envisions the unbearable brightness of the great machine, hears the even keening of an unimaginably sophisticated power plant. He is chanting under his breath; he, atheistic and reasonable, sings and sways; God, God, God, he breathes. On the back of his neck and his arms, the hair rises; his skin glows. He waits. "Come to me, come," he says. Prays. "I am here."

V

Messages, thought Loretta Hanes when first she woke on the morning of July 21, 1985. There's something I'm supposed to remember, she thought. Sleep was slowly clearing from her mind, letting other things back in. She was looking at her open bedroom window. I floated through that window like a performer in a magic act, she thought. What was it she should remember? She must have been given messages, information, some words to pass on. Otherwise, what was the point? But all she could remember was silence, voicelessness, her own and theirs. There were no messages. She listened: small, insignificant rustlings deep inside her ear, her skull. She didn't know what to think, that was the problem.

Wait. She had been stolen from her bed in the night by something she could not see. She had been given over into the arms of strangers, and they . . . had done things to her. Nothing bad—she had not been hurt or damaged in any way; they had taken care of her. She got out of bed and pulled her nightie off and saw that, naked, she looked the same as ever from head to foot. And yet her body repelled her. She hastily got into her bathrobe, then went into the bathroom and began running hot water into the tub. Immediately, in the way that children have, both Betsy and Kyle were at the door calling her.

"I'm having a bath," she told them. The voices of her children were strong and definite; they knew who she was, they knew she was Mommy. And who else could she be, after all, but herself? "Let us in," her children kept calling. "Let us in."

"In a minute," she said. "In just a minute." She had been looking at herself in the bathroom mirror; now she slipped into the tub and lay down under the hot water. Her long hair writhed around her face like the hair of a drowned person. She was drowned; she was a wraith; she was nothing. They must have had some kind of message for her, or they would not have chosen her specifically. Perhaps they had not chosen; perhaps they had simply grabbed at the nearest person they could find. No, no; she had been chosen, it had been her they wanted. Somewhere, at this moment, a sample of her blood was being investigated. And a fragment of cloth from the hem of her nightgown was under analysis, like the Shroud of Turin. She imagined the spacemen, their smooth skulls close together, examining the fibres, saying, in their non-language, This pollen is not from the same vicinity as the woman; this is from a plant that grows only in the south of China, how strange, what a problem. She imagined the cotton unravelling in their cold hands, bits of thread and lint sticking to their skinny fingers.

Then she remembered: She had bitten one of them. She really had. She felt herself blushing, and she stood up in the water and reached for a towel before stepping out of the tub. How had she come to do such a thing, to actually bite? Her mouth was flooded with the remembered taste, part bitter, part sweet. Oh, God, she had wanted to bite down harder and harder; she had restrained the urge with difficulty. It had been like sex, she thought now, so savage and intimate; she had wanted to consume the spaceman, to evoke a cry of passion, to make him cry out in pain, with tears and recriminations. He had stepped away from her, holding his injured hand, and the other spaceman had pivoted on his heel in surprise and then had examined his friend's hand carefully. Had they been frightened of her, for a moment? Had they been repelled? Or had they been drawn to her; had they wished to cover her with their pale, remote otherworldliness, their shadow-shapes? She saw the pale shape of her own body floating in the steamy mirror and felt again, fleetingly, as she had felt lying on that high, narrow table in the spaceship: fragile, delicate, important.

VI

Willis Byrne parks his Audi Fox outside the home of his friend Samantha Eberts. It is October. The maple in front of Samantha's house is a glorious gold. Her young son's red wagon lies tilted on its side in the marigold bed, where the flowers have been slightly darkened and crushed by the first night frosts. How well Willis feels, how fine and strong. He takes deep breaths and rubs his hand on the front of his sweater. Then he removes a copy of his new book from a box beside him on the passenger seat. His book, newly delivered from his publisher, is called *The River God*, although it is not strictly speaking about rivers or about gods; it is about spacemen, and abductions, and long, silver needles piercing the flesh of Willis Byrne and drawing out his dreams, his ambitions, his wish for love, his need to be loved, his human need for friendship. It is, in a way, about personal redemption and salvation, but it is not about religion, not about the prophet Elijah, although Willis sometimes feels he may have briefly danced the same dance as Elijah, his feet moving as fast and as powerfully as Elijah's. This book, Willis has said, when asked, is simply a book of poetry about his response to what he sees as being true in the world. It is possible, he has also said, although mainly to himself, that he has been chosen to receive some special form of revelation or insight, that he has in fact been set aside, as a member of a priesthood is chosen and set aside. But then, he is a poet, and so has already been, well, not chosen, but *picked*, in a sense . . . .

What matters, finally, he feels, are the fruits of his experience: his sense of well-being, the end to his loneliness in the form of Samantha and her six-year-old, both of them people he truly, truly likes and admires and wants to be with. His book, as well. Everything.

Even before he has a chance to ring the doorbell, Samantha opens the door. He hands her a bouquet of pink, white, and red carnations. They embrace; then Willis hands

Samantha his book, saying, "Fresh from the printer's, watch out, the ink's still wet."

She turns the book over and over in her hands, exclaiming at his picture on the jacket, the cover illustration, the paper, even the dedication, which reads: *To the strangers who lightened my journey*. "Oh Lord," she says. "This is so exciting. I never thought I'd be entertaining a real live poet in my house. *The River God*. Where'd you get the title from, Willis? Oh, I want to sit down right now and read this." She begins to read from the book:

> Go into water
> go into rain
> water-beast, sea-urchin
> Dwell in the small place
> the dark granite caves
> drowned
> Breathe air, breathe fire
> breathe my soul
> to death and back

"Wait a minute," Willis says, laughing. "Don't do that. I mean, don't just stand there reading my poems like that. You make me nervous. I'm sorry," he adds, seeing the hurt look on her face. "It's just, I don't know. I'd rather read them to you or something."

"Well, that's fine. You read them to me. I don't have a problem with that," she says, leading him into her living room. "You read. I'm waiting."

That night, Willis reads every single poem in his book to

Samantha. They go through two bottles of wine and a large bowl of popcorn, and Willis reads and reads. He has seldom felt more content. They are interrupted only once when Samantha's son wakes from a nightmare and she has to go and settle him down. "He was dreaming about his monsters again," she says to Willis. "Tall green meat-eating dinosaurs with bloody teeth. Too much TV."

"Ah," Willis says. He finishes a handful of popcorn, wipes his hand on his jeans, then turns a page and continues to read. When he has finished, Samantha gets up from the floor, where she has been reclining, her head on Willis's knee, and sits in a chair. It is very late. The clock on the mantle is ticking and ticking, the minutes falling into Willis's head and lying in neat rows like broken-off matchsticks.

"You know," Samantha says, "this is something I have never before told a living soul. When I was a little girl, about nine or ten years old, I saw the strangest sight. I was standing in my front yard, and it was just getting dark. I think this was in the summer, during summer vacation. I'd been playing outside, with my friends. And suddenly, over this mountain came three objects, three dark, saucer-shaped objects. They went past so quickly! I couldn't believe my eyes. I kept thinking, You did not see that, Samantha, you couldn't have. These objects were flying in a sort of V-shaped formation like ducks or geese, or those rare, beautiful black swans you hear of. Do you think I saw three UFOs, Willis?"

"No," says Willis. "I don't believe in UFOs. No sane person would. Everything has a rational explanation, Samantha. Spaceships, angels, shooting stars, spinning wheels of fire. Everything comes clear sooner or later. Sometimes what you see is just light, just a trick of the light, something happening at the far end of the spectrum, just past what the human eye can make out."

"Yes," says Samantha. "I believe that, too. It makes sense, doesn't it, Willis? When you think about it."

My
Glorious
Aunts

One of my aunts is introspective, methodical, serene of spirit, and passionate in her devotion to the solving of logic puzzles. Wherever she goes, she takes along at least one book of them, so that she can fiddle away at them while eating breakfast, while bathing, while waiting in her car at traffic lights, in the intervals between business meetings, even, I have heard, while carrying on an otherwise normal conversation. Logic puzzles have taught my aunt, she claims, that most of what happens in life is theory, not fact. It helps to know this, she says, pencil in hand, reading glasses poised on the tip of her exquisite nose.

This aunt's name is not Natasha. Natasha is another aunt altogether, who lives on a hobby farm with her fourth husband and raises Nubian goats. The goats are gentle and sympathetic and easy to be around. Natasha's house is built on a rise of ground facing south. She sits in a window, in the warmth of the sun, and plays the harpsichord. Natasha's four husbands were all, by a strange and probably unimportant

119

coincidence, of different nationalities. The first was French, the second was Belgian, the third was Polish, and the current husband is a Scot by the name of Alastair McAlastair. Alastair gives Natasha diamond eternity rings, sporty Japanese cars, fresh-cut flowers in January. He gives the goats their names: Ruby, Daisy, Bunny, Freckles, Sunny. Natasha and Alastair are happy together.

My Aunt Natasha is not a realtor. That is another aunt, Cynthia. (This is how you do logic puzzles: with negative information; by elimination.) Cynthia is the oldest of my glorious aunts, but she dresses young, in whatever appeals to her: mini-skirts, see-through blouses, leather pants. Black T-shirts, silver-studded leather collars, even. She lives in a luxury condo two blocks from a botanical research garden, which has encouraged her to grow lemon trees from seed, in tubs on her balcony, in summer.

Cynthia dated one of Natasha's ex-husbands, briefly, for a few months, long after he and Natasha had officially split up. This was the Polish husband, Stefan. Stefan was blue-eyed and handsome; he played the accordion like a wizard. At family gatherings—birthdays, wedding anniversaries— he played polkas, waltzes, mazurkas—especially mazurkas, in three-quarter time, very fast—and everyone would leap up and push back the furniture and begin to dance—it was impossible to resist. How Stefan enjoyed our prancing! He played and smiled, smiled and played endlessly, tapping his foot, which, as I recall, was always shod in gleaming black leather—a hussar he seemed to me, although of course he was not Hungarian, but Polish. And he was not particularly military-looking, in reality. Actually, he was unusually small, small-boned, delicate, with large, dreamy eyes.

Cynthia, the tallest of my aunts, five-eight-and-a-half, nearly six feet in the high heels she likes to wear, was so enraptured by Stefan's blue eyes, his dashing mazurkas, that she was, she said, scarcely aware of the difference in their heights. And really, it shouldn't have mattered, she says now. But at the time, she felt more and more like a giant; she began to stoop when she walked and to slide down onto her lumbar spine when she sat. It was painful; it was bad for her posture. And on top of all this was the fear that Natasha would find out about her and Stefan. They couldn't be seen together at family events. There was no music; there was no future for them.

After Cynthia broke up with Stefan, she didn't see anyone else for a full year, a definite record for her. Now she is going out with Brian, a radio announcer, a divorced father of two who does a morning show on an easy listening station. He is taller than Cynthia, a little on the heavy side, florid, expansive. Not my type, to be honest.

Cynthia, by the way, is not the aunt who does logic puzzles. Neither is Beverly.

Beverly is the aunt who has children. No one seems able to discourage her from having children—not her mother, who speaks sensibly to her about energy, and time, and money, resources that can be depleted all too easily; not her husband, who is an underpaid research assistant in a fledgling bio-technology firm. Five children! everyone was saying to Beverly; what a fine family, what a handful! And then practically before they'd finished speaking, my newest cousin arrived, young Byron, now five months old. Beverly plainly adores young Byron, as indeed she does all her children, especially when they are infants. She presses him firmly, protectively, possessively to her breast, and says, to her mother, "I will have as many children as necessary."

"As necessary!" says her mother. "What a word to use."

"Well," says Beverly, "you know what I mean." She looks around the room as if seeing for the first time two-year-old Katy, and three-year-old Gavin, both busy ripping pages from one of their father's scientific journals, and four-year-old Liza, and six-year-old George, who, mercifully, is sitting pacified in front of the TV. George is the most difficult of my cousins. Eight-year-old Tyrone is in his room, writing a novel. He is the most literary, so far. "But Mother, you had five children," Beverly, aggrieved, points out.

"Five is not six," says her mother with indignation.

Plainly there is no logic in either one of them: not my grandmother and not my Aunt Beverly.

This happens at my grandmother's house, at a reception following the christening of young Byron. Natasha sidles up to Cynthia and says, "Is it true that you are seeing Stefan?" Natasha is wearing a yellow dress, with a hem that comes nearly to her ankles. She has sandals on her feet and yellow daisies in her hair. Some of my aunts are whispering that perhaps Natasha is getting a little too countrified out there with the Nubian goats and the rude Alastair McAlastair. (The rustic, that is to say, as opposed to the impolite, Alastair McAlastair.)

Cynthia is wearing red silk, short and tight and daring, but undeniably stylish. She is standing near the buffet table, drinking champagne. Her new friend, Brian, is here some-where, chatting up the lady guests in his smooth, deep radio announcer's voice. Brian has been turning up at these family events lately. Not everyone is pleased. However, the presence of Brian makes Natasha's query about Stefan seem even stranger, if that is possible. Cynthia stares at her, taken aback, and then says, "Do you know, I haven't thought of Stefan in ages." Cynthia, because of her occupation as a realtor, is good at answering and not answering questions at the same time.

"You have no right to become involved with my husband, you know," Natasha says. She is obviously upset; she quivers; a daisy slips from her hair to the floor.

"Natasha, my dear, Stefan isn't your husband anymore," says Cynthia.

At that moment Brian appears, wiping his handsome, flushed face and saying that he wishes he and his ex—he calls his former wife his "ex"—had thought of getting their kids christened. "It's kind of a neat idea," he says to Cynthia.

A few people, family and guests, wince visibly at this remark. The doctrinal aspects of infant baptism might get overlooked in this family as much as in most, but the con-ventions are observed, *respect* is paid, to the tradition, the ceremony, at least. Of course, Brian's ingenuous remark might have passed unnoticed if everyone had not been listening so intently to Cynthia and Natasha.

"You shouldn't be seeing Stefan," Natasha says, stamping her sandalled foot upon my grandmother's oak floor. "Stefan and I were husband and wife, don't forget. We were legally married. While we were married, at least. He belonged to me. I mean, we belonged to each other. Oh, you know what I mean."

"Natasha dear," says Cynthia. "I don't. I don't know what you mean. I can tell you truthfully that I have not seen Stefan in years. Not in ever such a long time."

Alastair McAlastair, perhaps sensing calamity afoot in the room, perhaps merely inspired by the champagne he has been drinking, places his hands upon his broad chest, approximately over his heart, and intones: "As fair art thou, my bonnie lass, / So deep in luve am I, / And I will luve thee still my Dear, / Till a' the seas gang dry."

"Robert Burns," says Natasha, blushing. Alastair, who is indeed a fine-looking Scot, with thick black curls and red lips, concludes his recitation and bows to my grandmother, then to Natasha, then to Beverly, mother of young Byron, the newly baptized, who is fast asleep, his christening bonnet clutched in his fist. His fat, pink, dimpled fist, my grandmother would say. His brother George is blowing fruit punch through a straw onto the antipasto. By this time, no one cares.

Later, I follow Natasha into the bedroom she once, long ago when they were girls, shared with Cynthia and help her to comb her hair, which comes to her waist and smells of comfrey, wild thyme, nettles. Every now and then the comb catches on a strand of silver in Natasha's nut-brown curls. She twists the rings she wears upon her slender fingers and says, "I know Cynthia is seeing Stefan. I don't care what she says. Someone absolutely reliable saw them together at a French restaurant, eating *snails*." It is the snails that give this rumour veracity, it seems, as far as Natasha is concerned. Then Natasha smiles brilliantly up at me, and I bend and kiss her on the cheek and say, impulsively, with great feeling, "Dear, dear Aunt Natasha." When she and Alastair leave, we all stand on the front steps and wave goodbye, and someone, I think it is my mother, sighs wearily and says, "Oh God, this reminds me of one of Natasha's interminable weddings."

When my grandmother, whose name is Louise, was nine months pregnant with my Aunt Trisha, she slipped on an icy patch coming out of the public library and fell all the way down the stairs to the sidewalk. It was December, two days before Christmas. She landed at the feet of a Salvation Army captain who promptly burst into tears. The captain ran at once into the library to telephone for an ambulance, and while he was gone a thief stole his kettle full of donations. The thief paused to say, "Excuse me," as he stepped over Louise. A woman who had stopped to comfort Louise shouted, "Good luck to you too, sonny," at the thief. "It doesn't matter about the money," the Salvation Army captain said, coming gingerly down the library steps. "My books were due back today," said Louise. "I wanted to return them before I went into labour." "Well, of course you would," the woman agreed, patting Louise's hands. "I have three children myself," the captain said, as Louise was lifted into the ambulance on a stretcher. "What are their names?" she asked, and the captain just managed to say, before the doors were shut and the ambulance raced away, "The youngest is called Trisha." At least, that was what it sounded like to Louise, and when my aunt was born eight hours later at St. Joseph's Hospital, she was at once named Trisha, in honour of this unknown youngest child.

Louise, it turned out, had bruised her ribs, sprained her

wrist, and chipped her tailbone. The nurses said, "Oh, this is a miracle baby, for Christmas." The Salvation Army band came and played under the maternity ward windows on Christmas Eve. The three older girls, Cynthia, Diane, and Natasha, stood on the grass below and waved up at their mother, an unattainable face at a small window in a vast brick hospital. Poor children, they all had summer birthdays, when the ground was completely free of ice and no one stood on street corners ringing Christmas bells. "Miracle baby," they taunted, as soon as Trisha was old enough to be taunted. She didn't mind; she was a happy, level-headed little girl who loved school, where she excelled in mathematics and physical education. She did not particularly believe in miracles; she believed in logic and computations and in running very fast for long distances.

Aunt Trisha, of course, is the aunt who does logic puzzles. Although she claims to believe that most of what happens in life is theory, she lives like everyone else—as if facts are facts. She is an economist. She has serene grey eyes and cinnamon hair; she is married to Graham, who teaches chemistry at a community college. Their vacations are spent doing dangerous sports, like white-water rafting, spelunking, and mountaineering. So far, they have no children.

Natasha rises from her harpsichord, her skin glowing in the aftermath of a shower of baroque sixteenth notes—runs and trills and deftly executed ornaments. She is wearing a loose cotton shift with long, gathered sleeves and lace around the hem. The windows in this room are open, admitting a fragrant summer breeze and the sound of bells: The Nubian goats, each with a copper bell round its neck, are being herded from the barn down to the fields by Alastair McAlastair. My mother and I are here at Natasha's request. "I must, must, must see you," she said, on the phone.

My mother, in case you are getting confused, is Natasha's sister, Diane. The sisters go like this, in order of age: Cynthia, Diane, Natasha, Trisha, Beverly. Sometimes it seems like more, I know, but there really are only the five of them.

Natasha, padding around in bare feet, brews a pot of rosehip tea and serves it to us with paper-thin slices of lemon cake. She tells us her news: She and Alastair are going to Scotland in September to visit Alastair's mother. They will go fishing for salmon and trout and they will hike through the heather. Alastair's mother spins sheep's wool and then weaves it into blankets and sweaters. She has promised to teach Natasha how to spin and weave, as well. "That's nice of her, isn't it?" Natasha says uncertainly. She crumbles her uneaten lemon cake between her fingers.

"What I want," she says at last, "is for you to find out for me if Cynthia is seeing Stefan."

My mother says, "Oh, I think you can forget about that, Natasha. I don't think Cynthia is seeing Stefan at all. She's dating Brian."

"No one could seriously be dating Brian," says Natasha. "Obviously he is her alibi." She is sitting in front of us, on the floor. The light from the windows is behind her and there is a nimbus around her hair and skin, an effect of radiance, of glory. The problem is this, she says: She has had too many husbands—what could she have been thinking of? She can't even imagine. Now she feels burdened by these husbands, as if she were in fact married to them all at the same time. "Four husbands," she says. "Four." She has been imprudent, improvident, unwise, foolish. She should never have married, but if it was her fate to marry, and to marry to such excess, then she should never have allowed her marriages to end. She should have kept her husbands by her side, where she would know what they were up to, whether they were sad or happy, contented or miserable. And whom they were seeing. Or not seeing.

"All those vows," she sighs. "All those solemn promises. Promise after promise, all down the long, long years." She rises and goes to a window. She beckons us to her side. From here, we can see green fields bordered by fences, and hedges of blackberry bushes, and thistles. It is all pastoral and fetching in the extreme. The goats are browsing in the green, green fields and Alastair McAlastair, in khaki shorts and an open-necked shirt, is striding up towards the house. The breeze ruffles his black curls; he gazes directly up at us, or rather, at Natasha; he never seems to see anyone else. Natasha leans out of the window, her long hair spilling over the sill. There is something ever so slightly false in Natasha's behaviour, it seems to me. Or at least, the thought does enter my mind, but only for a moment. I brush it away, quickly, because she is, after all, my aunt, one of my aunts.

Cynthia tells me this story. It seems that one morning a call came to her office from a man who wanted to sell his house. He lived in Vancouver, and the house he wanted to sell was over here, on the island. "Waterfront property," he said.

"Worth a fortune." The house was rented out to a very reliable individual, a pediatrician, a single woman with two coal-black cats.

Why did this man add the detail of the two black cats so early in his conversation with Cynthia? "Who can say?" Cynthia says. "People get nervous when they contemplate selling property; they talk about everything and nothing at the same time." This man, this faceless voice on the telephone, actually stalled on the two black cats; he couldn't seem to talk about anything else. Both cats were spayed females, he said: clean, healthy animals. And of course, the pediatrician wouldn't allow a single flea on these animals. "You can imagine how fussy a doctor, a children's specialist, would be?" he asked Cynthia. The pediatrician didn't have the cats when he rented the house to her, the man added. His advertisement plainly said: No pets. But soon after she moved in, a friend had to find a new home for a pet cat or have it put down, so the pediatrician ("You can imagine how kind-hearted a pediatrician would be?" the man said, to Cynthia) took the cat in. Then, a mere two or three days later, an identical black cat turned up cold and starving on the doorstep, so the doctor took that one in, too. And the cats got along from the beginning like old friends, litter-mates. "Cats are extraordinary creatures, aren't they?" he said. "Yes," Cynthia said.

Eventually, this man got back to the subject of his property, which he described as comfortable, elegant, homey, with a jacuzzi in the bathroom, a rotisserie in the kitchen, and a glassed-in sun porch. "All this," he said, "on a level, sandy beach." And the view was magnificent. All day you could see the Coast Mountains, pale blue, with snow-capped peaks, and at night you could see the lights of ski-lifts sparkling like some new constellation in the eastern sky. When it rained, of course, you couldn't see much. The beach, the sea.

Three days later Cynthia met this man at the ferry terminal, as they had arranged on the phone, and drove him to the house he wanted to sell. He wasn't at all what she had expected. That is, she had expected an older man. He was about forty-five, her age, in fact. He wore glasses; he wasn't at all talkative, as he had been on the telephone. He sat in her car with his hands on his knees, saying nothing until the last possible moment, when he would suddenly shout, Oh, turn right here, or Quick, turn left, and she would have to pull hard on the wheel, skidding around corners. His name was Max. He was an artist. "Silk-screens, woodcuts, that sort of thing," he said. He didn't support himself as an artist, of course. Years ago, he had inherited money, and thanks to a friend who was an investment consultant, this money had grown and grown, like magic. "Amazing, isn't it," he said, "how money will respond to the right touch, the right sort of manipulation?"

"Yes," said Cynthia, who had her own kind of luck in this matter.

When they got to the house, Cynthia could see that in spite of Max's pride in it, there were problems. For example, the foundation was cracking, the front door needed refinishing, and there was a faint smell, maybe not detectable to everyone, but certainly obvious to someone who knew houses, of dry rot. Waterfront houses were highly sought after, but they were susceptible; the air was damp all the time; they had to be kept up, and you could see this house hadn't been kept up; it had been neglected. Also, Cynthia thought, there was something strange here: strange and oddly familiar at the same time. It wasn't that she had ever seen this house before; she hadn't. But there was something. She couldn't place it. It made her uneasy. The other thing that bothered her was the way Max kept getting too close. She would move and nearly bump into him, or she would step on his foot, and she found herself saying, Oh, pardon me, excuse me, I am sorry, until she felt like screaming. They were in the main room, a living room that measured twenty by seventeen feet, with a huge stone fireplace and a great bay of windows overlooking the sea. A pink negligee had been tossed over the arm of a chair. One black cat was asleep in the chair, and another was sitting on the sofa, giving them a cold and steady stare.

Cynthia edged away from the cat and from Max, and somehow managed to catch her foot in a thick, black strap which was, she saw, attached to an accordion, a large, handsome accordion decorated with silver flowers and silver braid. The accordion had been left on the floor, near the hearth. The black cat continued to stare at her. This was the oddest house; it made her feel so odd. The walls needed a coat of paint; the carpet was threadbare in places.

She was thinking that of course there were dozens, hundreds, of people who played accordions just like this one, silver flowers and all, and at the same time she was thinking, Oh, no, there aren't that many, not really. In her head she could hear music; fast, lively dance music; accordion music; Polish songs, beautiful, sad Polish mazurkas; she could see Stefan, his blue eyes, his nice smile which was always a little melancholy, too, a sad, sad smile. Everything seemed sad to her at that moment in Max's rented house on the beach, in the huge, echoing room with the pink negligee so carelessly draped over a chair. She already felt odd, on edge, fearful, and now she felt sad too.

"Well, of course it was a shock," Cynthia says now. We are sitting on her balcony, near the lemon trees. It is a bright, hot day. Cynthia is wearing a pink cotton sunsuit, and sunglasses which she keeps removing in order to rub her eyes as if she is very tired; in fact she has told me she hasn't been sleeping well lately. She tells me how she followed Max through his house, into the kitchen, where the morning newspaper was lying open on the table beside a piece of burnt toast and a half-empty cup of coffee. The house didn't look so fastidiously kept to her, no matter what Max believed about his wonderful tenant, the pediatrician. The garbage can was full; the flowered curtains on the window over the sink were stained around the edges. In the bathroom, a man's electric shaver had been left beside the sink, the shower curtain was drawn across the tub, and damp towels were lying around on the floor. The king-sized bed in the master bedroom was unmade, and on the dresser was a picture of Stefan playing his accordion. Cynthia remembered the picture; she had taken it herself. Stefan's beautiful smile had been directed specifically at her, Cynthia, not some stranger, not some woman who left her negligee lying around in the living room and never took out the garbage.

"So that's how you found out?" I say eagerly. "That's how you found out that Stefan knew this woman, the pediatrician?"

"I found out more than that. Stefan was in the house, he was there, hiding in the basement. Well, he may not have intended to hide, but he was down there, all right." My aunt replaces her sunglasses and unsmilingly considers the high glass walls of the botanical gardens, where it is possible to pay two dollars and fifty cents for a guided tour on weekday afternoons. One day I intend to go there, by myself, for a rest, sort of. In fact I may remain there for some time, solitary amid the glassy greenness; I may take root; I may grow leaves and put out cinnamon-scented flowers of my own, a biological oddity mysteriously devoid of relatives of any kind, including aunts. Meanwhile, I try my best to follow this story of Cynthia's; I concentrate on making sense out of what I hear. It is like trying to catch hold of a slippery end of ribbon in a high wind.

"Did you talk to him?" I ask.

"We exchanged a few words. He looked guilty, evasive. He couldn't meet my eyes. I had the feeling the whole house was laughing at me."

"Laughing, Aunt Cynthia?"

"Yes. It was, I don't know, as if the house knew that I knew Stefan and had arranged for me to go there. There was a sort of secretive feeling. And it wasn't the house it was supposed to be. Even Max, who owns the house, kept saying, It looks different, it needs a lot of work, redecorating, painting up. He was in a state of shock, in a way. He had thought his house was perfect, exceptional, a real mansion. Then I find Stefan down there in the basement, and I'm standing there staring at him, and he actually has the nerve to grin at me and say, 'Well, well, what a coincidence.'"

"A spooky coincidence," I agree, marvelling at the lives of my aunts, my glorious aunts, the things that happen, that they cause to happen, or walk into, or however it works, innocently, one supposes, and without guile.

ᕦ

Trisha was the one, she now calmly admits, who saw Cynthia and Stefan in the French restaurant, eating snails. "Oh, why not frogs' legs, I wonder?" says Cynthia. "I hate snails. The poor things are starved for ten days before they get cooked, and I hate that, it's cruel, it's like veal, only the opposite. I loathe snails. And even if I were in this restaurant, which I was not, how could you possibly have got close enough to see what was on my plate without my seeing you?"

And then she says, "Well, you might have seen Stefan, for all I know, but you sure as hell didn't see me there."

"It was you," says Trisha stubbornly. She is, I think, and so does my grandmother, the most stubborn of my aunts. She sets her mouth in a certain way and stares at you out of her long, intelligent eyes and that's that: You have to concede, she's right, her point of view is the right one. This is no doubt the result of doing all those logic puzzles and getting them right, and being good at math and sports. She thinks this whole situation is a logic puzzle: In theory, it may well have been Stefan in the French restaurant, and by a simple process of elimination and intuition it must have been Cynthia, because who else could it have been? Trisha considers this logical, but in my opinion she is no more logical than any of the rest of my aunts. In fact, sometimes I think I am the only one who is logical here, and that is because all I ever do is listen, and take things in, and refuse, most of the time, to get involved.

ᕦ

Natasha announces, suddenly, in August, that she is not going to Scotland with Alastair McAlastair in September, after all. She will not go fishing for salmon and trout, nor will she hike through the heather, nor will she learn to spin sheep's wool, nor will she weave it into sweaters and blankets. Alastair is gravely disappointed. A number of transatlantic telephone calls have to be made, so that Alastair can explain to his mother, whose name is Margaret, but who is called Daisy ("Never, never, tell my mother that we have a goat named Daisy," he has warned Natasha) that he will be coming to Scotland alone. "What on earth do you mean?" his mother at once demands. "Why won't you bring Natasha? How could you be so unthinking? I simply can't understand you, Alastair, it must be the connection. Get the operator, Alastair," she says, "and have her place this call again."

His mother hangs up; Alastair bangs his head against the wall in frustration. Then he throws himself on his knees in front of Natasha, having no pride left in himself whatsoever, and begs her to change her mind. She refuses. Before long, everyone is involved in trying to change Natasha's mind: my grandmother, my mother, my aunts, even, against what I consider my better sense, me. We all sit in a sort of circle around Natasha, who has become rather quiet and remote, and pale, and contained. She is keeping her thoughts to herself. The idea is that we will get Natasha to listen to Alastair and go on her holiday to Scotland, about which she was very excited only a short while ago, we point out. "Fresh salmon, fresh trout," we say enthusiastically. "*And* long romantic strolls through the hills, the heather, the highland heather. It'll be lovely."

"No," says Natasha at last, very certain of herself. Then she tells us that she is a conduit, through which fresh water flows: She is absolutely open and free and cleansed. She has had too many husbands, it is true, but now she is able to look back at these men, who are lined up she says, in her mind, on a narrow road winding through sunlit fields. She sees them, but they do not see her. They are searching for something. Perhaps for the peace she has found. Her husbands, she says, reeling off their names from the first to the last, the estimable Alastair McAlastair. Then she begins to sing under her breath, soft words you cannot catch no matter how hard you listen. As she sings, she plaits and unplaits her hair. We all look quickly, uneasily, at each other, and then we look away, stumped.

Here is what Natasha does: She drives into town early every morning, while Alastair is away in Scotland, and works at a soup kitchen in a downtown mission. The mission is run by a young man who started out in stock promotions and then went to prison for a time because of certain dishonest acts having to do with a large amount of unaccounted-for venture capital or something; there was a vague charge of aggravated assault, but that was dropped, and now, he says, it is time to make amends, time to start anew. When Natasha repeats these words, she does not blink; her gaze is steady and rapt and true.

There's no point in asking yourself why Natasha does these things. She just does; she is Natasha. She starts work at seven o'clock in the morning every day, buttering bread for sandwiches, stirring huge vats of vegetable and barley soup, sorting through piles of donated baby clothes. She also acts as secretary for the former stock promoter, arranging his appointments, typing up his correspondence, even drafting letters appealing for money—letters which will go out to his former associates in the stock market business: The ones, he says, who owe him. When he says this, he throws his head back and roars with laughter. Natasha laughs, too. They work exceedingly well together, she tells me.

Two or three times a week she speaks to Alastair on the telephone, and he tells her of his days spent hiking and fishing, his long, quiet evenings with his mother. He tells Natasha how much he misses her.

"I miss you, too," Natasha says briskly. Then she says, "Well, take care of yourself. See you soon, I expect."

I am staying here, with Natasha, to keep her company in Alastair's absence. She winks broadly at me as she says goodbye and blows little kisses into the telephone. Oh, she is devious, and willful, and naughty, and delicious. It is early, early in the morning, a late-summer dawn; the sky is clear as glass; a thin, pale crescent moon hangs above the dew-drenched fields. After Natasha has driven away, off to the soup kitchen, I go down to the field and talk to the Nubian goats, who gaze up at me out of their enormous, liquid brown eyes. "Well, that's Natasha," they seem to say. "When has anyone ever been able to understand Natasha?"

How quickly things happen in the lives of my glorious aunts; nothing remains settled or certain for long. Cynthia, for example, has broken up with Brian and has sold her luxury condominium near the botanical research garden, and she has packed up her two lush, green lemon trees in their red clay pots, and she has moved with them into Max's house by the sea. Max is there, too, of course. Instead of selling his house, Max gave his tenant notice, then replaced the carpeting, painted the walls, installed new gutters and downpipes, had an art studio made for himself and an office for Cynthia, and then they moved in, together, the two of them, Max and Cynthia. So much work, Cynthia says: so much dust, noise, confusion!

In the beginning, Cynthia acknowledges, she didn't care much for Max. He stood too close to her; she was always tripping over his feet. The two most endearing qualities he owns, his nearsightedness and his clumsiness, she mistook for aggression. How foolish of her! Also, Max had tried to blame her because the pediatrician turned out to have a man hidden away in the basement, but now he realizes, or seems to realize, that Cynthia of all people had nothing to do with this, even though she admitted to knowing the man. After all, she was as shocked as he was; more, even. They had gone downstairs, so Cynthia could see all the storage cupboards, and the furnace, and the new hot water tank, and there was Stefan, and they all stood gaping awkwardly at one another.

You know this man? You know this person? Who is he? What is he doing in my house? Max kept saying.

"Wait," says Cynthia to me. "There's more." Then she tells me that a few days later, she got a call from Stefan, who wanted to know if she would meet him somewhere for lunch. He wanted so much to see her, he said, so very much, and his voice over the phone was soft and persuasive, with that delightful accent, that dear, familiar accent. "Yes, yes," she said, and a date was set, and a place, a restaurant they had always liked when they were going around together. But when they got there, the restaurant was gone. In its place was a one-hour photo-finishing lab, with its automatic equipment spewing forth colour prints right in the window where you could watch them. Cynthia and Stefan stood there looking at pictures of birthday parties, bar mitzvahs, high school graduations appearing and disappearing on the conveyor belt, and Cynthia thought, Look, it's the same for everyone—Life. She was very moved; it was a moment of revelation, entirely unexpected. As she watched, she saw a picture of herself go past. In the picture, she was sitting on her balcony in the shade of her lemon trees, and each tree was loaded with star-shaped blossoms, pure white and shining. She clutched at Stefan's arm and pointed, but it was too late, the picture was gone. "I'm sorry, I thought I saw something," she said, taking her hand from his arm. In the window, she could see their reflections. She was tall and Stefan was not so tall.

They walked on for several blocks, coming at last to a small restaurant with lace curtains as thick and creamy-white as wedding cake icing draped all across a small bay window. They went in and sat down. Cynthia was thinking how at one time she and this man had been so close and now they were merely polite with one another. He took her coat; he held her chair for her. "What would you like?" he asked, opening the menu. "Oh, I don't mind," she said absently. "You order." Such indecisiveness was quite out of character for Cynthia, but she felt exhausted suddenly, and she was thinking, also, about Max, because at this point she was still unsure of him. What should I do? she was asking herself, every five seconds or so.

"Snails," Stefan was saying. He smiled at her in a way that was utterly familiar. "A real treat, something different," he said.

Now, Cynthia says to me, "Can you imagine what went through my mind? We were sitting in this little French restaurant, looking, I daresay, friendly, intimate, cosy, all of that, and in a little while we would be served a dish of snails. It was all turning out just as Trisha said, but it was happening months later, in the wrong time altogether. I was so shocked, so confused, that when they arrived, I ate the snails, which normally I detest. And then Stefan began going on and on about this relationship he had, this wonderful relationship, with Max's tenant, the pediatrician, whose name, it turned out, was Veronica. He met her while playing his accordion for a fund-raising event in the pediatrics unit of a hospital. He told me that he had the children and the nurses dancing, and that those who weren't able to dance were clapping their hands and singing. He said it was the most beautiful moment of his entire life. Veronica was captivated. She adores music, it seems, especially authentic folk music. I reminded him that Natasha was musical, although her tastes ran more to the classical. He said, 'All those pieces by Bach. So difficult, so complex, but beautiful too, of course.'"

In his eyes, Cynthia saw reflected seven Nubian goats, unnamed and unclaimed against a cloudless sky, patiently waiting for the dream of Natasha and Stefan to be replaced by the more accommodating, sturdier dream of Natasha and Alastair McAlastair. This happens, of course, in time. The goats step happily into their green fields; the future begins.

When Alastair returns from Scotland, he brings Natasha a warm cloak handwoven by his mother and coloured like the Highland hills, misty blue and mauve and forest green. Unknown to Natasha and Alastair, his mother has cannily taken the precaution of weaving steadfastness and fidelity into the very warp and woof of the fabric. This has a beneficial effect on Natasha, who loves the cloak and wears it everywhere. She has given up the soup kitchen, at least for the winter months. Snow covers the fields outside her windows; a fire burns in her hearth; she is content.

As for Max and Cynthia, they go out in the first snowfall of the year and walk along the beach outside their house. The two black cats, who were either left behind or have managed to find their way back home, accompany them. Not knowing the cats' names, they have renamed them Alice and Ermengarde. Max says he has coveted these cats since before he ever saw them, and now he knows they have at last assumed their rightful place in his heart, and, indeed, in his home.

An odd thing happens. I am travelling across town by bus, when I see, on the sidewalk in front of the main door of the Museum of Natural History, my grandmother and my Aunt Beverly. Of course, they are not alone. My grandmother is pushing young Byron's baby carriage, and the other children—there seem to be dozens of them, an uncountable number, each one more handsome and lively than the last—are in constant motion, running this way and that as Beverly grabs futilely at them. The wind is blowing; the sun is shining; all of these people, my family, and the buildings, the streets, the trees, are energized by motion and light; everything is glowing. I wave at them, pressing my face up against the window of the bus, but of course they don't see me; I don't expect them to, and it really doesn't matter; I enjoy the sensation of anonymity, something which, in this family, does not often occur, believe me. And anyway, how could they possibly see me? In a matter of seconds the bus moves on, the scene changes. I am on my way to meet Aunt Trisha for lunch. She phoned me up and simply said, "I miss you, dear niece, let's get together." That is how my aunts are, my glorious aunts. Sometimes I get almost scared; I think: Where am I in all this? Where is there room for me in such a family? I am overpowered; I am weak, weak with love and amazement. I look up at the sky, at the air above this city, which is, I now see, like a seamless handwoven garment without flaw, conferring upon us all certain gifts, the things we most wish and hunger for: comfort, peace, security, love.

Living
In
Trees

Linda stands beneath the tree house, her arms around Adam and Tessa. Jon, who is two, sits on his haunches and pokes in the mud with a stick. Chris is taking readings from their skin, hair, and clothing with a light meter. He pauses to flick a stray strand of hair off Linda's forehead.

"We are standing right in the mud here," she says.

"Nice mud," Chris says. He fishes in his pocket for a tissue and hands it to Jon. "Wipe your nose, son," he says.

Linda takes the tissue away from Jon and holds his head still while she wipes his nose. Then she says, "What about Lyle?" She shouts, in the direction of the house, "Lyle, hurry up."

Chris squints into the camera, which he has set up on a tripod on a plank of wood, to keep it out of the mud. "Don't move. Smile, everybody. That's great. That's perfect."

"Wait, Chris," Linda holds up her hand. "Lyle has to be in the picture, too."

Chris groans and straightens up. They all watch as Lyle

walks up the trail from the house, his shoulders hunched, black hightop sneakers unlaced and flapping at his ankles.

"You give him a call, Chris," Linda says. "He won't be shy if he thinks you want him in the picture."

"Christ," says Chris. He goes over to Tessa and smooths the collar on her blouse. It's a blouse Linda made, with blue daisies embroidered on the collar. The blue is meant to match Tessa's eyes. Linda believes it does match, Tessa says it does not. "You going to be in this shot, Lyle baby?" Chris shouts, without bothering to glance in Lyle's direction.

They all wait. It is quiet enough to hear the wind in the cedars, the surf rolling in along the beach, which is not far from the house.

"You can all quit smiling," Chris says, not that they are smiling any longer, "until I tell you when." He waves his arms. "Come on, Lyle," he shouts. "The kids want you in the picture. Tessa wants you to stand next to her."

Tessa, startled, steps back onto Linda's foot.

"Oh, Tessa," Linda says. "Now I've got mud all over my sock."

Lyle, inching slowly closer, says, "You don't want me in your picture. I'll wreck it."

"I do," says Linda. "We all do. Don't we?" she appeals to the children, who say nothing. "Come on, Lyle," she says. "Be a sport." She smiles encouragingly, and when he gets near enough, she reaches out and takes him by the hand. Then she turns him toward the camera. "Look at the camera, Lyle," she says, and he lifts his head and blinks.

"Now," says Chris. "I want everybody smiling their heads off. Smile, Jon, 'atta boy."

But instead of smiling, Jon sneezes. Tessa swings around

to look at him. Adam shrugs dramatically and rolls his eyes. A Rhode Island Red runs squawking from the hen house, her wings spread in fright, directly into what becomes, at that moment, the foreground of the picture. Lyle, surprised by the hen, has thrown his arms up and screwed his eyes shut. This will all appear in the photograph, which is meant to commemorate the completion of the children's tree house. It will be a photograph of blurred, smudged features; windmilling arms. A failure, Chris will say, blaming it on Lyle. You can't blame Lyle, Linda will say, for something a stupid chicken did. Linda is the only one smiling in the photograph. Her smile is crooked and distracted and rather goofy, but she likes it. She thinks this picture says something true and unequivocal about herself and her family and even about Lyle, the stranger who should not have been there, but was.

Linda and Chris live with their children, Adam, Tessa and Jon, in the rain forest on the Esowista Peninsula on Vancouver Island. They live beside the open Pacific Ocean. Their doorstep is almost on the beach, in fact, and in the winter, after a good storm, they find all sorts of debris—driftwood, Japanese glass fishing floats, ropes of seaweed, other less interesting and less appealing flotsam such as plastic bleach bottles and beer cans—deposited only a few feet from their property line. The geographical location of their house is important to them because of the sea, and also because of the clean air, the forest, and the proximity of a large national park, which Chris says will keep at least some of the worst aspects of progress, so-called progress, from encroaching.

Chris and Linda built their house by hand. They have lived in it for five years; they lived here when their youngest child, Jon, was born. And now Chris has built a tree house for the children. And Lyle has appeared, coincidentally with the completion of the tree house, not that the two things are connected. Lyle is like something rather sad and unfortunate that the sea has dredged up and dumped at their feet after one of those winter storms.

"What's wrong with him, exactly?" Chris wants to know. "He makes me uneasy. Why does he do that?"

"Poor Lyle," Linda says. "He doesn't mean anything. He's just Lyle, I guess." She laughs uncertainly because, to be honest, she doesn't know how to explain her cousin, her long lost, half-forgotten cousin. When Lyle was five years old, she tells Chris, he was in a serious car accident with his parents. His father was killed, his mother was injured. After the accident, Lyle stopped talking for nearly a year. His mother worried that he had suffered damage to his brain, but that wasn't the case. His physical injuries had been minor, almost negligible, but obviously something had gone wrong. He had nightmares and couldn't sleep, and he developed an enormous, insatiable appetite for food, so that by the time he was ten years old he weighed one hundred and fifty pounds. He was ten the summer he stayed at Linda's house. The idea was, as far as Linda can remember, that Linda and Lyle would be company for each other and Lyle's mother would have a break from him at the same time. What Lyle's mother did that summer, as it turned out, was meet a man who became, a few weeks later, her second husband. Late in August, Lyle moved with his mother and his new stepfather to Winnipeg and Linda didn't see him again for years.

146

Lyle had a hobby the summer he stayed with Linda and her family: He collected snakes. He captured them and kept them in jars and in old fish tanks in the basement of Linda's house. He talked to his snakes. Every morning he set off on expeditions to find more specimens, as he called them. Linda went along with him sometimes, down to the creek, which had dried to a trickle that summer. Lyle would get down on his belly, very serious. He wore a white hat to keep the sun off his head. His eyes became dark and reptilian and superior: He knew about snakes, how to catch them, what they ate, where they slept. When he grew up, he said, he was going to study snakes in Africa and South America. He was going to be a herpetologist. "Oh, sure," Linda said. Now that she is herself a mother, she can look back and find Lyle's desire to be a herpetologist commendable, even endearing, but back then, when she was eleven years old, she believed Lyle was either bragging or lying. Everything he did made her angry. He had nightmares and woke everyone up with his screaming. He had to have a night-light; one of her parents had to sit on his bed holding his pudgy hand and telling him, There's nothing in your room, Lyle. You just had a bad dream.

"So, what are your nightmares about, Lyle?" she asked him one day when they were walking back up from the creek. "Do you dream about monsters? Witches with green hair? Mean old ghosts?"

"I don't dream about ghosts," he said. "I'm not a stupid baby." He was carrying a pickle jar containing a newly-acquired garter snake and some willow twigs. His face was shiny and red from the heat.

"I guess you dream about snakes," she said. "Smelly old

snakes crawling all over your blankets and getting up your nose, right, Lyle?"

"Asshole," he whispered.

"What did you say?" she shrieked. Lyle repeated the word, emphasizing both syllables. Then he lumbered off, his thighs bouncing together. The grass flattened and parted in his wake. Linda ran after him, yelling, "You swore, you swore." Oblivious, he plodded on.

Why does she remember this incident in such detail? She doesn't come off very well in it. Surely that summer contained as much amicability as anger? She and Lyle used to watch old black-and-white movies on TV when it was too hot to go outside. They drank Kool Aid and ate Dad's cookies in the living room with the curtains closed to keep out the sun. They traded comic books and walked together to the corner store for bubble gum and pop. They were like normal kids on summer vacation. Close to normal, anyway.

"At least try to be nice to him," she says now, to Chris. "He's only here for a little while."

"I should hope," Chris says, pulling a face and hunching his shoulders in what she supposes is meant to be an imitation of Lyle's usual stance.

∽

At first she thinks, Lyle? Lyle who? The voice on the telephone is slightly familiar to her, but she can't match it, or the name Lyle, with anyone she knows. "I'm sorry," she keeps saying, and then at last she understands, with a curious sinking of energy, so that she has to pull a chair toward her and sit down. Oh, she thinks: Lyle. My cousin, Lyle.

Yes, she says at last, this is Linda. Lyle tells her he is at a pay phone outside the Co-op store in the village. "Stay there," she tells him. "Don't move; I'll be there."

"Can you hear me?" Lyle shouts into the phone. He tells her that he intended to take the boat from Port Alberni, but he slept in at his hotel. The boat left at eight in the morning. So he got on the bus. He hadn't known how long the bus trip would be; he almost got sick. The road was terrible. He was sure they were going to crash. "But now I'm here," he says. "This is your cousin. Your cousin Lyle."

Yes, yes, Linda says to herself as she gets her coat and the keys to the van. This is nothing unusual; they've had unexpected company arrive before; this is nothing. Chris is at work up in the tree house; she can see him through the kitchen window. She decides not to tell him why she's driving into the village. Let him be as surprised by Lyle as she was. She goes outside and shouts up at him to keep an eye on the kids, who are in the house. "Don't forget, will you?" she calls. He nods, waves a hand, then goes back to hammering. Did he hear a word she said? He has a great natural avocation as a day-dreamer, although he denies that this is true. She climbs into the van and backs down the drive to the road.

This is your cousin, Lyle, she hears, as if Lyle were whispering in her ear. Come and get me.

What Chris especially loves about this tree house is the way it appears to grow out of the tree itself, so that the two seem to become a distinct organic entity. He would have loved a tree house when he was a child. Now, he's thrilled that he is able to give his own children what he missed out on. They will play here, creating for themselves new worlds where they will be free to act out tales of heroism and mystery. Their minds will become rich and elastic. The tree will do this for them. He catches the edge of childhood in his mind, a feeling like Christmas morning, and at the same moment he glances up at the tree, which is straight and tall as a cathedral spire, its highest branches scraping the calm, grey March sky. He adores this tree in what he considers a mystical fashion. That is, he gets a strong sense of wonder when he contemplates the fact that he and this tree are made up of the same amino acids; their nucleo-proteins are absolutely identical. Or so he has read somewhere. Hallelujah! he sometimes wants to cry out, in praise of the tree.

As he reaches for a section of planking, he hears Linda calling to him, but he doesn't quite manage to catch her words. He waves absently, then watches her back the van down the lane, and he sees, not the van, but the thick, wild, complicated and utterly natural forest growth on either side of the lane: pussy willows with their soft, silver animal-fur buds beneath the taller, darker trees, the fir and cedar and hemlock. The smell of damp earth, of cold spring mud mixed in with the rich, heady salt tang of the ocean, permeates the air, and he breathes it in, deeply, thinking: I am at home here. This is all mine.

It is March, and the tree house is nearly done, and there is the spring and summer to look forward to, and life, this life he has arranged for himself, is good, it really is. It pleases him.

ᗡ

"I had to get away to some place new," Lyle says, in the van. He stares out the window, as if wondering if this place is new enough, if it is going to do. Linda is driving home along the peninsula road after picking Lyle up in the village, and there is nothing to see but the dank, twisted vegetation of the rain forest. Lyle, who had been large at ten, is now an immense giant of a man. His body seems to give off a lot of heat, so that the van's windows keep fogging over. Linda plays around with the vents and the defogger; then she rolls her window down. Lyle looks as if he's been travelling for a long time. He's wearing jeans and a parka with plaid lining that shows through a rip under one sleeve. His hair is worn long, tied back with what appears to be a shoelace. When Linda caught sight of him, waiting exactly where she had told him to wait outside the Co-op, she thought: Oh, no. He looks like someone who needs to be cleaned up and talked to, and fed and comforted. I have enough to do already, with three kids and Chris.

He says, when Linda asks him how he's feeling, that he is actually much better now. He just needed to get out in the fresh air, after that bus trip. "Whew!" he says. He didn't know the bus would take so long, or that the road would be so bad. He looked down one time, and there was nothing but empty space. What a freaky sensation—one wrong move, and crash, you're at the bottom of a mountain. He sure isn't looking forward to the trip back, he says.

Linda shifts down to turn onto the road that leads to the beach where she and Chris live. Up until a few years ago, hardly anyone else lived here, but now thin columns of smoke from house chimneys rise between the trees at fairly regular intervals. Chris hates this; he wonders how far people will have to go, eventually, to get away from progress, from other people. Well, this is as far as I'm going, Linda always replies. Lyle, catching sight of the sea through a clearing in the trees, the breakers rolling in along the white sand beach, turns to her; his face, which up until now has worn a single expression, which she can only think of as morose, or at best sombre, is split by a huge, delighted grin.

"You live on a beach?" he says. "Oh, wow."

When she stops in front of her house, Lyle hides his chin in his coat collar and begins to rummage through his pockets. His face is scarlet. Chris comes out onto the porch, with Jon in his arms. Adam and Tessa, wearing warm wool sweaters but with no socks or shoes on their feet, are right behind him. They assemble themselves neatly at the top of the stairs, composed and watchful. They match each other, Linda sees; they match each other and the house and the forest. An alliance; a group. If she were Lyle, she'd feel shy too. In fact she does feel strangely shy, awkward. She keeps her hands on the steering wheel, waiting.

Then Chris comes down the steps and walks around to Linda's side of the van. "Company, Linda?" he says. Lyle, perhaps because Chris is no longer between him and the house, opens his door and slides out. He carries his suitcase— he is travelling with a scuffed brown leather suitcase—up to the porch and sets it down, then says to Adam and Tessa, "Hold out your hands. This isn't a trick or anything. I've got a present for you."

When, hesitantly, Adam and Tessa extend their hands, Lyle places something in each palm. Linda gets out of the van and says, "What have you got there?" to the children. They open their hands for her to see: a quarter each.

Lyle says, pointing at Jon, who is watching with interest from his father's arms, "Does he want one, too?"

"Oh, no, Lyle. Thanks, but no. He'd probably swallow it or something."

Lyle slips the last quarter back into his pocket and says, "You have kids, Linda. That's really neat. I was saving these quarters for phone calls, but that's okay." Then he picks up his suitcase and waits patiently for Linda to invite him into her house.

∽

Who is he? Who is he? Adam wants to know. Linda is preparing dinner and setting the table. Adam and Tessa are getting in the way.

"He's my cousin. Here, carry these," she says, handing Adam the salt and pepper shakers.

"What's a cousin?" Adam wants to know.

Linda looks at him. He really doesn't know. "A cousin is the son or daughter of your mother or father's sister or brother." She doesn't have a sister or a brother; neither does Chris. These children of hers do not have a cousin. Quickly she adds, "Some people have a lot of cousins and others don't. Families have different shapes and sizes. Everyone is different."

"Oh," Adam says, placing the salt shaker on the very edge of the table, then nudging it forward with his finger.

When they sit down to eat, Lyle insists on keeping his parka on. The children stare at him. Even though he looks uncomfortable and hot, he digs in with a good appetite. Every now and then a seemingly involuntary grunt issues from his throat, which causes Tessa to widen her eyes in alarm. The children have pushed their chairs down to the far end of the table, away from Lyle. They did this of one accord, surreptitiously, their eyes meekly downcast. Adam catches Linda's eye, points his fork at Lyle, and wrinkles his nose. Linda shakes her head at him. Chris eats, but doesn't say anything. Linda has never known such a silent meal. Clearly, it is time for some lessons on hospitality, being kind and thoughtful to others. But she says nothing. Chris, who has always said, Our door will be open to passersby, we will be a friendly, welcoming household, says nothing. The meal continues. Lyle's pale, fleshy lower lip is smeared with spaghetti sauce, which causes Adam to stare and then scrub at his own mouth with exaggerated and excessive care. Lyle doesn't notice; his eyes are hooded and without expression. Or perhaps they are expressive, in a way Linda does not understand, of avarice and greed and an instinctual sort of gluttony. Perhaps that is why they all feel so uneasy? She does not know. "Pass the bread, please," she says at last to Chris, more to break the silence than anything.

Later, when she and Chris have finished washing up the dishes and she is alone, wiping off the counter, Lyle comes into the kitchen and looks out the window. She hears him suck in his breath. "What is that?" he says urgently, pointing out the window at the tree house, which is barely visible in the March dusk. It is hanging amid the trees, its windows dark and secret, its steep roof rising into the overhanging branches like the fairy-tale dwelling of some forest creature.

"What is that?" Lyle asks, wringing his hands. "Can I see it?" Without waiting for an answer, he pulls the door open and heads outside. Linda doesn't follow. She has to get the kids into bed and find sheets to make up the cot for Lyle in the spare room where she has her sewing machine and the loom, from the time when she was interested in weaving. It is almost an hour later, and dark, when Lyle comes back inside. According to Chris, who has been watching him from the porch, he has been standing at the foot of the fir tree all this time, staring up at the tree house. His eyes are bright, his face cheerful. He looks like someone who has had a vision or has unexpectedly been given a gift.

"Linda," he says. "You have a tree house. I think that's so neat."

Later that night, in their bedroom, Chris says to Linda, "How could you possibly forget that you have a cousin? How could anyone forget a cousin?"

Linda, tugging her sweater off over her head, says, "I didn't forget, exactly." Is it possible, she wonders, that she has never even mentioned Lyle to Chris? Yes, she decides; it is possible. When she and Chris met, one thing that drew them together was the knowledge that they had both grown up without brothers or sisters, they had both suffered through solitary, isolated childhoods. Chris had said, sounding partly aggrieved and partly proud, "You know, I don't even have a cousin, not even one cousin, anywhere in my family." And Linda quite likely said, Well, neither do I. In fact she knows that's what she said. So that they could be the same. The two of them against the world. Chris likes that; he likes to be against the world. That is a big part of why they live here, supposedly removed from the world and the evils of the world. They have constructed, with their children, their own world, their own society. Chris can say it better. He has theories, dreams. He speaks of sanctuary, of safe havens, of refuge, and he believes that without corrupting influences like television and the movies, his children will grow up with no notion of violence, of pollution, of any form of pollution, physical or mental. When they first came here to live, he used to run out to the water's edge every morning before breakfast, and he would scream at the surf, scream and scream, sometimes until his throat bled and he was voiceless for the rest of the day. This helped to clear his system, he said, of society, of that world "out there." Now he is a milder man, it seems. He folds his blankets neatly across his thin, hairless chest and says, again, "How can you forget a cousin?" He seems amused. "Are you sure he's your cousin?" he asks. "And not some weirdo who just got loose from the nut house?"

Adam is in grade two at school and Tessa is in kindergarten. Normally, they leave each morning on the school bus at the top of the road to the beach, but this week is spring break, and they are at home. Chris is introducing them to the tree house, getting them used to going safely up and down the ladder. He tells them they have to hold on with both hands and they must never attempt to carry anything, food or toys, up the ladder. He has rigged up a special wooden box on a rope and pulley for that. The problem is, Adam and Tessa are not strong enough to work the pulley. "Try again," Chris keeps saying, demonstrating where they should place their hands and how they should brace their feet and shoulders.

Linda has the camera; she has been taking shots of Adam and Tessa climbing the ladder, looking out the windows of the tree house, and now learning, or trying to learn, how to pull toys and books and things to eat up in the wooden box.

"Maybe we should put something in the box," she says to Chris. "A toy or an apple, so it will make more sense to them." Tessa and Adam peer down at her, and at Jon, who is tugging at her coat. He wants to be up there in the tree house too. Linda points the camera down at him, then swings around and catches Lyle in the lens as he chucks handfuls of feed at the chickens. He loves to feed the chickens.

It is now five, no, six, days since he arrived. Every morning he gets up very early, before anyone else, and makes up the cot he sleeps on, pulling the blankets tight and smooth and plumping up his pillows. He keeps his brown leather suitcase on the floor at the foot of the cot, as if he needs ready reference to it. He has one change of clothes with him, so every second day he uses the washer and dryer to do his laundry. He showers and shaves and straightens up the bathroom, picking up towels and socks left behind by the children. He delights in the sound of surf on the beach and sometimes sits for hours, even in the rain and fog, on a log at about the high tide mark, listening and watching. Sometimes he walks miles and miles along the beach, all alone, picking up shells and fragments of coloured glass polished by the sea, and these he shows Linda before storing them in a shoebox in his room. He helps Linda make bread, something he has never done before in his life, he says happily. He kneads the dough, rolls it out. Rain strikes the kitchen window. A basket of fresh eggs, gathered earlier from the hen house by Lyle, sits on the counter. Very deliberately, his slow, strong hands punch and mold and roll out the bread dough. Adam and Tessa hang around the kitchen, playing with bits of left-over dough, waiting for the bread to emerge, golden, steaming hot, fragrant, from the oven. They watch as Lyle spreads butter and Linda's home-made blackberry jam on thick slices for them. "I should have been a baker," Lyle says proudly, shoving a second, then a third piece of bread into his mouth, wiping melted butter from his chin.

"You must be anxious to get going," Chris says to him from time to time. "What's your next stop after this?" To Linda, he says, "You're being too nice to him, that's the problem."

"Well, he is my cousin," she says. She begins to remind him of Lyle's history, his unfortunate history: the car accident, the death of his father, his mother's remarriage.

"Well, I don't think an accident at the age of five can entirely account for Lyle," Chris says flatly. When she tells Chris about Lyle talking to the snakes in his snake collection, down in the basement of her house, he says, "I collected snakes, too, when I was a kid. There's nothing in the least unusual about collecting snakes, or butterflies or whatever. Tadpoles. Didn't you ever collect tadpoles, Linda?"

"Yes, I collected tadpoles, for a science project or something. I had a reason for collecting tadpoles, it wasn't an obsession. But that's not the point. The point is, don't we have some kind of responsibility to him now that he's here?"

"I suppose so," Chris says. And then he says, "Well, no, I don't think we do. We don't. Of course we don't."

"Oh, yes, we do," says Linda, not wanting Chris to have the last word in this. But do they? Even after coming to what feels like the end of the earth to find peace and refuge, she and Chris may not understand how to give these things to a person in need of them. Linda thinks of Lyle at ten years of age, with his pickle-jar garter snake. She recalls herself that same year, running after him, her hair long and yellow as Tessa's is now, calling, You swore, you swore, her anger completely out of proportion, it now seems, to what Lyle had said to her. Lyle has forgotten by now. He tells her at least once a day, it seems, how he bought a bus ticket in Winnipeg and set out to find her, knowing only that she still lived somewhere on Vancouver Island. "I didn't know if I would find you or not, Linda," he says.

"Well, you did, Lyle," she always replies. "You didn't have any trouble finding me at all, did you?"

They are walking along the beach, she and Lyle. It is the first day of April, and the fog, persistent for days, seems at last to be breaking up. There is even a patch of blue up there, she sees. As they walk, Lyle says something Linda can't quite make out over the roar of the surf. They are heading in a long, slow, oblique line from the house to the water. Lyle hangs back; he kicks at the sand. It is the first time Linda has accompanied Lyle on one of his walks on the beach. She cups her hand to her ear and yells, "I can't hear you Lyle."

He draws in his breath and yells, "I ran away."

Linda stares at him, horrified, thinking that he is about to tell her that, just as Chris suggested, he has escaped from an institution of some kind, an asylum. The loony-bin. She sees the escape clearly in her mind: Lyle hiking his leg over a stone prison wall, dropping with an "ouf" of astonishment on the other side which turns out to be an empty road that leads directly to the west coast of the country and his cousin Linda.

Then, gradually, he makes her understand that in fact he has run away from a scheduled appointment with a psychologist he's been seeing. The psychologist has been helping him to come to grips with a lack of direction in his life. "The main problem I have," Lyle says, "is in not being able to sleep. It's extremely debilitating. I get so wiped out. I can't hold down a job, I can't study, I can't even think straight. I got some pills, and they helped a bit, and then the doctor said, 'Try it without pills. You don't want to get addicted to sleeping pills.' So I tried, but it didn't work. I have this continual racy feeling in the bones of my leg."

As if to demonstrate, Lyle shuffles his feet madly back and forth on the sand, in a sort of high-speed moon-walk.

"Oh, Lyle," Linda says, trying not to laugh. The sand under his feet makes a whistling sound and he stops, listens, and then looks at Linda, disbelieving. Linda nods her head and begins sliding her own feet back and forth on the sand, which is so fine that it rises in a grainy fog around her shoes. "The sand is singing," she shouts. The wind catches her words and Lyle, not sure of what he has heard, looks at her in confusion. At that moment the sun breaks gloriously through the fog and the water sparkles and the sand is suddenly too white and bright to even look at. Linda zooms her feet around on the sand. She feels warmed through by the sun: her skin, her heart, her soul.

"The sand is singing," she shouts jubilantly at Lyle, who grins widely and says, "Whish, whush, whish," and does his strange moon-walk on the shining moonscape of the beach.

〇

One morning several days later Tessa wakes Linda up by urgently pinching her arm just above her elbow. "Ouch," Linda says. "What are you doing? What is it?" She feels as if she has been dumped out of one dream into another. Tessa is a pale, silver sprite floating up near the ceiling. Then she floats down and gently says into Linda's ear, "Jon's outside. He's outside in his sleepy suit." She means pyjamas: Jon is outside in his blue fleece pyjamas.

Linda looks at the clock. It is six. She gets out of bed and reaches for her housecoat. Chris is asleep, his arm thrown across his eyes. Linda checks Jon's room first, where she sees that his crib is indeed empty and even his pink blanket, without which he will not sleep, is missing. She runs downstairs and opens the front door and goes out onto the porch, into the cool, misty dawn, and sees, almost at once, Lyle, in his pyjamas and his unlaced hightop sneakers, halfway up the ladder to the tree house with Jon, wrapped in his pink blanket, tucked under his arm.

"Get down from there," she calls, gathering up the hem of her nightgown and stepping carefully across the boards Chris has put down over the worst of the mud. It rained heavily again in the night, and rainwater has collected on the papery leaves of the salmonberry bushes and on the roof of the hen house and in Jon's red wagon, left beside the footpath. All this rain water gleams like liquid mercury in the dull dawn light.

She reaches the ladder and places her hand on a lower rung. "Get down," she says, very firm. Lyle begins to make his way unsteadily down the ladder. "Careful," she says. "Careful." Jon's blue eyes stare at her over the top of Lyle's shoulder. She stares back. As soon as she can reach she pulls

Jon away from Lyle and holds him so tightly that he squirms and whines and demands to be put down. Her son, her baby, her handsome boy, she is thinking, sentimental and outraged at the same time.

"He had a nightmare," Lyle is saying. "He was scared. He called me to his room. He couldn't get back to sleep."

It is possible, she thinks, to make too much of this. Already the image of Lyle hauling himself up the ladder with Jon is fading in her mind. She should ask Lyle what he was doing, what he thought he was doing, but she can't, because she can't bear to think how her questions might be answered, or not answered. All she says, finally, is, "Do you know what time it is?" Then she says, "Oh, never mind, never mind." She settles Jon's weight in her arms and prepares to walk back to the house.

Lyle is not listening to her anyway. His attention is, she can see, on the tree house, which is directly overhead. It hangs there in the grey morning light like a picture from a dream, a small dream of castles and enchanted forests and make-believe. It seems to Linda that Lyle's feet are slowly rising above the ground, and his body, normally so heavy and awkward, is assuming the grace of an angel. Eventually, she supposes, he will float all the way up to the tree house and then what? He will live there. And they will never, never be rid of him.

☞

Chris climbs up into the tree house with his carpentry tools. He worries that the tree house, which measures nine feet by ten, is not quite large enough, considering that eventually,

162

when Jon is a little older, three children will be playing in it. But the roof is steep, with exposed rafters, and so there is a feeling of roominess and the light is quite wonderfully diffuse and mysterious. There are three small windows in all, and Linda has promised to make curtains for them when she has time. On the other side of the windows are the branches of the fir tree, deep green and heavy, swaying gently in the wind and beaded with drops of moisture from a shower earlier that morning. The idea comes to him, at that moment, that the branches are the feathered wings of angels, which will descend in a solemn sweep and enfold him lovingly, tenderly. This is an unusual thought, but he follows it; he imagines Adam and Tessa sleeping up here in the summer, high above the ground, themselves angels floating in the clouds. These images are appealing and at the same time disconcerting, as if his children, asleep in the clouds, will be forever beyond his reach. And in that case he would lose them, and he wouldn't want that to happen, ever. This, he suddenly understands, is the danger of living in trees. Like the young boy who climbed the beanstalk, you might well go on climbing higher and higher until you found yourself in a land where you did not belong, where you were at all times in imminent unforeseeable danger.

He thinks of the giant, the malevolent giant, at the top of the beanstalk, and at the same moment he sees Lyle walking over to the storage shed near the hen house. Lyle looks close enough to a wicked giant to be one, with his hood pulled over his head and his pant legs stuffed messily into thick grey socks. As Chris watches he disappears into the storage shed, then reappears carrying a bucket of feed for the chickens, which cluck and flock enthusiastically to his feet. This is another example, Linda would say, of just how much help Lyle is getting to be. He feeds the chickens, bakes bread, chops wood, keeps the fire going, minds the kids. I taught him how to do all these things. Good for you, Chris thinks. Every day they take time to argue about Lyle: When is he going? Chris wants to know. Soon, Linda says; any day now. But the days pass. Chris gets angry, he can't help it, and then Linda says, "You're not jealous, are you?" Of all things, Chris most hates to be called jealous. He remembers how people used to say, Oh, an only child, he must be selfish, he must be spoiled. What idiots they were: He has grown into a perfectly well-adjusted adult. It isn't necessary, in his opinion, to be constantly surrounded by people and noise. He prefers solitude. He has what he wants: his own land, his family, his children. He has things arranged in a way that pleases him.

He watches as Lyle returns the feed bucket to the shed and walks back to the house. Before going up the steps, he pauses and scrapes the mud off his shoes onto the bottom step. Chris thinks: Soon, just from seeing the things he does, I will be as crazy as he is. Of course, the mud can easily be washed away, that's not the real problem. The real problem is Lyle. Lyle is out of place; he doesn't belong here. Chris made this, all of it; even the trees, he feels, grew out of his heart, out of his great need for peace and distance from the world, and here is Lyle, wiping his big muddy feet on the steps. It's too much, Chris thinks. It has to stop.

Yesterday, and the day before, Linda tried to get Lyle's mother on the telephone. Lyle gave her his number, then

164

watched as she dialed. She let the phone ring and ring, but no one answered. "Probably shopping," he said in a disinterested tone. "She loves shopping." Linda hung up and tried again several hours later, still with no luck, and then again the next morning. Finally, Lyle told her that his mother and Dan, which was what he called his stepfather, had gone to Florida with friends. They were renting an apartment near the beach in Miami or some place, he thinks, and unless they had tried contacting him they had no idea he was not at home. He didn't even know he was coming here himself, he says, until he actually had the bus ticket in his hand.

"Yes," said Linda, exasperated. "But why didn't you tell me there was no one there before I tried phoning?"

Lyle shrugged: He didn't know.

Do not imagine, Linda tells herself, any of these things: Do not imagine that Lyle has murdered his mother and stepfather and left their bodies in the cellar of their Winnipeg home. Do not imagine that he has robbed a corner store, or been caught exposing himself to children outside a school. Because it's a test, in a way. If you begin to imagine these wicked things about Lyle, then you fail the test. Do not imagine that, as Chris flippantly suggested, Lyle has run away from an institution of some kind. Because he hasn't. The worst he's done, and he told her this himself, is miss an appointment with his psychologist, and what's so bad about that? It's all in your mind, Linda, she tells herself. It's a test, and if you don't want to fail the test, then don't allow yourself to dwell on what is not true.

Of course, no matter what tests Linda sets for herself, no matter how determined she is to be fair, kind, understanding, patient, trusting, there will come a time. A time when Lyle will step over an invisible mark that has been drawn directly in his path by her and Chris. Or by life. Or by Lyle himself. It doesn't matter who put the mark there. He will step on it anyway, and that will be that. Everyone knows this, even, Linda suspects, Lyle himself. Otherwise, why would he go out searching for this invisible mark, unless simply to get it over with.

One day, Lyle takes Tessa and Jon with him to meet Adam when he gets off the school bus. Kindergarten is only half a day, and Tessa is home already. They leave at three o'clock, Lyle pulling Jon in his red wagon, and by four they are still not back. Chris keeps looking out the window and at the clock on the kitchen wall. "Goddamn," he says. "He isn't responsible. He's a fruitcake." He means Lyle, naturally. "Why did you let him go off with the kids like that?"

"He always takes the kids for walks," Linda says. She rinses her hands under the kitchen tap. She has been peeling the skin off chicken pieces, for supper. She flicks her hands dry over the sink, then gets her yellow rain slicker and hat. It seems to her that it is taking a long time to warm up this spring. And every day, around this time, it rains. "I'll find them," she says to Chris, who is staring gloomily out the window, drawing, she imagines, certain invisible lines across his field of vision. Outside, she hesitates for a moment on the porch, listening to the surf pounding in along the shore. Although it is a sound she should be used to by now, it never fails to astonish her with its strength and insistence. She has, in the past, played with the idea that before she and Chris arrived with their tools for building and implements for digging and planting in the soil, there was only silence, nothing moving, not even the wind in the slender spaces between the tall trees. It took their coming here, with all their hope and optimism, to set the tides going, to encourage the strong west winds. What nonsense, she now thinks: The sea and the wind have never noticed either the absence or the presence of Chris and Linda and their children. The sea doesn't care; why should it? She is the one who cares; she is the one who listens. And Lyle, who has confided in her that now he doesn't mind his insomnia, because when he lies awake at night he can always listen to the ocean. He would rather listen to the ocean than sleep, he now says, even if he were given a choice.

She walks away from the sea, up towards the road, then along the road, past the place where the school bus picks up and drops off the children, then down the road again, toward the house. Just as she begins to worry that perhaps something is wrong, she catches sight of Lyle and all three of her children crouched down in a clearing in the trees, and staring at the ground. She must have walked right by them the first time.

"I was calling you," she says as she approaches them.

"We didn't hear you," Adam says without looking up.

Lyle, his face flushed and wet with rain, says, "Linda. Linda, look at this."

Linda crouches down between Adam and Tessa. Jon is sitting in his red wagon, his thumb stuck in his mouth. On the trail, heading in a slow east-west direction, is a slug, an ordinary brown spotted slug, the kind Linda routinely plucks out of her vegetable garden and drowns in bowls of stale beer, a practice she read about in a gardening book. Tessa picks up a twig and prods the slug in what might be called the stomach area.

"Don't touch it," Lyle says sharply, batting Tessa's hand away. "You'll hurt it."

"I wasn't going to hurt it," Tessa cries. "You're mean, Lyle." Tessa is easily offended. She is wearing the blouse she wore the day the photograph was taken under the tree house, the blouse embroidered with daisies that do in fact exactly match Tessa's blue eyes, now bright with anger and tears.

"It is beautiful, isn't it?" Lyle whispers, his nose inches from the slug.

"Beautiful!" Adam crows. "Beautiful!"

Adam and Tessa leap to their feet and begin dancing around. "Lyle loves slugs, Lyle loves slugs," they chant. "Lover-boy Lyle," Adam shouts, and Linda catches him by the arm and says, "Enough, enough." They must all go right home, no nonsense, she tells them. She has to put the chicken in the oven, she says, and Adam doubles over and says, "Chicken, yech." Then he and Tessa take off down the road. Linda follows with Lyle, who is pulling Jon in the red wagon.

"I'm sorry," she says to Lyle. "They were being rude."

"I know," Lyle says placidly. "Kids are rude sometimes." Carefully he pulls the wagon around a pothole, moving with a ponderous, irreproachable dignity that Linda thinks must surely be new to him. Acquired when? she wonders, and how? And then she thinks: Here, of course. She sees at once how useful they have been to Lyle, how therapeutic. It is something in them, she thinks, something Lyle has simply absorbed and made good use of. She feels proud of herself, and of her wholesome, normal family. She is actually thinking this, feeling self-congratulatory and pleased with herself and with Lyle as they approach the house, where Chris is waiting on the porch.

"Where the hell have you been?" he demands. Then he

runs down the stairs and grabs Lyle roughly by his coat collar and begins shaking him and spluttering "You, you, you," in such a wild and incoherent way Linda can only watch in disbelief. Then Chris pulls back his arm and lands a solid punch on Lyle's nose. There is blood; there are screams, from herself, from Lyle, from Adam and Tessa and Jon, who have unfortunately witnessed all this.

"You broke my nose," Lyle mutters thickly. He collapses into the mud, legs extended. His hair, wet from a sudden, fresh shower of rain, is plastered to his head.

"No, no," Linda says. "It's probably not broken." The children are crying; Chris is stalking around, cradling his sore knuckles and telling the children to be quiet. "Come into the house and I'll get you an ice-pack," she says to Lyle. Cold comfort, she thinks, amassing names to use later on Chris: bully, selfish, spoiled brat, hysteric.

In the house, she bathes Lyle's face with warm water and then gets him to hold a bag of crushed ice over his nose. "You're going to have two lovely shiners," she says, using a tone that comes in handy when the children have stepped on nails or pinched their fingers in doors.

Chris pulls up a chair and sits down. "That wasn't like me," he begins. "I've never done anything like that before."

"Lyle's had enough apologies for one day, thank you," Linda says.

Later, after dinner, which is of course late, the chicken suspiciously pink in places and the boiled potatoes crisp, Lyle disappears. For a while, Linda and Chris assume he's in his room, but when they look he isn't there.

"The tree house," Chris says, heading for the door.

"Wait," Linda says. "Leave him there."

169

"It's cold. He can't stay outside."

"It's what he wants," she says. "Let him do what he wants." From the window she can see the tree house cradled in the wings—wings? she thinks—branches of the fir. She is getting the same sense of power and strength from this tree that she got earlier listening to the surf rolling along the shore. Everything has its own power and sufficiency and will work out for the best in the end, she thinks. She believes that Lyle is sustained through the cold, starless night by thoughts identical to these. Sustained and comforted. Lyle loves plants and animals, especially, as she has witnessed for herself, those creatures large enough to be visible to the naked eye, but small enough to be at risk from a misplaced step, a heavy rainfall, a child's curious, probing touch.

Early the next morning, Chris talks a shivering, shocked, ashamed-looking Lyle out of the tree house and into the warm kitchen, where he feeds him oatmeal porridge, and toast spread with fireweed honey, and mugs of hot strong coffee. After awhile, Lyle stops shivering. Chris tells him how sorry he is for what happened. He doesn't usually have a bad temper, but he'd been worried—parents do worry about their children, he says. He hopes he hasn't ruined Lyle's visit, which in any case must be about over by now. Lyle's eyes are bloodshot, darkened by bruises. His nose looks puffy and sore. Linda catches his eyes for a moment, but he looks away and begins tracing the outline of his coffee spoon on the tablecloth.

"You can't stay here indefinitely, after all. You have your own life to get back to," Chris says. "You have your friends and your family to get back to. You can't just stay here, Lyle. It wouldn't be right."

Linda notices that Chris doesn't explain why it wouldn't be right. He just gets up and walks away, leaving Lyle with his coffee spoon and toast crumbs. To make matters worse it's a cold day, with the wind howling in from the south-west and huge breakers crashing in along the shore.

Later, Lyle irons his clean shirt and jeans and hangs them neatly on the back of the closet door in the sewing room. Linda does the housework in silence, wishing that she could find words to smooth everything over and make the situation tolerable, at least for herself. Lyle's expression, although wounded, is one of forbearance, as if there is a lot he could say but is holding back.

The first year Linda and Chris lived on the west coast, they had to leave their house when a tsunami warning was issued following an earthquake in Alaska. The earthquake had been seven point something on the Richter Scale but no one had been seriously injured, and perhaps because of this the warning seemed more like a friendly joke than anything. Linda and Chris calmly strapped Adam and Tessa, who were babies at the time, into their infant car seats and drove to the national park, where they met up with other people who had either evacuated their homes or who were simply curious. Some, of course, were people on holiday, camping in the park. They all straggled up a hill to higher ground to get a good view of the sea, which was where disaster would come from, if it came. It was a beautiful, warm May afternoon, the sea unusually flat and peaceful. Surf rolled in lazily along the endless white sands. Birds sang in the trees. The idea of a tidal wave occurring here seemed absurd. And yet, Linda began to dwell on the idea of her new house and its contents, all the furniture and baby clothes, the dishes and the pictures on the walls, caught up and swept away by a wall of cold sea water. She thought about it until she believed it was inevitable. Chris had promised they would be safe on the west coast, they would be protected from the random, unpredictable violence of modern urban life, but they were evidently not safe at all, they were in as much danger as anyone, anywhere.

The tsunami had been predicted for two o'clock at the latest, and as that hour approached, Linda, along with everyone else, shifted her attention to the sea. At exactly two, a number of people observed a dark line they believed marked the position of the tsunami as it moved in along the surface of the ocean. Before the line reached shore, however, it was gone. Linda thought she had seen it and so did Chris. After awhile, everyone agreed that there had been a dark, ominously dark, line and that it had travelled at an incredible rate of speed, wearing itself out long before it reached land. This may have been the case, for all Linda knows. She believes now that there had been nothing to see. She believes they all invented the dark line to fulfill their expectations, so that they could go home safe but not entirely disappointed.

That, she thinks, is how it is with Lyle. She and Chris have been standing on a high point of land, so to speak, looking down on Lyle and seeing the idea of evil, of wrongness, of wrongdoing, more clearly than they have seen Lyle himself. They expected disaster and when none actually came they began making fairly minor occurrences seem more serious than they really were. Everyone who ever meets Lyle will do this, she fears. She did it to him when they were children.

How can she ever make amends? She thinks of Lyle shuffling his feet in the singing sand at the edge of the incoming tide. She thinks of him crouched on the trail, raindrops dripping off his hair into his eyes as he observes a slug's slow progress from nowhere to nowhere.

Lyle is gone. He left while they were all away in the village shopping for food and new shoes for Adam and Tessa. When they returned, they at once perceived an emptiness behind the closed doors and windows of their home. "He's gone," they said to each other, going through the silent rooms, staring at the place at the foot of Lyle's neatly made-up bed where his suitcase had rested for a length of time they seem unable now to calculate. "He's gone, isn't he?" they said. Adam ran into his room and slammed his door shut. "He'll come back and visit us another time," Chris tried to say through the door. "He'll come back soon, you'll see."

All Lyle seems to have left behind is his shell collection, and Linda opens the box and picks up a clamshell and a sand dollar. "He had a good time here, you know," she says to Chris. She thinks of how Lyle was made to let his snakes go at the end of the summer he spent at her parents' house. He went outside and tipped the glass tanks and jars on their sides and prodded the snakes out of their lethargy. Captivity made them sleepy, he told Linda: They no longer even dreamed of being free. He wouldn't have kept them much longer anyway, he said.

This is your cousin, Lyle, she hears in her mind, and at the same time she has the oddest sense that Lyle was never here at all. He was a dream she had, or imagined she had, a dark, troubled line racing madly across the surface of her mind, then vanishing, spent and worn-out.

Then she realizes that proof of Lyle's time with them exists irrefutably in the photograph Chris took beneath the tree house, on one of the first days Lyle spent with them. The photograph is pinned up on the kitchen wall. In it, Lyle has his eyes shut and his arms up as if he's afraid of being hit with something, which, as it turned out, wasn't such a farfetched notion. Actually, he looks no stranger than any of them, all thrown off-balance, wild with confusion. And above them is the tree house, lodged high in the green, sheltering branches of the tree as if tossed there by the sea. She places her thumb over Lyle's face in the photograph for a moment. With or without Lyle, the rest of them look just the same. Thirty years, fifty years from now, Linda thinks, Chris's tree house will have rotted away in the west coast rains. A hundred years of winter storms and a slight change in the geography of the coastline and even their house will be gone. A tsunami won't be needed to accomplish this degree of destruction, sadly enough. Only time will be needed.

In the
Dead Room

On the first day of school in September, Claire read to her students "The Cask of Amontillado" by Edgar Allan Poe. "'The thousand injuries of Fortunato I had borne as I best could, but when he ventured upon insult I vowed revenge,'" she began. The story wasn't exactly part of the curriculum, but Claire didn't use it for study; she used it as a treat for the class, a way of easing them into the rigours (in her opinion, her classes were rigorous) of grade eleven English and a new school year. Also, she loved reading aloud; she had once been told that there was a pleasant, indeed almost mesmerizing, quality to her reading voice, and she believed, she hoped, that this was true.

"'It was about dusk, one evening during the supreme madness of the carnival season, that I encountered my friend,'" she read, pleasantly aware, from the quality of the silence in the room, that she had the attention of a majority of her students. This was the part of the story that she herself most enjoyed. Here it was that Montresor, whom she saw as paradoxically fair and bland of countenance, in spite of his wickedness, began to cast the dark nets that would inextricably bind poor Fortunato.

And the words "carnival season" delighted her. She wanted to come out from behind her desk and beseech these young people: Only listen to what is suggested here. Think of this Italian town, hot, dark, lit with torches, all the citizens drunk on wine and their own merriment. Think of Fortunato dressed in his motley, his cap jingling with bells. Plainly, he's out for a good time. Imagine yourself there with him. Imagine all of us transported to that night. What would happen? What might we witness?

At three-thirty, after her last class, Claire went downstairs to the staff room and sat down, exhausted, with her daybook open on her lap. Her throat was sore from reading aloud. She couldn't even think about the next day's classes; she closed her eyes and tried to relax, to slow her pulse and quiet her breathing. A man, another teacher, came in and set his briefcase down on the floor, then gave it a sharp kick into the corner. He filled the kettle with water and put it on to boil, then stood staring out the window, whistling. Claire didn't know his name. This was her first day at this school; she knew almost no one, except for Inez, who taught sewing and cooking. And Inez wasn't likely to introduce her to whatever social life went on among the school's staff, Claire suspected. Inez had nothing good to say about any of her male colleagues, and she was not, she claimed, on speaking terms with most of the women. Claire had met Inez in August at the beach, when she sat near her, not quite by accident, to dry off after a swim. Inez had removed her straw hat and her sunglasses while she studied Claire. "I wouldn't swim in that water if you paid me," she said. When Claire told Inez that she had just moved to the town and had a job teaching at the high school, Inez said, "Oh God, why here, of all places?" She laughed bitterly, saying there must have been other places, other teaching jobs. "But this is a nice town," Claire protested. "It's right on the sea, and it's small, and old-fashioned, and picturesque, in a way. I feel at home here already." (This was only partly true; Claire was also lonely, homesick.) In any case, Inez merely snorted and became absorbed in applying suntan oil to her shoulders.

Claire could hardly have come out with the truth, which was that she first encountered this town in a dream, months before she saw it in real life. In her dream she flew (it had seemed to her that she was flying) directly over the blue harbour where tall ocean-going freighters lay anchored at the sawmill docks, over the very beach on which she and Inez sat talking, over the flat tar-and-gravel roof of the high school, over the green playing fields, the small houses set back from the narrow streets, the very smokestacks and lumber yards of the sawmill. It was such a vivid dream, full of colour and a sense of high adventure. And then, when she arrived for her job interview and saw it all just as she had dreamt, only from a more normal perspective, what else could she think but that her coming here was foreordained, an event over which she had little, if any, control.

She rented a house from a widow who had gone to Scotland to stay with her sister for a year. Before leaving, the widow showed Claire through the house as if making introductions: This is the Royal Albert china; this is the dishwasher, new last year; this is the wallpaper I chose to go with the new drapes; this is a shell Sidney brought back from our trip to Hawaii. Sidney was the late husband. The house was large and comfortable and a five-minute walk from the school. "Look how lucky I am," Claire said to Inez, showing her over the house, giving her the widow's spiel. "The TV's only a year old, it's got remote control, it gets thirty different channels." Claire and Inez got into the habit of staying up late nights, watching TV and heating frozen pizza in the widow's microwave oven. They also went through her photograph album, and her dresser drawers, looking for outmoded birth control devices, or anything else of a sexual or sinister nature. But the widow had cannily packed away her personal belongings.

"Such a secretive woman," Inez said, banging shut a drawer. "I wonder what she had to hide?"

Claire and Inez were in one of the upstairs bedrooms, long unused, unless, as Inez suggested, the widow had been in the habit of bringing men up here. Young men, handsome young men, not terribly bright, with slightly dirty fingernails and bad taste in shoes and ties. Inez pretended to be the widow. The widow would try to reform the young men; she would show them her late husband's ties, his shoes. "He went to good schools," Inez, as the widow, said. "He worked in a bank."

Claire straightened the curtains at the bedroom window, surreptitiously checking out the house across the street as she did so, trying to see over the hedge, through the branches of the trees. She saw that the car was gone from the garage. Probably no one was at home. Inez, still as the widow, was saying, "You're nay a patch on my bonny lad, but you'll do, in a pinch." "Would you shut up," Claire said. "You're incorrigible." "I know," said Inez happily, marching out of the room, thumping down the widow's uncarpeted stairs.

The weather stayed fine into late October, so that Claire and Inez were able to sit outside on the widow's patio, chatting and making up exams. It seemed impossible, to Claire, that the first two months of the school year were nearly over; soon it would be winter. Winged seeds from a maple tree were whirling through the air and skittering across the patio floor. Inez was stretched out on a chaise lounge, her feet and legs bare, admiring the scarlet polish she had just put on her toenails. She was off on her favourite theme again: the unwholesome nature of the town; more than that, the absolutely monstrous nature of the town. "Like a monster, it swallows you up," she said. "It devours you." She always did the very best she could to encourage her students to move on, to leave here and make something real out of themselves. It was a tragedy that most of the kids went all the way through school and then ended up working at the sawmill and marrying young and having kids, repeating the whole cycle, generation after generation. "Such a sacrifice," she said, "such a waste. And not only the kids, come to that." When she thought about it, when she considered all the years she'd already spent here, and the years presumably still to come, she felt, frankly, as if she were suffocating.

Inez alternated between warning Claire about the town and warning her about William, who lived across the street, in the house Claire had spied on from the upstairs window. Inez had caught her looking out, pretending to fiddle with the curtains. "You're interested in him, aren't you? You can't fool me," Inez said.

"Well, at least he's friendly," Claire said. "He always says good morning and he's invited me over for coffee a couple of times."

"That was totally out of character, believe me," said Inez. "William Johnson is not the neighbourly type. He's not 'just folks'. He's a big snob and he goes around thinking women should throw themselves at his feet." Inez wouldn't get mixed up with the man, that was for sure. "So be warned," she said to Claire. "He's probably after you for free babysitting."

William had two daughters, Natalie, eleven, and Pamela, eight. They were pretty, delicate children with long brown hair and huge dark-brown eyes. William was fair and robust in appearance; therefore, Claire reasoned, the girls must take after their mother, who was entirely absent from the scene. As far as Claire had been able to tell on her brief visits to the house, there wasn't even a photograph of her around. And William never mentioned her, not even when speaking to his children. Claire, who had gathered from Inez that there had been a divorce, or at least a separation, some time ago, complied with the unvoiced ban on the subject, never once alluding to a possible mother for the children, a wife for William.

Natalie was studying piano, and Pamela was studying the flute. William said that this was a rule of his, that each girl should play at least one instrument proficiently. The music was important, of course, he said, as was the acquisition of a new skill, but most important of all was the discipline developed while learning to play an instrument. "What greater gift could be given a child," he asked, "than the gift of self-discipline?" "Well, yes," Claire had responded, uncertainly. Natalie practised on an upright grand piano, a Heintzman, in the living room, while Pamela played the flute in her father's study.

William told Claire that Natalie was a good little pianist; she might even make a career for herself out of music. Pamela on the other hand had been started on the piano, as had her sister, at the age of four, but she had this appalling stutter. "No, really," he said. "In her hands. She stutters all over the keyboard. I don't know how else to describe it. A hesitancy, in her playing. It was a great disappointment, you know, for her as well as for me. Then we switched her to the flute, and that seems to be working out very well. But poor old Pamela. She has a darned hard time keeping up with her sister." It was what happened in families, in siblings; it had to be watched out for, compensated for, he said.

Claire had met the girls before she met their father. They came to her door, the day after she moved in. They wanted to see inside her house. Claire showed them everything, including Sidney's sea shell from Hawaii. Natalie held it to her ear, listening for the sound of the sea, and then Pamela did the same. They were quiet little girls. The tips of their fingers were pink, moist. They looked to Claire like children from the nineteenth century: pale, intense, polite—withdrawn, even. Miniature adults. On the second-to-last day of the summer holidays, Claire took them for the first of many walks along the beach below their house. Pamela tossed pebble after pebble into the waves, and Natalie and Claire overturned large wet rocks and observed the frantic scuttling of dozens of shiny black crabs deprived of shelter. The air smelled richly of the sea, and white gulls flew overhead, mewling. Claire enjoyed herself very much, down there on the beach, and although she tried not to, she began to think of herself spending more and more time with these little girls, mothering them, looking after them; part of the family, of the household, married, possibly, to their father. This was self-indulgent, unwarranted fantasizing, of course; she embarrassed and even shocked herself with such thoughts. Thank goodness Inez knew nothing of what went on in her mind; Inez would be full of scorn. Inez would, in truth, be horrified.

∽

Inez informed Claire that she, Inez, was not at all the same person she had been eighteen months, two years, earlier. She'd changed herself, her looks, her attitude towards life, dramatically. For one thing, she used to have very long hair, but she'd had it all chopped off. She had just had it cut again, as a matter of fact; now there was practically nothing left. "Do you think it's too short?" she asked, and without waiting for an answer went on to say she was changing fundamentally, from the inside out; she was working on the level of her very cells, as she put it. She had converted to a new style of eating: lentils, soya beans, brown rice, raw vegetables. She'd lost weight. She was continuing to lose weight. "Oh, I know what it is," she said. "It is the great neurosis of the age, to concentrate all your will on the food you put in your mouth. Food has to make up for everything now, because we've lost so much, haven't we? When you think about it. I mean, the earth is poisoned, the ground is full of chemicals, the ozone layer is vanishing. We might as well face facts."

Did Claire have any idea, for example, that the cancer rate in this area, right here in this town, was much higher than it ought to be? Much, much higher than the national average. A study had been done; the results had been quite conclusive, although no one had done a thing about it. But it was true. If you lived here long enough, you could see for yourself.

"See what?" Claire demanded. The way Inez talked made Claire feel chilled, depressed, resentful. Inez always seemed to be implying that she had some kind of special access to information denied everyone else. "See what for yourself?"

Inez shrugged. "Oh well," she said. "All your friends getting sick, people dying one after the other." She named names, she gave examples. The former principal's wife; her neighbour's husband, two doors down; a teenager from the school the year before last.

It was the sawmill, she said. The sawmill poured toxic garbage into the air, and then everyone breathed it in. And the pulp mill, which was only a few miles away, pumped the most disgusting chemicals straight into the ocean. "They don't give a shit," said Inez angrily. The chemicals got into the fish and the people ate the fish. There was nothing anyone could do, or would do. "Cowards," she said. "We are all cowards."

Inez was in fact experimenting with eating nothing, did Claire know that? She felt fine eating very little, she said. The truth was, it wasn't necessary to eat a lot to survive. She had found this out for herself.

It was usually Friday evenings, at the end of a week of teaching, that Claire and Inez got together, and Claire found herself listening through a haze of fatigue to Inez's extraordinary revelations. They sipped wine and watched TV and Inez became increasingly restless. She seemed in fact febrile; she ran her fingers through her cropped hair until it stood straight out around her head, like an impish demented halo, and she talked.

When she first taught at the high school, and this was going back a few years, Inez said, she had to teach the girls in Home Economics how to pack a proper lunch for a working man. This was part of the curriculum. She instructed them in the making of bologna sandwiches: thick slabs of bologna on slices of white bread spread with margarine, for economy, and prepared mustard, for flavour. The margarine had to be whipped in a small white dish, so that it would spread easily. These things were important in order to keep the working man happy, the class was told. A man didn't like to bite into a sandwich that wasn't buttered right up to the crust. The girls had to wrap the sandwiches in wax paper with the ends tucked in just so. And then the sandwiches went into a lunch bucket along with freshly baked oatmeal cookies, or a slice of chocolate cake, and a thermos of hot, sweet tea.

But was there not something seductive in all this, Inez said. Didn't it make an appeal to the senses, to the heart, the thought of those wax paper-wrapped sandwiches tucked into metal lunch buckets? It was so elemental, she said: domestic life stripped to the basics, or at least the basics North American style. She could fall into a trance and picture it all: the house, the children, the souped-up Chevy in the driveway, the husband coming up the road in his work boots and hard hat. She could see the trikes left out in the front yard, yes, and the few daffodils coming up along the edge of the sidewalk; she could smell the floor wax, see the clean cloth spread on the kitchen table. The pub on Saturday nights, the drive into the country on Sundays in the candy-apple red Chevrolet; two kids in the back seat.

"You make it sound rather attractive," said Claire.

"Well, for some maybe. But it sure isn't for me." Then she said, reflectively, soberly, "For me, it would be a living hell."

Claire allowed for a moment of silence when she had finished reading "The Cask of Amontillado," and then she plunged the class into an open (she hoped) discussion.

"What was the story about?"

"Revenge."

"Trickery."

"Being buried alive."

"Yes. And this was a favourite theme with Edgar Allan Poe. Being buried alive."

"But why did this guy—Montresor—want to kill Fortunato in the first place?"

"Well," said Claire, "we aren't told. We aren't given that information. We are simply told that he felt he had suffered insults of an unspecified nature at Fortunato's hands and had, therefore, vowed to take revenge. But why this particular form of revenge? It's hardly common practice, is it, to brick someone up and leave him to die? He could have chosen some other form of punishment, but he chose this one. Can anyone tell why?"

"He wanted Fortunato to know what was happening to him? He wanted Fortunato to know that he was being buried alive?"

"Yes," said Claire. "Yes. Of course. 'It is equally unredressed when the avenger fails to make himself felt as such to him who has done the wrong.'

"Which simply means that retribution would mean nothing, at least not in Montresor's nasty mind, if Fortunato were not, at every moment, aware of what was about to happen to him."

"Yeah, but maybe Fortunato deserved what happened to him."

"Perhaps," said Claire. "But still, Montresor is hardly shown to be a particularly charitable individual, is he? We don't *like* him, do we? We can't possibly like this man." She smiled at her class. It delighted her to see how willingly they grappled with the difficult ideas presented in this dark little tale: confinement, punishment, retribution, revenge.

The sawmill, which was the single industry in the town, was antiquated and dirty, and its days were numbered, although few were aware of that fact for the moment. Black smoke poured out of its twin smokestacks into the blue sky, adding a hint, a small, innocuous hint, of purple, of indigo, of heliotrope, of sootiness. A smudged sky. Claire asked William if there were harmful substances coming from the mill. He looked at her askance, when she asked this, and said, "Substances?"

"Chemicals," she said. "Combinations of chemicals?" She became unsure, apologetic. William was a chemical engineer at the mill, and she thought he, if anyone, should know. But what did a chemical engineer do? She pictured him locked away in a sort of medieval laboratory full of bubbling liquids, exudations. She saw him pouring beakers full of nameless fluids into fires; the smoke—rising straight up the chimneys and into the air, into the streets, in through house windows—disseminated like a series of infinitely small, scattered messages telling of something new, unheard-of.

William looked at her and said, "You're not one of those, surely?"

He meant an environmentalist. Or whatever fashionable word was being used these days, he drawled. She shook her head; she didn't think so. She hadn't given it much thought. She had just been concerned, curious, seeing the smoke.

He made her come away from his living room window, with its excellent view of the pretty harbour and the streams of effluent from the mill. They sat down and he said, "Now, look around you. Tell me what you see."

She saw nothing unusual. William's comfortable, slightly overstuffed living room: sofas, armchairs, Oriental rugs, draperies. The piano, some plants, books in shelves. On the walls were framed portraits, excluding any of William's wife, and some unremarkable oil paintings, pastoral scenes, dark in tone. William spread his arms dramatically. "This profusion," he said. "These accumulations." There was even a layer of dust on everything, and he knew it. The flute teacher, when he had first come to give Pamela her lesson, had examined the room in dismay and then had informed William that the room was completely unsuitable. The flute could not be played, he had said, in a dead room.

"He was very earnest," William said. "And very critical." It seemed that sound was muffled, deadened, in such a room. The flute required certain external acoustical conditions, a certain liveliness to the air. Well, so did all musical instruments, he supposed, but the flute was apparently especially sensitive.

"I cannot remember," William said, "if the opposite of a dead room is a light room or a live room. In any case, Pamela now practises in my study, where things are more suitable, according to the flute teacher." William laughed. "But my room, my nice living room. The dead room. It does give me a strange feeling, at times, to look at this room in those terms."

Claire was invited to stay to dinner, and after dinner she helped with the washing up and with getting the children ready for bed. She accompanied them up the stairs and sat on the end of Natalie's bed, reading to them a fairy tale about a princess locked in a high tower. The girls shared a room, with a window open to the sound of the sea. Gothic, Claire thought, the whole atmosphere of the house. If she lived here, if she had these children in her care, she would lighten the tone of their lives a little, she would paint and wallpaper the walls and make new, bright covers for the beds as a start. She would let them both stay up later at night. She kissed them and said "Good night Natalie, good night Pamela" and adjusted their closet door and turned out some lights and left on others as she was instructed. Then she went back downstairs and joined William for tea in the living room. A fire burned in the grate. William put on a recording of classical music, something sprightly with many sharp trills and quick, breathless runs. She found it distracting, like a child's rhyme repeated until it had lost all meaning. Then he came over to her and put his hand on her arm and asked her not to go home, but to stay the night with him.

No? Yes? How should she respond? Did she properly understand what was being asked of her? Outside, she knew, it was cold and dark, and the widow's house, across the street, was also cold and dark. Into her mind came images from her long-ago dream, with its contradictory enigma and clarity. A dream of flying was a sexual dream, it occurred to her now. Was that Freud? Jung? Her arms spread like wings, her feet trailing behind. The sky blue, the sea blue, the roofs of the houses coloured like bits of glass, like the smooth rosy glass she and Natalie and Pamela often found scattered along the beach, in among the rocks.

○

"She was someone I knew," Inez said, with some reluctance.

"Who?" said Claire.

"Their mother, of course," said Inez. "Who do you think? His wife. William's wife, Barbara Johnson. She came up to me one day while I was shopping and said that she needed someone to talk to. I hardly knew her at the time. But she seemed desperate, so I said she could come to my house. It seemed urgent enough; she was very upset. She just needed to talk, she kept saying. She wouldn't even take off her coat at first, or sit down. She said that her husband was keeping her prisoner in her own house. But anyone could see that wasn't, strictly speaking, true. I mean, she'd been out shopping, and there she was, standing in front of me in my living room.

"She said that he criticized everything she did, he told her she was lax with the children, an indifferent mother.

"I said to her, 'Well, do you think you're an indifferent mother?' She gave me this perfectly furious look and pulled her coat off and threw it on the floor. Then she pushed her sweater sleeve up and showed me a bruise on her arm. 'There, see this?' she said. 'He did this to me.'

"Then she said that it didn't matter, it was all her own

189

fault. And besides, he had only hit her once. She knew she could be exasperating; she knew she was enough to make him lose his temper."

"What did you do?" Claire asked.

Inez shrugged. "I didn't do anything right then," she said.

This was at Claire's house. Inez had dropped by on her way home from school, bringing with her a box of iced almond tarts, a product of Foods and Nutrition 12, left over from a parents' visiting day. They would have a tea party, she said, and be festive. She arranged the cakes on one of the widow's Royal Albert plates. "This is the kind of thing we teach our boys and girls to make now," she said. "No more bologna sandwiches. Although men and women still go to work. I wonder what it means? Here, have one," she said. And then: "Does he ever mention Barbara to you?"

"No," Claire said.

After they had both had tea and eaten the almond tarts, Inez complained that she felt unwell, weak. Almond tarts were the wrong kind of food for her. They had too much sugar. Sometimes she honestly thought she might be hypoglycemic. Or something like that—she was sure she had some kind of disorder. She went to lie down on the couch in the living room. Claire slowly washed up the teacups and tried to picture, not for the first time, what William's wife looked like. She saw a girl not much older than Natalie, although Barbara was of course a grown woman about the same age as Inez. But still, the image persisted, and was enlarged upon: William's wife was a thin, finely wrought young woman with long dark hair and sombre brown eyes, like Natalie and Pamela. Claire saw her, pale and determined, brushing her fingers across the keys of the Heintzman, staring moodily out at the sea, weeping in childish frustration. She was a prisoner in her own house; she had a bruise on her arm.

And what was true, and what was not true?

The awful thing was, Claire discussed Inez with William. She didn't mean to, and she wished she could refrain, but how William loved to hear of Inez, of how she had cropped her hair and wore nothing but black—shapeless black skirts, black sweaters unravelling at the wrists. Of how thin she had become, through not eating. "Self-abnegation," said William with a sneer. "Self-denial. It is a sickness, a compulsive need for attention." Did Claire know that Inez had once been arrested, for throwing a stone at a police car? There had been a demonstration of some kind at the gates to the mill yard, and the police had been called, and somehow, in the jostling and shoving, a stone had been thrown. By Inez, who was picked up by the police and driven away.

"She means well, though," Claire said. "She feels these things strongly."

"Inez is a hysteric," William said. He said he was familiar with her kind. (Claire thought fleetingly of the wife, Barbara, the bruised arm, the appeal for help made to a stranger in a supermarket.)

Inez, William went on, was the kind of person who managed to get hold of half the facts, or less; she was a little educated on certain matters, but not enough. She got her information from questionable left-wing tracts, communist literature, he wouldn't be surprised. It was like a religion to her; she was a fanatic. He advised Claire to be careful; she would get the same kind of reputation Inez had; it would rub off on her. Then he said, still speaking of Inez: "She is perfectly capable of influencing people, you know, of taking over their lives, bending them to her point of view. I know this from personal experience, unfortunately. She and my wife were great friends. Were you aware of that?"

"Oh," said Claire. This was, as far as she could remember, the first time William had spoken of his wife. She flushed, as if he'd mentioned something indecent, made a terribly revealing confession. "Well, yes," she said at last. "I knew they were friends. Yes, I did know that."

"Great friends," she repeated later to Inez. "He said that you were great friends. Was he telling the truth?"

"Yes, I suppose he was. We were friends."

"But you told me that you hardly knew her."

"What's the difference?"

Claire was sitting on a table in the sewing room. Inez was behind her desk, marking examination papers. It was four-thirty in the afternoon. Outside the open classroom door, the janitor was pushing a broom over the hall floor.

"But you lied to me," Claire said.

"I didn't *lie* to you."

"You did."

"Now you know why. I didn't want to get into this: You said this, you said that, William said, I said. All that nonsense. I've been through it before and that was enough, believe me. Anyway, he could be the liar, for all you know."

"But you just said he was telling the truth." Claire saw the smile on Inez's face, the smile she couldn't quite hide, even though she bent over her work and put her hand to her head. A secret smile, like a sign she was giving Claire, that Claire could not understand and would not likely ever be able to understand.

But even so, Claire and Inez remained friends. Inez talked,

occasionally, about William and his wife, the gradual erosion of their marriage, the sadness in Barbara's eyes, the gossip that circulated around the town. And Claire, while continuing to listen to Inez, also went on telling William about her. Inez was going steadily downhill, in her opinion, she told him. She was starving herself; her ideas were getting more and more disorganized. Claire was worried; she was concerned for Inez, as any friend would be. To Inez she said, "He dotes on those children. It can't be good for them. He doesn't ever give them a minute alone, he doesn't let them think for themselves." And Inez said, "Well, if you had ever seen Barbara with her children, you would know how shocking it was that she went off and left them. She was completely devoted to them. Every bit as much as he is, if not more. It just shows, she was willing to do anything to get away from him."

This was one evening, at Inez's house. Inez gave out these opinions about Barbara and William as if she had held on to them for a long, long time and was only now dispensing them, slowly, in the form of dark, gritty messages that blew in the windows and settled on the furniture, every bit as unpleasant and as persistent as the soot from the mill.

"When she came back here to get the children, William wouldn't let her in the house. He locked the doors, and she had to stand outside, banging on them with her fists and shouting. He wouldn't let her see the children; he wouldn't let the children see her. There was a court case, over custody. I sat in the courtroom, to give Barbara some kind of support. I think that's how he came to know she was a friend of mine. William, being well-off, had the best lawyers he could get his hands on. And the facts were on his side—she had gone off and left the children. I told her, 'Tell the court that William can be violent.' But she said the bruise on her arm had disappeared a long time ago, and who would believe her anyway? She might have walked into a wall; she might have pinched herself in her sleep."

"William isn't violent," Claire said. "That's crazy."

"Is it?"

"Yes, it is."

"Well, there you and Barbara agree. That's what she finally said, that William isn't the violent type."

William was strict with his children. Yes, Claire thought that could be said: He was strict. He was careful with Natalie and Pamela, very particular about the way they behaved, how they spoke, their manners. He made them say please and thank you. He saw to it that they had music lessons, dance lessons, lessons in French and in swimming. He sat beside Natalie at the piano for hours while she practised for examinations, and if she made a fuss, if she began to cry in frustration, in exhaustion, he handed her a Kleenex and said, One more time, Natalie, one more time from the beginning. The metronome ticked out a rhythm that was exactly suited to the rhythm of the house. Slow music, measured out, with something quicker rising secretly out of the melody in the right hand. And the child's thin back bent over the keyboard: Da da da da, up and down the scale.

But let it be admitted that William had his bad moods. He had a temper. Claire will say nothing of this to Inez, but one day William asked her to stay with Pamela while he took Natalie to the doctor. Natalie, it seemed, had a mild case of impetigo on her chin. "Can you imagine?" said William when they got back. "I have told her over and over to wash her hands properly, with soap, with hot water and soap, before meals, when she comes home from school, after going to the washroom, and never to touch her face with her hands. I've told her this countless times. She's not a baby anymore, for God's sake. You'd think she could practise a little elementary hygiene."

He removed a bottle of prescription medicine from a pharmacy bag and slammed it down on the counter. "A simple enough thing to remember, isn't it, Natalie, to wash your bloody hands?" he roared. The child's face crumpled. Pamela slid from her place at the table and backed toward the kitchen door.

Then William calmed down; he was fine. Claire had taken it upon herself to put a chicken casserole in the oven earlier, while she was waiting for William and Natalie to get back, and she ended up staying to dinner. That was how it was, by that time. Claire was almost one of the family; she was usually at ease in this household. Except on this occasion she felt subdued, rebuked. She felt as if she had been struck on the side of her head, the left side, but no one had been struck, not her and not Natalie.

Claire ate at William's table, she witnessed his temper, his sudden, rough, nearly abusive temper, if that were not going too far, and what was more she slept (yes, it was true, it was possibly true that while flying omniscient, prophetic, triumphant over the town, she had in fact descended to the warm heart, the most secret, comforting centre of its being) in his bed. And whatever else she might deny, or attempt to deny, it was true that on any number of occasions during that year she sat with him through long, quiet companionable evenings in the dead room.

ᕔ

Without intending to, she became persistent when discussing "The Cask of Amontillado" with her English class. She hadn't meant to return to the story after that first day and yet she did, she went back to it at least once, in the days following the Christmas vacation. "Do you remember?" she asked her class. And then, "Do you really understand?" She stood over them; she walked back and forth in front of their desks. "Do you really have any idea what it would be like," she said, "to be incarcerated in that way?" She stressed particularly the description of the "still interior crypt or recess" to which Montresor led the unhappy, the unfortunate, Fortunato. She read out with slow and thorough emphasis: "'. . . in depth about four feet, in width three, in height six or seven.'"

"Think about it," she urged. "Think about being imprisoned in such a place." She realized that she was trembling slightly, that there was a tremor in her voice. Again, with great insistence, she appealed to her students: "Imagine yourself bricked up, with no chance of escape, in the dampness, in that small, dark, wretched space, the walls hanging in nitre . . . ."

Several of her students shifted uncomfortably in their desks; their eyes evaded hers. Drained, she leaned against her own desk. Her heart was beating rapidly, as if she had run a great distance. This was not like her; it wasn't her teaching style at all. Class dismissed, she tried to say. The class is over, you can go.

ᕔ

A letter arrived, from the widow, announcing the date she would be returning from Scotland. This was in the spring, nearly eight months into the school year. At about the same time, Claire heard from the school board that her contract, which was only a temporary one, would not be renewed. Budgets were being trimmed; classes would have to be consolidated. This was at the beginning of a recession that would affect the sawmill and the entire town, changing both forever, but Claire did not know this at the time. She sat, stunned, on the edge of her bed with the official notification from the school board in her hand and wondered if, as William had predicted, her friendship with Inez had alarmed the board, that Inez's reputation had "rubbed off" on her. Or, worse still, had someone on the board found out about those times when she left William's house at dawn, sneaking across the road to the safety of the widow's house? This was a small town; everyone knew, Inez always said, what everyone else was doing. In spite of this, Claire managed to keep the letter from the board a secret. She did tell Inez, however, that the widow had written to say she would be back at the end of June.

"Oh, what a shame," Inez said. "You need the house more than she does. Why can't the old biddy stay in Scotland?" What they should do, she said, was talk the widow into selling them her house. "All those bedrooms upstairs," she said. "We could stock them with handsome young men, like the widow did." Of course, the widow could live with them, too, if she wished. Inez and Claire were not greedy women, she said.

Claire did not tell Inez that she would soon be out of a job, and she didn't tell William, either. In May, on the Victoria

Day weekend, she went with William and the girls to watch a parade. The girls wore new spring dresses, with puffed sleeves and lace collars, and new shoes. William told them about Queen Victoria, who, he said, had liked to go trout fishing in dresses with skirts three yards wide. He bought ice-cream cones for the two girls and for himself and Claire; then they walked around town, saying, Hello, hello, to everyone they met. They threaded their way in and out of the crowds, in and out of other family groupings, young couples with their children. Claire caught several of her students staring at her curiously. Yes, she wanted to say, this is me, here I am with this handsome man and these lovely children. She waved at them brightly. "Having a good time?" she called.

The sawmill was closed for the day; the lumber yards were quiet. Claire said to William that she missed hearing the mill whistle sound for shift changes, and Pamela said "will mistle" and made them laugh. Claire thought that at last she had discovered the town she had flown over in her dream. The small town that had parades and people calling to one another across the street. Festivities and merriment; adventure.

William took a picture of Claire standing with the girls in the park. Behind them was a wooden replica of the water wheel that had powered the first sawmill, built on this site in 1880, according to the plaque. "When Victoria was queen," William said. Claire took a Kleenex out of her purse and wiped ice cream from the corner of Pamela's mouth.

"What a wonderful day," she said to William when he pulled into his driveway. She got out of the car. Natalie and Pamela tumbled out after her and grabbed her by the hands. Across the street the slightest of winds was tumbling pink blossoms out of the Japanese plum trees in the widow's front yard.

"Don't go," Pamela and Natalie shouted at her. "Don't go."

"Claire must go home," said William. "She needs a rest from this noisy family. Say goodbye to Claire, Natalie. Pamela. Goodbye, Claire."

"Goodbye," Claire responded. She had chocolate ice cream on the front of her dress, she saw. Her hands were sticky and her hair was in her eyes. And her nose felt burned by the sun. She must look a mess, she thought. "Goodbye," she said, stooping to kiss Natalie and Pamela. "See you later," she said to William happily. Then she walked across the road through the storm of pink blossoms, which were already slightly bruised and fading.

Finally she told Inez, "You know, I won't be teaching here in September. I'll be unemployed again, damn it."

Inez threw her arms around Claire's neck. "That's good news, don't feel bad about that," she said. "All my friends are so lucky. They get to leave this damnable place sooner or later."

Claire said that surely Inez could leave as well. Why didn't they both leave? They could join CUSO or something, whatever it was one joined, and teach in Africa. They could travel around and get odd jobs. She made these proposals enthusiastically, almost seriously. But Inez flatly said no. Other people could leave, but not her. She had come to the rather depressing conclusion a long time ago that she was meant to stay right here. She was condemned to stay here, in a sense, by circumstance, by indolence, by her own bad luck, by whatever. She would grow old here. Older, she said. She'd get so she didn't know anything better, or different, existed.

In June, Claire invited some of the teachers from the school, the ones she'd become more or less friendly with, to a party at the widow's house. It was Midsummer Night, as it happened. Inez came, even though she said she usually avoided what she called staff meetings with booze. She stood on the doorstep dressed in her usual black, with silver chains around her neck and spoon-shaped silver earrings dangling from her ears; she stamped her feet and hugged herself as if it were the middle of winter. Claire dragged her inside. Almost everyone Claire had invited turned up, with the exception of William. Whenever the doorbell rang, she thought it would be him, but it never was. She was wearing a new cream-coloured dress with a finely pleated skirt and pearl buttons. Too dressy for this occasion perhaps, but it suited her, she thought. The sad truth was she had bought it because she thought it was the kind of dress William would like and approve of, and he wasn't here to see it. Or to see her. She went upstairs to the spare bedroom and parted the curtains slightly. The lights were on at William's house. The curtains were pulled across the window. There was a full moon in the sky. She went back downstairs. It got to be eleven o'clock, eleven-thirty, and finally she gave up on him. Several times she went to the phone in the hall and lifted the receiver to call him, but then she made herself put the phone down and go back to the party. It was getting to be a boisterous party. Someone was playing a guitar and singing. Someone had a Polaroid camera and was taking pictures. Claire kept one of these, a shot of Inez lying on the floor with her arms crossed over her skinny black-clad chest and five grinning men sitting around her. It was a curious pose. What had been going on? Claire wondered. It seemed to her the picture had been meant to convey something essential about Inez, about this town, about Claire's tenuous, temporary place in the town, but what exactly? Obviously, it was nothing more than a silly moment, Inez clowning around. She thought of Inez throwing rocks, sticking her neck out, being obstreperous, getting herself laughed at. She feels things strongly, Claire had said once to William, in Inez's defence. But didn't everyone? she now added, to herself. In any case, she kept the photograph for a long time, placing it in her album beside the picture of herself with Pamela and Natalie on Victoria Day, and underneath she wrote the year and the name of the town.

The next morning, a Saturday morning, Claire kept going to the phone and then deciding she should finish cleaning up the house before talking to William. What if the widow walked in right now? What if she saw the state of the carpets? Claire got out the vacuum cleaner. Then she put the dishwasher on. She scrubbed a stain from some spilled beer out of the widow's floral slipcovers. She got up off the floor and dialed William's number. Her hand was trembling, but she made her voice bright. "I'm sorry you couldn't make it last night," she said.

"Noisy affairs aren't in my line," he said. Then he began to complain about the noise, saying that the sound of her drunken guests leaving her house had kept him awake into the early hours of the morning. "Well, I'm sorry," she said, stung. "That's all right. I won't be around to bother you for much longer." And that was how she came to tell him that she was going away.

"Oh," he said. "Well, I'm sorry to hear that. We must have

dinner before you leave. We must arrange something." And they did, in fact, have dinner together a number of times, once alone, without William's children, at a restaurant. They sat across the table from each other and chatted and smiled, but behind William's words and gestures there seemed to Claire to be a clear rebuke: She had done something wrong. She waited for an explanation of some kind, but none was forthcoming. What have I done? she wanted to say. Why are you so angry with me? Then she thought, Nothing I do or don't do would be right, in his eyes. Inez would love to witness this, she thought. My discomfiture. My shame. Didn't I warn you? Inez would say. Claire smiled at William. She ordered dessert; she ate with apparent enjoyment. "What a lovely meal," she said as William slipped her coat around her shoulders.

She waited for him to ask her to stay in touch, to send him her new address. She waited for him to wish her luck. He did none of these things. His smile remained perfectly polite and, it seemed to her, perfectly cold. She could not get past this coldness or his elegant good manners. And after she had moved away, it was not William she missed but Natalie and Pamela. She found herself wondering if they missed her. Did they ask their father why Claire wasn't there to cook their dinner, to read them a story at bedtime? Possibly they absorbed the new situation quite well. After all, by now they would have it figured out: the locked door; the sealed walls; the transgressor receiving (for whatever reason) a suitable punishment.

ᖆ

For a long time after leaving the town and establishing herself elsewhere, Claire continued to hear from Inez. She received letters containing news of the town and of William. "I imagine you will want to hear the latest about *him*," Inez wrote. The biggest news came when the sawmill closed down at the height of the recession. Inez said that there was no money in the town, the poverty was appalling, a food bank had been started up, and then a soup kitchen. "How is this possible, in this day and age?" Inez wrote, but on the whole she sounded more jubilant than sorry. "People are pulling together," she said, "life is simpler, more real. And listen to this: The air is clean, you can breathe! Incidentally, William has moved away." He had evidently got himself transferred to a larger town, to a newer, more efficient mill owned by the same company. "Trust him," said Inez. His house was empty; it had been put up for sale.

Claire tried to imagine poverty and joblessness added to the previous sins of the town and failed. It saddened her to think that the mill whistle would no longer signal the shift changes four times a day; men would not stream out of their houses, with lunch buckets under their arms, heading down the streets in amicable silence toward the clouds of black smoke issuing from the smokestacks.

At her new school, in a town miles away, Claire opened a different book each September and tried out different stories on her new classes. One year she read "The Lottery" by Shirley Jackson, and then she tried "The Magic Barrel" by Bernard Malamud. None seemed as suitable as "The Cask of Amontillado," or as capable of drawing the attention of the class. No other story lent itself so well to the cadences of her voice, which, when things were going well, seemed to lift the words right off the printed page, imposing their excitement and danger on the otherwise sullen September air of the classroom. When she read "The Cask of Amontillado" she had them; she had her class; they were hers. But the story was now forbidden to her, bound as it was in her mind with the town, the town she had actually flown over in her dreams, an angel, a seer, before she ever saw it in real life. It seemed to her now to have been a place composed of small, closed-off rooms that permitted no escape. Or, if you did escape, if you did manage to break your way free, you would emerge into the light of day only to discover there was no way back, no way to find again the route you had travelled.

Vargas

Marjorie and Celia were sisters, all that remained of a family that had once owned the world's third, or fourth, largest shipping line. Marjorie, who was older by two years, was born in 1916. Now, in what they referred to deprecatingly as their old age, they had come to live on a small west coast island. They owned the island: It had been left to them years earlier, almost incidentally, along with a reasonably lively portfolio of stocks and bonds, a Georgian-style mansion in Shaughnessy Heights in Vancouver, an apartment building they had never seen, and would likely never see, in Pittsburgh, and a defunct horse-racing track in south-western Ontario. The family home in Sussex had been disposed of long ago, as had a ranch in Brazil, south of Rio de Janeiro.

Every evening, Marjorie and Celia walked to the edge of the sea and watched the sun set behind an extinct volcano which was now heavily forested and a deep violet-blue in the twilight. Its cone slumped inward like an underbaked soufflé. At the foot of the volcano, which was on another island much larger than theirs, a Catholic mission bell chimed at nine o'clock unfailingly. The music of the bell travelled across the water and manifested itself in the waves rolling in along the beach and in the ornately skeletal driftwood, the rotting bull-whip kelp, the empty clamshells.

Once the sun had set, they went up to the house for Ovaltine and biscuits. They sat at an open window, through which came unceasingly the roar of the surf and from time to time the sound of a gillnetter rounding the point, headed for the government dock in the village up the inlet. Marjorie and Celia spent only the summer months on the island. In August they went back to their house in Shaughnessy Heights, where they belonged to clubs, played bridge, went to the movies and the symphony.

During their first few days on the island, Marjorie had felt, to her dismay, uneasy, frightened. She pleaded with Celia to leave at once, to go home with her, citing as reasons the almost unworkable antique water pump beside the rust-stained kitchen sink, the kerosene lamps set out on the sideboard in place of electric light, the outdoor plumbing, the woodstove. She told Celia that she simply hadn't considered the impact such obviously primitive and unmanageable, yes, plainly unmanageable, conditions would have on her. She couldn't cope, she said; obviously neither one of them would, in the long run, be able to cope. They must go home, now, before they got into real trouble.

This was not at all like Marjorie; Celia didn't know what to do. "Wait," she told Marjorie. "Give it another day, a week, two weeks; you'll get used to it." Celia, unlike Marjorie, was enjoying herself, getting out of bed early every morning to light the woodstove, cooking oatmeal, mucking about outside in a sweater and blue jeans, beachcombing, she claimed. Come with me, put on your boots, put on your warm sweater, let me show you the beach, she would say, until finally, reluctantly, Marjorie followed her down to the beach and along the edge of the forest, as far as the next bay and the one after that. This was an extreme, astonishing reversal of their usual roles.

"You obviously spent too long in the damned Girl Guides," Marjorie said. She didn't know how she could explain to Celia that she mistrusted this island and, moreover, mistrusted her *self*, her existence, on this island. Who was she, at least while here? Something reduced, made plain. A bag of bones left to dry under the hot sun, flesh assaulted by wasps and mosquitoes. The sea pulled at the blood in her veins, and not pleasantly, but with compulsion. She was forced to remain in her body, a creature of itches and burns and aching joints, aching muscles. All she wanted out of life, all she had ever insisted upon, she now realized, was the mind, the intelligence, the ability to reside utterly within her own thoughts, privately, without distraction, if she wished. This was possible in the city, but on the island she was cruelly exposed; her thoughts disintegrated, along with everything else. She aged; she was crumbling fast, decaying; her mind was fuzzy; her skin itched and itched. To no avail, she rubbed medicated lotions on her insect bites and bathed her sore feet in tepid water.

⌒

When Marjorie and Celia first came to their island, they detected signs of occupation, signs that someone else was around the place. They arrived by water taxi, from the village, and the water taxi operator gave them a hand bringing their luggage up to the house. They had seen the house before, of course, and certain preparations had been made. So they weren't entirely surprised that the grass had been freshly mown, or that someone had deadheaded the old blooms on the tea rose near the front steps. "How wonderful," Celia said, "that roses grow here at all, in such wildness." The house was dark, woodsy: definitely rustic. Near the front door was a brass plate, recently polished, inscribed: The Lodge. They entered and had the immediate impression that someone had exited by the back door. At least, Marjorie sensed something. Who was here? she kept saying. To be here alone was bad enough; to be alone with someone unknown, unseen, was much worse.

Celia was flinging open doors. She stepped out into the back porch. "Would you look at this," she said, "here's everything we need." Kindling, piles of wood in the woodbox. As if the seven dwarves had been secretly hard at work, she said. Well, of course, she quickly added, undoubtedly their lawyers had hired someone to see to these details. Marjorie was busy with the implications: Someone was here, teasing them, standing in the forest laughing his guts out. She knew it was a man. The stranger was a man, a maniac with an ax, with an ax for chopping wood and chopping up old ladies. She slept with a kitchen carving knife under her pillow, a precaution she considered sensible. This went on for days.

Then they discovered Edmund. Or rather, Celia discovered him, in a clearing above a sheltered cove, around a point of land. She had gone exploring on her own, against Marjorie's advice, or what would have been Marjorie's advice, had she known. She had come upon two living creatures: a blue heron standing in the shallows (the tide was low) and a man kneeling on a tarpaulin. The heron, startled, took off. The man stayed. When he saw her, he got to his feet. That was how Celia told the story. He had been cleaning engine parts, spark plugs and so on. Behind him, in the trees, was a cedar shack with a stove-pipe sticking out of the roof, and a vegetable garden surrounded by chicken wire. He wasn't young; he had white hair, worn long, in a ponytail. Celia told Marjorie she thought this was a nice touch. "He looked like a pirate," she said.

"Oh, a pirate," Marjorie said. "Isn't that nice. Who spoke first?"

"I can't remember," said Celia, although she could. She had.

"I hope you asked him what the hell he's doing on our land." Marjorie was standing at the kitchen table, peeling hard-boiled eggs. Her fingers, covered in fragments of shell, felt predatory, armoured. She felt that way all over: defensive and territorial. The stranger was unmasked, but he was still the stranger. "Who is he?" she wanted to know. "Who the hell is he?"

"He lives here," said Celia. "His name is Edmund." The wonderful thing, she said, was that he had two boats, one large and one small. He said they could borrow the small boat, and one day he would take them out for a cruise in the big boat. Also, she said, he collected sea shells and labelled them according to genus and so on; then he shipped them away to schools and colleges.

"My sea shells," Marjorie said. She was almost blind with fury. This was her island; it was to be her and Celia living alone in these unlikely circumstances, being brave and self-sufficient, provoking admiration. She had forgotten her aversion to the island; she believed now that she had been perfectly happy until Edmund had been discovered. He was the one who had chopped the wood and kindling for them; he was the one who had polished the brass plate beside the front door and pruned the rose bush.

"See, no mystery," Celia said happily.

She invited Edmund to tea at the lodge. They sat on the verandah and Edmund stared out to sea and tapped his fingers on his knees and nodded mutely every time Celia said, "Would you like a biscuit? Would you like more tea?"

He hadn't meant to hide, he said to Marjorie after awhile. He just hadn't wanted to intrude on their privacy. Or that was what Marjorie made of his mumbling.

Before he left, however, Edmund found his voice long enough to tell them a bit of local history. About forty years ago, a man living on another island had attempted to swim across the narrow channel that separated his home from what was now theirs. People assumed he was enjoying his swim; no one knew he was in trouble. His body had washed up on shore on an April afternoon. Right down there on that stretch of beach.

Celia kept saying, "Oh, my goodness" and "How horrible" and staring bug-eyed at the beach, where nothing much was going on at the moment. It was a peaceful afternoon: blue skies, white gulls chasing the odd fishing boat. Behind, or under, this peacefulness, Marjorie detected something else: disasters, memories of disasters, boats adrift, storms, high seas. She buttoned her sweater and reached for her teacup, looking for comfort.

ᴏ

Marjorie's initial apprehension concerning life on this primitive island receded, leaving behind a residual uneasiness. She
tried to describe this to Celia, saying it was something she
had never experienced before; she had been lost, anxious, ill
at ease, as had everyone, but this was different, this was
worse; she didn't understand this in the least.

Then, on one of the days they took the water taxi to the
village, Celia bought Marjorie a notebook and a pen in the
Co-op and told her to keep a journal. "Don't humour me,"
Marjorie said at once, annoyed. Self-indulgent people kept
journals, she snapped; politicians kept journals, and stage
actors, and housewives. Then, perhaps simply because the
notebook was there, lying on a table, and there was nothing
else to do—it was raining all the time, it was foggy, the wind
was blowing—she set about writing her memoirs.

"Oh God, look at this," she said. "I can't stop. I had no
idea I could be so verbose." She was writing, with great
enthusiasm, about her twenty-second birthday trip by cruise
ship to Rio de Janeiro. She found herself slipping right back
in her mind to that time, getting more and more engrossed
in that cruise to Rio all those years ago.

Then she happened to discover that immediately behind
their island was another island which bore the name Vargas.
This was the most amazing coincidence—she was in the
process of writing about Getulio Vargas, who had been the
president of Brazil in 1938, the year she'd been in Rio. She
was writing about him because she remembered how
Darleen, her dear friend from those days, had passionately
despised Vargas and had been rendered impossibly bold, or

211

foolish, as a result of her delusion that he was personally persecuting her family. She had tracked him down, cornered him, on a street in Rio de Janeiro; she had gone right up to him and said his name. Or so she had claimed, to Marjorie. And now it seemed that Vargas was here, in the form of a remote, uninhabited island. This strange, unexpected symmetry comforted Marjorie immensely. Her fear vanished; she could even say, to herself at least, that it was her fate to come here; it was the rounding out of her life, even as she committed this life to the impartial lined pages of her notebook. Not of course that Spanish place names were uncommon on this coast. At times she even believed that the rain forests of the southern hemisphere had, with extraordinary determination, managed to link up with the rain forests of the northern hemisphere in a sort of Manifest Destiny of the spirit.

Some mornings Marjorie woke to a wall of white fog pressed against her bedroom window like a blank page waiting to be written on. My life, my life, thought Marjorie: one bold stroke, a slash across the page. Where I was born, my name, my parents' names. What happened next. Her dreams were filled with memories, the past rushing through her head along with strange images, faces she had never seen—nothing made sense. The fog frightened her, it was so absolute. It cut the island off completely. By afternoon, however, it would be burned away by the sun; everything would be blue sky, blue water, green trees, purple mountains, until the fog settled in again at evening.

One night, Marjorie, unable to sleep, got up and went out

into the fog. She was deep in thought, or perhaps she was actually fast asleep and dreaming. She was remembering her twenty-second birthday party on the cruise ship and how the ship's handsome Finnish captain had presented her with a mauve orchid. He pinned it to her evening gown while the band played "Happy Birthday" and everyone applauded. Her parents, who were not on the cruise, had sent along a gift: a ruby ring. And a card that said, "We know you don't care for jewellery, darling, but we couldn't think what else!" The cruise was supposed to have been her birthday present, but perhaps her parents had forgotten this. That was the night she had met Darleen, who became her best friend.

Marjorie began to waltz around on the grass, pretending she was on a ship's deck under a starry southern sky. That had been on the Atlantic, and now she was here, surrounded by the Pacific. Perhaps her life had a special affinity for the oceans, and water was naturally her element. Something drowned-looking was at that moment floating through the trees by the woodshed. The figure was distinguishable in the darkness by its pale clothing and by its face, which was featureless and white. She stepped forward and the figure disappeared into the trees.

"Come here, you," she cried. She ran across the grass. "Don't hide," she said, grabbing onto a tree branch. "I want to talk to you." She was twenty-two again; the figure in the trees was her friend Darleen, elusive as ever.

No sound came from the trees; no movement. "Damned troglodyte," she shouted. "Bloody sneak." She was half playing a game. She knew who was hiding in the trees; not Darleen, of course.

She went back into the house, up to her room, where she

wrapped herself in the quilt from the bed. She began to invent a scenario: She ran lightly toward the forest. The mist cleared; the moon shone down. A man stepped from the trees; they nearly collided. She in her party frock, he in the sort of open-necked, full-sleeved shirt Errol Flynn wore in the movies. He halted her flight with a firm restraining hand on her arm.

Marjorie committed herself to the writing of her memoirs, a practice, she felt, of great benefit to her nerves and her mind. She sat, wearing dark glasses and a straw hat, in a canvas deck chair in the shade of an enormous cedar. "February, 1938," she boldly wrote. "Our ship sailed from New York Harbour for Rio de Janeiro. By the time we got to Rio, it was discovered that something had gone wrong with the engine, or with the propeller shaft, and we had to stay in port for two weeks, a week longer than had been scheduled. The weather was hot, and people kept saying how lucky we were to have the ocean breezes. In Rio, they said, the heat would be beyond endurance. In the mornings, the passengers went swimming; in the evenings they danced or played bridge. I danced with the captain. I played bridge with the Marlowes, among others."

Marjorie stopped writing and thought of the Marlowes. They were a married couple, old friends of Marjorie's mother. "If you have any problems, go to the Marlowes," her mother had said. Mr. Marlowe, splashing in the deep end of the ship's pool, had merrily slapped Marjorie on the seat of her bathing suit as she climbed out. Darleen, sunning herself in a deck chair, said, "Isn't he disgusting?" Darleen had dark, curly hair; olive skin; large, expressive brown eyes. She was the same age as Marjorie, but seemed, to Marjorie, much older. Darlene's mother was Brazilian and her father was German. She was born in Brazil and had grown up there, but she was currently living in New York with her parents, who were, she said, in self-imposed exile. Her parents were sending her on this cruise before she forgot the city of her birth, beautiful Rio de Janeiro, she explained as she diligently smoothed tanning oil on her knees. Her perfect knees, Marjorie thought enviously, tucking her legs out of sight under her chair.

It was illegal now to speak German in Brazil, Darleen said. The German schools had all been closed. It was because of events in Germany, she added, sweeping her hair up off her neck with her arm, then letting it fall smoothly into place. Next to Darleen, Marjorie felt gauche, clumsy, pale, like a slug. She had had her hair cut in a bob, short, to the earlobes. Now she hated it. Darleen whispered: "Let's go into Rio. Let's go have some fun, the two of us." Marjorie believed she could hear and even feel the noise and heat of the city reverberating through the deck of the ship. She chose at that moment to stop thinking for herself. Before she could fully comprehend what was happening, she and Darleen, dressed like school-girls in straw hats and short white gloves, were standing alone at the foot of the Avenida Rio Branco, which led straight into the city.

In August, Marjorie and Celia circumnavigated their island in Edmund's eleven-foot boat with a four-and-a-half horse-power outboard. The sky was overcast after several days of sun; a band of dark cloud had affixed itself to the volcano.

Marjorie and Celia were wearing bright yellow hooded slickers. Marjorie instructed Celia to sit in the exact centre of the boat while she sat in the stern and steered. She called out to Celia things she was to pay attention to: a birch tree curving out over the water, a log shaped like the prow of a Viking ship, an eagle landing on a snag near the shore. And even the colour of the sea, which was in places a deep, placid green, and in other places a frothy pearl-white. On and on they went, the bow of the boat nosing the solid bulk of the island.

"How lovely this is!" Celia called, over the noise of the engine.

On the south side of their island, they came upon Edmund's shack. "Halloo," Celia called, waving her arms. Then she stood up and the boat rocked violently.

"Have you lost your senses?" Marjorie barked, cutting back on the throttle. Celia sat down and folded her hands in her lap. They were in any case moving past Edmund's place.

"I forgot," said Celia.

Marjorie frowned and said Edmund wouldn't want to see her sinking his boat; then she opened up the throttle and they shot ahead. They were rounding a point, heading into a slight wind. "Steady on," she said. Far out, there were whitecaps and green swells. And the horizon, like a chalk line. Also, ahead and to their left, was Vargas Island. Vargas Island, with its splendid long beaches and its dark forests and its Spanish name. Sometimes Marjorie truly believed this island had travelled toward her from a great distance, lugging its name along with it and saying, Marjorie, Marjorie, wait up.

♋

One night Celia, unable to sleep, got up to make herself a hot drink. But the fire had gone out in the woodstove. She couldn't have what she wanted, which was hot milk sweetened with honey. She marched out of the house and down to the beach, where she sat on a log. It was a cold night and she thought with satisfaction that she would probably get sick. So what? If she couldn't have a hot drink when she wanted, everything could go to hell. That was how she felt.

She sat for a time; then she began to think of her late husband. To be truthful, she scarcely remembered him. He had been an RAF pilot and his plane had gone down over the English Channel in 1943. She had been married for only six years out of her entire life. At eighteen she had been a bride, and at twenty she had been pregnant, a child with yet another child tucked inside: an egg within a faceless egg. Her child had been stillborn. Her husband had died. Celia did not know what to make of these events. Life was cold and taxing and, like the sea, possessed of a vicious undertow that eventually took everything off.

The sea ran up and lapped at her feet. It was teasing her. Love me, the sea said. Put your arms around me; lie down in me; I will sing you to sleep. Pretending it was not full of drowned ships, dead sailors. Edmund knew all the history of this area, the boats that had gone under, snagged on reefs, capsized in fierce storms. The captains and sailors and Indian warriors who had done each other in by sword, by gunfire, by disease. Even that poor drowned man Edmund had spoken of, whose body had washed up on this very beach, possibly where she was now sitting.

Celia rose stiffly to her feet. She had come outside in her slippers, and now they were soaking wet and full of sand. Her hair was damp from the night air. She felt pale, small, smaller than a shell, a broken periwinkle shell. Marjorie would tell her she was crazy, but then Marjorie was the one who imagined she had seen Edmund skulking behind the wood-shed in the night fog. Edmund was not the type to skulk; Marjorie should know better. Once, Edmund had served Celia Chinese tea, when she had, on impulse, walked over to his house. He had given her a lesson on the Latin names for sea shells: Siliqua patula, which was nothing more than a razor clam; collisella pelta, a kind of limpet. And littorina, the periwinkle. She had touched them and repeated their names. Chinese tea and the sun striking the water on the other side of the window. She hadn't breathed a word of this to Marjorie, though. Marjorie didn't need to know every-thing.

Marjorie and Celia took the water taxi up the inlet to the village. They waited for its arrival exactly as if they were at a bus stop in town, checking the time and fussing with their hats and scarves, pencilling in additions to their grocery list. Then, when they got to the village, they went directly up the hill from the government fishing dock to the Co-op. Marjorie saw that the locals paid attention to them without ever directly addressing them. They knew who they were all right: the women from Vancouver, the women—well, they probably said "old ladies"—who owned that island. Celia said, "Oh, Marjorie, no one pays us the least bit of attention." She plucked items from the shelves in the Co-op, going, she told the clerks, strictly for things that didn't need to be boiled, fried or baked. "We have no electricity," she told the cashier. "We are roughing it, fools that we are."

Marjorie went outside and saw the water taxi operator coming out of a beer parlour. He waved and pointed down the hill toward the dock, indicating, she assumed, that he would wait for them there. This town, Marjorie was thinking. The road leading up from the water, the church, the disarray; kids and dogs, men in plaid jackets smoking in doorways, blue mountains leaning insistently into the middle distance. It made her think of Rio, of Darleen. Her past, her history, was somehow emanating from these mountains, like smoke drifting ominously out of a supposedly dormant volcano.

Celia appeared then, with two bags of groceries. Marjorie took one of them, and they walked together down to the dock. A wind was getting up, the water in the inlet was flecked with white. Waves slapped against the side of the water taxi. This is just another damned west coast village with a Spanish name, Marjorie told herself, everything leading downhill to the dock, to the waves, and, eventually, to the cold, dark ocean floor.

Marjorie sat on the verandah with a blanket wrapped around her legs and her notebook on her lap. She wrote: "We went to a sidewalk café and drank papaya juice." She was trying to remember exactly what had happened after she and Darleen had left the ship and gone into Rio de Janeiro. No one seemed to have noticed their leaving, but then passengers were getting on and off the ship all the time. In the city it was hot, noisy, crowded. Carnival time, Darleen explained blithely. Then she became quiet. She kept looking behind her, as if afraid of being followed. Her face was pale under the brim of her hat; she kept pressing her gloved hands together. Marjorie had felt either frightened for Darleen, or frightened *of* her, which was ridiculous. "After we finished our drinks, which tasted awful to me, too thick and sweet, we walked up and down the streets, up and down . . ."

She and Darleen had taken a room in a hotel two blocks from the beach. They had been audacious in their behaviour. Marjorie thought: Now the adventure begins. She was on her own, nearly, in a city where you were expected to be naughty and reckless. Even crossing the street was a gamble with your life. The first morning, she woke early, before Darleen, and quickly dressed. She tried to brush her hair into a more sophisticated style, then gave up. She would never look like Darleen, she thought, no matter what she did to herself. Then Darleen woke up, yawning and stretching and rubbing her eyes. Her first words were, "I must get to church."

"Church?" Marjorie said. She felt dazed watching Darleen dress, then grab up her purse and gloves. Marjorie, not knowing what else to do, ran after her, downstairs and out into the street. They walked until they came to a cathedral with a long flight of steps leading up to the doors. Darleen went inside. She had been serious, then, Marjorie thought, astonished; she went down the steps, then up, then down again. No sound came from the interior of the church. A man came up to Marjorie and spoke suggestively to her in Portuguese, winking and smacking his lips—a desperately poor-looking man, with a black cigarette dangling from his mouth. He reminded Marjorie of Mr. Marlowe, not that Mr. Marlowe smoked black cigarettes. She

220

was in a panic. She should have gone into the cathedral with Darleen, she thought, never mind not being a Catholic. She went down the steps and stood on the pavement, which was patterned in black and white diamonds repeating endlessly, lines extending forever. She felt ready to fall on her face. And the mountains were actually closing in on her; they were about to topple; she would be crushed. When Darleen finally emerged from the cathedral, she laughed. She said that all strangers believed the mountains were falling, but it was an illusion, it almost never happened. "Except occasionally, to nice English girls," she said. In the shade of a Brazil tree, Darleen stopped, took off her hat, and shook out her hair. "In Rio, I revert," she said, self-importantly, Marjorie thought. "I attend Mass. I go back to my childhood. Rio has that effect on me."

"My family owns a ranch just south of here," said Marjorie, waving her hand in the direction of the Brazil tree's highest branches. In fact, Marjorie had visited this ranch only once and had glimpsed a few horses, miles off. She wanted to make Darleen think that Rio meant something personal to her, too, that there were connections between her and this city.

Marjorie sat in the sun (she was on a small island that had not even one tree for shade; it was really nothing more than a large rock) and ate wild strawberries. The strawberries were sweet and fragrant; they grew on small, dense plants with leaves the exact blue-green colour of the sea. Edmund had brought her and Celia here in his boat, *The Gull's Wing*. She could see Celia and Edmund gathering strawberries in a bucket Edmund was carrying, the two of them clinging to the side of the rock, their heads bent close—the best of friends. Celia had let her hair hang down her back in what was surely a most unsuitable style for someone her age, and yet, somehow, she managed to look youthful, refined, adorable. That was Celia: the pretty sister. The one who got married, not that marriage was everything. Marjorie had been Celia's maid of honour at a showy society wedding held, as it happened, two days before Marjorie's twentieth birthday in February, 1936. It was a day of wind and sleet; the train of Celia's dress had dragged in the wet and mud. No one remembered Marjorie's birthday, at least not until the day was long past, and then her parents had promised the South American cruise for the following year as compensation, only it had to be postponed until the year after that. Marjorie was at Oxford in 1937. She was studying history; she was good at history. She liked the perspective time gave to events—nothing happened alone or without consequence, and nothing ever really changed; different names and faces arrived and left, but the same events kept occurring. Which was depressing perhaps, but also reassuring.

She picked a strawberry, then let it fall from her fingers. It sparkled in the sun, a brilliant red, like her ruby ring, the one she had worn all the time she was in Rio. Then, she had given it away to Darleen, casually, quickly, as if it meant nothing. But to her the gesture did have meaning—it was like a promise. She had thought it was a promise.

Celia and Edmund were moving farther along the side of the island, being slow and careful. Edmund would go first, then he would turn and give Celia his hand. To Marjorie, their progress suggested two mollusks painstakingly arising from the deep. Celia, the smaller, sprier female mollusk, was determined to pick enough berries for dessert.

This was not the first time Marjorie and Celia had come here with Edmund. And, as on their previous trips in The Gull's Wing, they had first sailed past the drowned man's island. The drowned man had lived alone on a small, heavily-wooded, pudding-shaped island that had a reputation for disaster and misfortune that went back much further than his unfortunate history. There were stories that the Indians had buried the victims of evil spirits on the island, or had not buried them but had left them alive, barely alive, to die. Marjorie believed the first but not the second possibility.

She and Celia had stood quietly at the side of the boat, watching for the slight clearing in the trees that marked the former site of the drowned man's house. Edmund remembered the house, although it had been falling down, neglected and vandalized, when he first saw it. He said it had been tall and narrow, with too many windows and too many stairs—the house of an eccentric, a madman. He spoke with an edge to his voice that sounded to Marjorie like contempt, and she thought, I know why—because the drowned man is him. He could turn into that drowned man, dead and gone, unremembered, except as an interesting bit of local lore. Yes, she thought with triumph, That is who Edmund is—the drowned man. But then, what did she know? It was not absolutely impossible that Edmund had children, grandchildren, a wife, even, living elsewhere.

Then Edmund had pointed out another island, where yet another man had lived alone, building himself a house, planting a garden, before returning to his former life. Marjorie laughed. "Is the west coast littered with old hermits?" she

223

asked. Edmund was at the wheel, taking the boat cautiously around a kelp bed, pretending he couldn't hear her. Marjorie and Celia leaned over the side of the boat, watching the kelp, golden in the green water, moving back and forth in the current, like the hair of someone swimming beneath the waves, or someone not swimming, but drowned.

Now Celia was clambering up the rocks, saying, "Wait till you see how much we got." Her face was flushed and she was panting. Edmund took a handkerchief from his pocket and wiped his face.

"We're all going to come down with sunstroke," Marjorie said, and meant it. She felt awful. She tried to stand, and everything shimmered and went dark in front of her. When her vision cleared, she saw that she was looking directly at the Catholic mission, which seemed to have floated across the water in her direction. She thought she could make out someone raking the lawn. She could see the bell tower and the main entrance. Then she saw a canoe moving through the water toward the mission. Two young native men were rowing, and their passengers, two priests dressed in black cassocks, raised their ghostly hands and pointed at the mission, where Darleen had appeared, luminous and youthful, in the doorway and was now running lightly down the steps. "Don't worry," Darleen was calling to Marjorie, "it's all an illusion, the mountains won't fall, nothing will hurt you, nothing will hurt a nice English girl like you."

ᘐ

Marjorie insisted she had sunstroke, but Celia told her she was only overtired. If it had been Edmund sick, it would have been different, Marjorie thought, the sympathy would have been unrestrained. Celia brought her tea and oatmeal biscuits. Marjorie lay on the couch. Edmund tentatively offered her a book on sea shells. Marjorie leafed impatiently through it, looking at the glossy colour plates, and saying, "Nature's very repetitive, isn't it?" She was pleased that he looked startled. She could see he wanted to get his precious book away from her, but she held onto it, turning the pages. Celia and Edmund had only got tanned out in the hot sun: silver hair, blue eyes, brown skin, a fetching combination. As soon as Edmund left the room, Marjorie let his book fall to the floor with a thump. Celia brought her aspirin and another cup of tea. "Does the tea taste funny to you?" Marjorie wanted to know. "It tastes peculiar to me."

"No, no, of course not." Celia and Edmund were having tea in the kitchen and washing the strawberries. The tea tastes of cedar, Marjorie thought. She imagined giant cedar roots working their way into their well. The image seemed to possess her; she couldn't get rid of it, or of the taste in her mouth.

Again and again, in her mind, she saw Darleen coming down the steps outside the Catholic mission; then the scene would change, and it was Darleen coming out of the cathedral in Rio de Janeiro. Darleen was trying to tell her something. Was there something Marjorie needed to learn, to understand? The pain in her head was not at all imaginary. She felt unhappy, confused. Then she began to think of the hotel she and Darleen had stayed at in Rio. It was surrounded by new highrise buildings, testimonials to the vigour and energy of the new president. But from the window in their hotel room, Marjorie looked down into the courtyard of a house built in an eighteenth-century baroque style, with green wooden shutters and wrought-iron rococo balconies. No matter how diligently she watched, or at what hour of the day or night, she failed to see a single person, man or woman, on the balconies or at the windows. All around was movement, traffic, noise, but the house was possessed of an extraordinary silence. To herself, Marjorie began to call it the House of Ghosts.

One morning, Marjorie had woken to find Darleen gone, the sheets on her bed thrown back and one of her scarves lying twisted on the floor. How upsetting the sight of the empty bed had been, the absence of Darleen. She bathed and dressed and sat by the window, looking down on the House of Ghosts until she began to believe that Darleen was trapped inside, a prisoner. This seemed to her not unlikely—she had heard of cults in Rio, of spiritists, even of human sacrifice, especially at this time of the year when everyone seemed to be going mad because of Carnival. The maid came to make the beds, and Marjorie gathered up her gloves and bag and went down to the hotel restaurant, where she sat over coffee and a huge orange split in half and served with a knife and fork. She felt conspicuous and lonely without Darleen, and she thought longingly of the ship, even of the Marlowes. She thought of Mr. Marlowe as being merely jocular and affectionate, with his playful slaps.

Then Darleen appeared at the door and came over and flopped in the chair beside Marjorie. She was wearing a tan silk dress, a hat with a satin ribbon, a corsage of small yellow flowers. "I spoke to him," she announced. Her eyes were bright; she unpinned her corsage and picked absently at the flowers.

By "him" she meant Getulio Vargas. She had met him, she

had spoken to him. No, he had spoken to her. It was common knowledge, she told Marjorie, that every morning Vargas walked alone to Cattete Palace, where he had his office. So she went to a particular street and waited. And after awhile, he came by. He lifted his hat and said, "Good morning, what a fine day, what splendid weather." He had a very expansive style of speaking, Darleen said. She could see he had an eye for young women. With the slightest encouragement, she was sure, he would have tried to pick her up. He would have invited her to meet him for lunch.

She laughed. "Vargas spoke to me," she said. "The great Vargas." She said that she hated him, he looked like a fat lizard sunning himself on a rock. He had a cruel mouth, a slash in his face. Because of Vargas, her father had lost his government job. Because of Vargas, her parents were in exile in the States and everything was a mess.

Marjorie picked up her fork and stared at her orange, a small, juicy Brazilian sun. No, it looked like an egg yolk, disgusting. She pushed it away. Overhead, the ceiling fans revolved slowly, but the room didn't get any cooler. The other people seemed to be leering at her; they had a bizarre aspect, as if already masked and costumed for Carnival.

Darleen clasped Marjorie's hand across the table. Her skin was warm, moist, and had a deep, spicy fragrance. "I knew I would find Vargas today," she said. "I prayed that I would find him, and my prayers were answered." She reached across the table and touched her fingers lightly to Marjorie's lips, a gentle touch that nevertheless brought tears to Marjorie's eyes—it was too gentle, it hurt her. She had been left alone, she had been frightened, but now she was fine, she felt so much better. Then Darleen went back to pulling the corsage apart. "Oh, but you aren't having any fun, are you?" she said, looking up at last. "I promised you fun in Rio, didn't I?"

Later Darleen took Marjorie to a samba school, a number of which existed, Darleen said, specifically to turn the populace into good dancers in time for Carnival. Marjorie and Darleen sat on chairs in a long, narrow gymnasium, and a woman in a red satin dress with a ruffled skirt put her hand on her waist and rotated her hips as she gave rapid instructions in Portuguese to the floorboards. Across the room, a woman in a green sequined turban got to her feet, winked at Marjorie, and gyrated her hips wildly—it was all very immodest, even exhibitionist, Marjorie thought—in imitation of the instructor. At this time, Marjorie realized that she was probably not going to have a good time in Rio, after all.

What amazed Marjorie about Edmund was that he seemed to have dealt even more ineffectually with life than had she and Celia. They at least had never withdrawn to an island permanently—they had both gone out into the world and accomplished something. Their summers here were more an experiment than anything: Could they do it?

The question Marjorie wanted to put to Edmund was: How long have you lived here? She never did find out. Once, he told them that The Lodge had been, years ago, a sort of hotel, a resort. There had been an Italian chef, whose speciality had been octopus on a bed of dandelion greens. He told them this while he was dining on Celia's speciality: a leg of lamb with mint sauce from a bottle.

"A hotel?" Marjorie said doubtfully. "We didn't know anything about that." She looked around as if expecting to see paying guests stepping out from behind the sideboard.

"Octopus," said Celia. "How wonderful. On dandelion greens."

"When exactly was this?" Marjorie was eager for dates, names.

Edmund began to speak, then stopped, then said, "In the fifties, I believe."

"Ah. So you were living here in the fifties, then?"

"Was I?"

"Let me get this straight," said Marjorie. "You were here when The Lodge was a hotel?"

"Oh no. No. I came later." He cut a small piece of lamb, then put down his knife and fork.

"Don't be so inquisitive," Celia cried.

"I was only interested," Marjorie said. She was wondering if Celia had intended the lamb to be so pink, or if the oven had not been hot enough. Edmund, who perhaps felt that she and Celia were waiting expectantly for some kind of revelation from him, began to talk about how he had been overseas during the war. He had been in Holland, in 1945, for the liberation.

Celia wiped her hands on her napkin, then used it to wipe her nose. "Oh," she said. "Were you in the war?" Then she told Edmund about her husband, the pilot whose plane had been shot down. "War is terrible," she said. Marjorie thought: Oh God, history as seen by the innocent bystander.

Later, when Edmund had gone home, she found her notebook and took it at once into the kitchen and threw it into the stove. The stove might not have been hot enough for the leg of lamb, but it handled her so-called memoirs with ease. The thing was, she had changed her mind about writing them. Who would be interested? She had no children, no nieces or nephews. In any case, history was meant to be made up of facts, or the approximation of facts, and look where her own memories had taken her: into wild imaginings, fantasy, speculation. A samba school in Rio de Janeiro. Mr. Marlowe, that blameless Englishman, swatting her on the bum. And Darleen. What had she expected from Darleen, that pious, church-going young woman with the beautiful eyes and the political fixations? Adventure? High-living? Dancing and men and romance? No, no. The truth was she had been looking for devotion; she had been looking for friendship, the real kind, that lasted for decades.

In a way, she envied Celia, the one who had got married, the one who had friends. Even weird, mumbling Edmund followed Celia around absolutely everywhere, saying things like, Watch your step, Let me carry that for you, Be careful on those rocks. Handing her in and out of boats, picking strawberries for her. No one did that kind of thing for Marjorie.

Then she began to remember how just before she had left on her cruise, in 1938, her mother had telephoned her to say, "I have some very bad news, poor Celia has lost the baby." At first Marjorie, not having seen or talked with Celia for months, was completely confused, unable to connect her sister with this news. Lost what? she almost said. Then, she remembered that, of course, Celia had been pregnant, and she tried to find a suitable response, a sympathetic word, but nothing came. She had no gift for sentiment. "Poor Celia," she said briskly to her mother, and as soon as she put the phone down, she went to order flowers. How hard she was then, and clean-edged, severe.

She believed, then as now, that what mattered in the end were names, dates, declarations of war, famous treaties, famous battles; the deaths and births of monarchs, the passings of presidents. She had started her memoirs in that spirit: "My sister and I are all that remains of a large, prosperous family. We own an island, a house in the city, various other properties of little actual use or interest." (She was thinking of the horse-racing track in Ontario, the apartment building in Pittsburgh.) But she had got sidetracked at a certain point— 1938, the birthday cruise, Darleen, Rio de Janeiro—and now she had burned her notebook.

Or perhaps it was that out of her entire life, only the time in Rio with Darleen mattered. Was that possible? She sat on a chair on the verandah, with a blanket over her knees, watching the cold, silver Pacific, waiting for her vanished life to reassert itself in her memory. All she could think of was that hotel room in Rio, an image which became increasingly vivid, taking on the nature of a hallucination. She was looking out the window, down into the House of Ghosts, observing Darleen, who was with the great President Vargas himself. Darleen was saying, "I hold you completely accountable. You are to blame entirely."

Vargas kept saying, No, no. His skin had an oily sheen, not at all pleasant to look at. In the room was a parrot in a cage, and the walls were hidden behind thick draperies patterned with green leaves. Darleen drew these aside, revealing French doors, which she opened. She stepped out onto a balcony, and the wrought-iron railing gave way, and she fell a great distance into the sea. Marjorie, horrified, felt herself slipping through her open hotel window headfirst into the water. She saw Vargas out on the balcony, waving his arms like a madman. "Save those girls," he was crying. The water was cold and tumultuous: Nothing could save them. Marjorie put her arms around Darleen and tried to pull her along in the water. She was sure Darleen was not breathing, although her eyes were open and as dark and malevolent as the sea. The movement of the water turned Darleen's face toward Marjorie, and her lips closed on Marjorie's face in a cold kiss: Goodbye, goodbye.

Of course, there had been no water beneath either her hotel window, or any of the balconies that festooned the House of Ghosts, which in any case was not the House of Ghosts, but an ordinary Brazilian residence. Darleen had not drowned, and neither had she. Yet the dream seemed conclusive: a retelling.

Getulio Vargas, she now thought. President of Brazil from 1930 to 1945. In 1937, he gave Brazil a new constitution and made himself into the kind of benign tyrant who liked to walk alone every morning savouring the air and chatting to young women. In 1945, he resigned; in 1954, he killed himself in Rio de Janeiro. These were the few facts known to Marjorie. She imagined a few more: that Vargas, alone in the House of Ghosts, with its green shutters and rococo balconies, could not find his way out. That none of the doors yielded to his touch; none of the windows swung open. The patterned draperies billowed and lunged, and their lush green leaves consumed inordinate amounts of oxygen. The parrot danced angrily in his cage. Vargas gasped and choked.

There was, it seemed, simply no way to get out, to get free. Not for him, anyway.

∽

She never did see Darleen again, after the cruise. When the ship docked in New York, they said goodbye and exchanged addresses. "Please, please, please, keep in touch," Marjorie said. Darleen was wearing a navy blue coat with a sailor collar. Her father was meeting her, she said, and Marjorie exclaimed, "Oh, mine too," as if this were the greatest coincidence imaginable. It was at this moment that Marjorie pulled off her ruby ring and put it firmly in Darleen's hand. She and Darleen would go on being friends forever, she believed. They would discover similar tastes in music, books, and food. They would live together, just the two of them, in a quiet village somewhere, in New Zealand, for example, or Australia. Both places appealed to Marjorie equally well. They would keep a dog. They would continue to travel on Marjorie's father's ships, for free, and they would meet interesting, intelligent people all over the world. Marjorie wanted to pile these plans for the future into Darleen's hands along with the ring, but there was no opportunity to speak properly, and Darleen scarcely opened her mouth; she didn't even say goodbye. Marjorie thought it was the shock, the grief, of parting, just as they had started to be friends, but then months went by and she heard nothing, and then years went by, and she kept wondering, Was it something I said, something I did? Then she began not to think about Darleen. There was the war, and the years following the war, which she persisted in seeing through a haze, some things true,

233

others possibly true, possibly false. Now she was beginning to understand that even without exactitude there was at least completeness, finitude.

∽

When Marjorie first came to this island, she had the impression that she had lived here as a young child. Celia said, "You're crazy, you never lived here before, certainly not as a child." But Marjorie distinctly remembered going down to the beach every morning, early, with a bucket and a spade. It must have been about 1920. She had worn one of those heavy, knitted bathing costumes, with legs and sleeves, and she had espadrilles on her feet and a bucket and a spade in her hands. Her hair was cut straight across her forehead, in exactly the same unbecoming style she had worn at twenty-two. She remembered seeing the sun glinting on the bell tower on the Catholic mission. She must have heard the bell; she must have looked out across the water, her attention utterly caught, held, by the ringing of the bell. A woman who might well have been her mother sat on a log reading, waiting patiently as Marjorie gathered up shells and sand dollars and put them into the bucket. Marjorie produced as evidence of these long lost childhood summers a small crescent-shaped scar on her knee, which she now stubbornly attributed to a fall she'd had, climbing over driftwood on this beach, on this island. "You are silly," Celia said, when Marjorie pulled up her pant leg to show her the scar.

"But wouldn't it be an amazing thing if it were true?" said Marjorie, who had nearly, by this time, convinced herself.

"Ah yes," said Celia. "If."

The
Winter
Train

W hen Adele was seven years old, in 1954, she travelled
by train from Vancouver to Edmonton with her mother and
her three-year-old brother, Andrew. At first, she refused to
get on the train; she stood on the platform screaming No,
no, no, until a porter lifted her off her feet and carried her
up the steps to her mother. Her mother opened her purse and
gave the porter a fifty-cent tip. The porter winked at Adele as
if she were the worst child he had ever seen. Her mother
snapped her purse shut and then grabbed Adele by one hand
and Andrew by the other and made them go with her into
the train. Once inside, Adele saw that the train was exactly
as she had feared: a separate world, infinite in only one
direction: the future. Her mother made her sit down beside
Andrew, who was clutching his stuffed bear, Mina. Andrew
and Mina stared apprehensively at Adele, as if expecting
another storm. But now Adele was occupied; she was watching the other passengers remove their hats and coats and
unfold their newspapers before settling into their seats. She

and Andrew were the only children. Then a woman came down the corridor and took a seat directly across the aisle from Adele. She was wearing a fur coat, and her hair, long and darkly red, fell in a smooth, shining wave over the coat's fur collar. As Adele watched, this woman pulled her gloves off slowly, one finger at a time, and folded them together on her lap. Then she folded her hands on the gloves and crossed her legs. She wore black suede pumps with very high heels and bows and cut-out holes at the toes. Once, for two seconds, Adele had held a brilliant butterfly on her finger, and she felt now as she had then—as if the insect's soft wings were dissolving into the warmth of her heart. Now, without stopping to consider, Adele slid from her seat and crossed the aisle to sit beside the woman. Behind her, her mother was saying, "Come back here, Adele. Come here right now." But how could she? The woman glanced at Adele and smiled; then went back to looking out the window at the dark December sky.

The train began to move. The past, in the form of people left behind at the station, in the form of buildings and trees—the entire city of Vancouver—dropped away like a stone thrown from a great height; the present moment was nothing; it was so small and fleeting that it was of no importance at all. And the future, Adele thought, was out there somewhere, racing along in front of the train at a hundred miles an hour.

Adele tried to sit quietly, so that she wouldn't disturb the woman, but her arm kept creeping closer and closer to the woman's arm; soon it would be impossible to avoid contact. Adele was wearing her new winter coat, blue with a darker blue velvet collar. The woman's coat was a deep, rich, brown fur with fine strands in it of black and silver. Adele wanted desperately to touch the fur, to stroke it as if it were a live animal, a beautiful animal, asleep, but she managed to refrain. Instead she folded her hands in her lap exactly as the woman's hands were folded, and then she concentrated on the clatter of the train on the track, not an angry sound, but not peaceful, either. She began to remember that her teacher had told the class that a train was called an iron horse. She tried to imagine an immense grey horse galloping over the land, but she could tell there was more to a train than that. There was more to know about a train. For one thing, the train was much more powerful than a horse and more dignified in the way it negotiated its determined path without hindrance or fear. Also, she thought, a horse had only its own soul and its own heart, whereas a train held within it so many separate hearts, each with its own dreams and ideas. Including, of course, her own heart and that of the beautiful woman in the fur coat.

It was December, and the country she and her mother and brother were going to was the country called winter. Her mother had told her that by the time they reached Edmonton there would be snow everywhere—on the streets, on the roofs of all the houses. And they were not going merely as visitors who could turn around and go home again, but to stay, for months, perhaps for years. Adele's father had joined the Air Force. He had done this precipitately, according to Adele's mother, who had pressed the palms of her hands fiercely against her eyes before locking the door of their house, now emptied of all their belongings, for the last time. Everything they owned had been packed up and was waiting to be shipped to Edmonton. Adele's father would meet them when they got there; then they would drive to the Air Force base, where they would live. Adele pictured steel-grey airplanes, the sky a whirling mass of blades and guns, and bombs, as in the war.

Adele's teacher, Miss Bayard, had told the class that as soon as one war ended, another threatened. That was why, she said, the entire grade two class must stand on guard, diligently. "Stand on guard," Miss Bayard sang out each morning before school started. "Shoulders back, arms straight," she said. The class sang, and Adele fixed her attention on the fir trees at the edge of the playground, a small forest that did not in the least resemble the true north, which was surely mysteriously white and endless and blinding, with polar bears, and houses carved from ice sparkling under a sun that was unable to leave the sky, even at midnight when everyone slept.

When Adele had told Miss Bayard that she was moving to Alberta, Miss Bayard instructed the class to draw pictures of the sea and the mountains—two geographical features missing completely in Alberta. Adele could take her drawing with her to show her new friends what they were missing, said Miss Bayard. Adele attacked her paper in a frenzy: the sea, the mountains, the sea, the mountains. Miss Bayard stared in dismay at her picture, and Adele knew why: Her sea rolled extravagantly across the paper; the mountains were fierce jagged peaks, the colour of mud. As soon as Miss Bayard walked away, Adele crumpled her picture up and shoved it into her desk. Her mother had not told her that the sea and the mountains would be absent in Alberta.

In any case, Adele suspected that the children where she was going would not care about mountains and water. They would be interested only in what they already had—winter, and the dangerous, shining things that went with winter—skate blades, icicles, snowballs, sleighs with steel runners. Adele didn't even know how to skate; she hated snow, which was cold and wet and got inside her boots and could, according to her mother, give her pneumonia.

The woman's name was Helen. She took Adele's hand as if Adele were grown up and said, "It's a pleasure to meet you." Adele didn't know what to say. Helen had small, very white teeth, something Adele especially noticed because she had recently lost one of her front teeth. It had been loose; then it had come out while she was eating an ice-cream cone, and she had swallowed it. Helen told Adele she was going home to Edmonton after spending some time with her fiancé's family in Vancouver. Her fiancé was a soldier; he had been in Korea. Soon, he was getting out of the army for good, and then they would get married. So saying, she turned a ring on her finger, and Adele, astonished, saw a figure inside the diamond—a lost prince, a soldier, like the bee trapped in amber she had once seen in a museum. Helen moved her hand, and the lost prince disappeared in a blaze of light. Adele leaned back, bemused, and Helen took her hand again and said, "What a cold hand." She rubbed Adele's fingers briskly, and Adele sneaked a look sideways at her mother and Andrew. Andrew was asleep, his chin resting on Mina's round head, and her mother was turning the pages of a magazine, pretending she couldn't see Adele. The train was quiet, muted; the passengers spoke to one another, when they spoke, in whispers. Later, it became dark very quickly, an early December darkness, and the windows were mirrors reflecting the dazed faces of the passengers, who at once set aside their newspapers and their books in order to contemplate this new and interesting fact: night on the train. Adele, fascinated, stared at the pale, oval reflection of Helen's face and the smaller, inquisitive face of Adele, waiting for whatever was going to happen next to happen.

Then Adele's mother, holding Andrew by the hand, appeared at Adele's side. It was time for dinner, she said. Then she said, "Won't it be fun, eating on the train?" She said this partly for Andrew, it seemed, who was pulling on her hand, trying to sit on the floor. Adele said, "I'm staying here," and slid down as far as she could in the seat. Having discovered Helen, she wasn't going to leave her, ever. Her mother was a stranger to her, she thought. Helen stood up and began introducing herself to Adele's mother, and at the same time Adele's mother was apologizing for her daughter's behaviour. "She's stubborn," she said, "she's such a handful." Helen said, "Oh, I love children." Then, miraculously, it was arranged: Adele was to eat dinner with Helen, who would otherwise be on her own. Adele was so excited she forgot, momentarily, to breathe; she sucked in her cheeks and made a dire face at Andrew, who clutched his bear tightly to his chest and stared at her, afraid.

In the dining car, Helen took off her fur coat and draped it over the back of her chair, where it looked suddenly bereft and sad, all the life gone out of it. She was wearing a blouse with a lace collar and a pleated tartan skirt, the exact kind of skirt Adele intended to wear every day of her life when she was grown up. "Have you ever been through the Rocky Mountains before?" Helen asked. Then she told Adele a story of how she had once been driving through Banff and a black bear had positioned himself in the middle of the road, so that she had to stop. The bear came around to her side of the car, and she opened her window just enough to slip him a peanut butter-and-jam sandwich. He ate it in one bite, then said, "How's about another sandwich, lady?"

"Is that true?" Adele said.

"Oh, yes," said Helen. "His voice was a bit gruff, but I understood every word." Adele looked at her plate, which the waiter had just set in front of her. Roast beef, mashed potatoes, peas, and gravy. The worst food in the world, in Adele's mind. Several tables away, her mother was cutting Andrew's roast beef into small pieces for him. But she was keeping an eye on Adele at the same time.

"My fiancé and I," Helen said, "are trying to decide whether we'll go to Lake Louise for our honeymoon, or to Niagara Falls. Either one would be fine with me, I told him. Adele, don't you like your dinner?"

Adele was listening to the train. She could hear it gathering strength, like a horse, drawing air deep into its chest, then exhaling, driving its hooves into the thin metal surface of the night.

"Adele, Adele," said Helen. "Are you a black bear, by any chance?"

"Yes," said Adele, mesmerized. "I am."

"I thought so," Helen nodded. "Black bears always have

so much appetite, no matter what." She pointed at Adele's plate, and Adele, infatuated with her black bear self, began to eat ravenously, until half of everything on her plate was gone, and Helen smiled at her and lit a cigarette and sat back and said, "Good for you, kid."

At a certain time that night, all the people on the train seemed to vanish as if they had never existed. In place of seats there were beds, hidden by thick maroon curtains. Porters came around with blankets and pillows and they kept saying, "Good night," and, "Have a good sleep," as if all the passengers were children. Adele's mother showed her how to climb into a bunk above the bed where she and Andrew were going to sleep. Adele lay behind the thick, dark curtain like a doll in a box. For a long time she lay there, her eyes open, listening to the train and remembering how she had stood on the station platform crying because she didn't want to get on. Perhaps she was still there, alone in the dark, and this was a different Adele, a girl she didn't even know, one who was brave and strong, like a black bear. The train was chanting the same words over and over: You can't leave me here, you can't leave me. They sounded like the words her mother had said when Adele's father joined the Air Force. "What are you doing? Are you crazy?" Then the house was empty; toys and lamps, books and dishes were disappearing into boxes.

On Remembrance Day, at school, Miss Bayard had handed out red poppies and said, "Remember our fighting men." Then she made Adele stand up and tell the class where her father had gone. She made it sound as if Adele's father had gone into the past, to a place where the war was still going on. "There is always conflict," Miss Bayard said severely. Then she spoke about the war that was going on now, which was a new kind of war: a Cold War. Adele, alarmed, thought of snow and ice, airplanes circling a white frozen earth, people on the ground motionless, like ice-statues. "Do you know what the communists would do to a little thing like Adele?" said Miss Bayard to the class. "They would send her to work in a factory. Even though she is a child. That is what the communists are like."

When Adele told her mother about this, she replied, "Miss Bayard has communists under her bed." Adele pictured Miss Bayard lying on top of her bed in her housecoat, afraid to put her foot over the side in case a communist grabbed her ankle. She pictured the communists cramped and impatient, waiting for Miss Bayard to make a move, playing cards to pass the time.

Outside the classroom windows, Adele saw that the sky was full of clouds that tore themselves apart and re-formed in the shapes of Canada, England, Germany, Russia. It was plainly up to Adele to keep the clouds at peace by not taking her eyes off them for a minute. If she did, the wind would take over, the clouds would collide, war would break out. "War," said Miss Bayard dramatically, her grey hair unravelling around her head, her arms in the air.

∽

That night on the train, when Adele at last fell asleep, she dreamed of a cabin in a field of snow. She and Andrew were inside the cabin, alone and afraid, like the children in a fairy tale. They were waiting to be rescued. Adele threw open the door and saw the moon, a planet white with snow, like the earth, with a solitary set of footprints crossing its surface. Adele understood that these footprints belonged to the lost prince, Helen's fiancé. The lost prince had left Korea; he was walking determinedly across the moon; soon he would arrive, resolute and handsome, at the door of the cabin, with Helen, wearing boots and her famous fur coat, behind him. They would bring with them a basket of food and a sleigh pulled by white dogs. Get on the sleigh, Helen would say, but Andrew would begin to cry: He was afraid of the dogs, he was afraid of the sleigh. Get on the sleigh, Helen would say again, and the lost prince would say, You'll freeze to death if you stay here. It doesn't matter, Adele would tell them. Her eyes would close; she would be unable to stay awake. We don't want to go with you, she would say to Helen and the lost prince. We just don't want to go.

The strange thing was, when Adele and her mother and brother got to Edmonton, it turned out there wasn't a house ready for them on the Air Force base, and they had to stay in a cabin much like the one in her dream. The cabin was situated miles off the base, in a field of snow, and at night the roof creaked and snapped and Adele and Andrew lay awake, terrified. Andrew was afraid of the dark. Adele told him a trick she knew: If he closed his eyes for a long time, then opened them, the darkness would seem less dark. "Try it," she kept saying. And when he closed his eyes, he fell asleep, every time. Then she was the only one awake, listening to what sounded like wolves howling, off in the distance. Wolves, she thought. She heard them getting closer, stepping so lightly on the frozen surface of the snow their paws left no mark.

244

ᴖ

Adele would finally move with her family into a house on the base. On the very day they moved in, a jet flew over and broke the sound barrier, causing everyone to run outside to see what had happened. Adele pressed her hands to her ears: She felt as if a bomb had gone off in her face. She was afraid that war had broken out, just as Miss Bayard had predicted. But it wasn't a war; it was the Air Force; it was life on the Air Force base. And on another day, her father flew over their house in a helicopter shaped like a glass bubble. She could see him sitting inside the bubble, in his Air Force parka, but he couldn't see her, she knew: She was hidden in the cold blue shadow of a house that was the same as a hundred other houses on both sides of a hundred streets, going on forever. Children poured out of the houses in a long line, bundled in snowsuits with hoods, and with scarves wrapped around their faces. Adele couldn't see their eyes or their mouths, but she could hear them. They were saying, Who are you? Who are you? She turned away, shy. Who was she? A black bear, a child left behind in Vancouver, afraid to get on a train. But all of this came later, after they got to Edmonton, after they moved onto the base.

ᴖ

On the morning of the second and last day on the train, Adele couldn't stop running. She ran up and down the corridor between the seats, annoying her mother and the other passengers, who shook their heads and examined their watches. How much more of this child? they seemed to be saying. The train was suffused with a harsh white light Adele interpreted as the light of winter. She had arrived, not intentionally, at the true north: the place behind the fir trees at the edge of the school yard. She should be at school, looking at the fir trees through the classroom window. She shouldn't be here. She should be getting ready for a spelling test, numbering her sheet of paper from one to ten with a fresh, sharp pencil. But she would never be there again, in Miss Bayard's classroom. She was the only one who wasn't where she belonged: in school. This thought made her run even faster from one end of the car to the other. She pretended she couldn't hear when her mother begged her to stop. Then Helen caught her by the hand and said, "Sit down." Adele sat. Helen was wearing a green dress, and her hair curled smoothly over her shoulders. Her fur coat lay on the seat beside her, like a bear deep in hibernation.

Helen unwrapped a stick of Juicy Fruit gum and gave it to Adele. "The next time I travel on this train, I'll be married," Helen said. "I'll have a different name. Won't that be strange?"

"I can't skate," said Adele. This seemed to her the greatest misfortune: How could she go to live in a world of frost and ice if she didn't even know how to skate? I will never get off this train, Adele told herself: Never, never, never.

Helen said, "Adele, pay attention to me." Slowly she lifted her hair away from the side of her face and said, "See this?" She had frozen her face solid, she said, learning how to skate on the pond behind her house when she was Adele's age. She had been so stubborn: She refused to give up until she could skate a certain distance, from one point to another, without falling down. And now she had this mark, a dead white patch, where her skin had frozen. Adele looked and saw nothing; then she looked more closely and saw a star that turned into a snowflake as she watched, a beautiful, ice-white snowflake, painted forever on Helen's face. Adele wanted the same mark on her own face; she wished for it fervently. "You'll learn how to skate," Helen told her. "I know you will. You'll be a good little skater."

Outside, the land floated past: a road, a house, a line of trees, a field. A land without a sea, without mountains. Then a porter came down the aisle, saying, "Not long now," and Helen sighed and smoothed the skirt of her dress and said, "Oh, thank goodness." She helped Adele into her blue winter coat and buttoned it up to her chin. Adele's mother was dressing Andrew in his coat, scarf, and mittens, wrapping him up so that he could hardly move. Then he began to cry, saying he had lost Mina, his bear, so Adele and Helen began looking for it, and Helen found the bear under Adele's mother's coat and gave it to Andrew, who smiled, cheerful again. Adele thought, Is this the way a journey by train ends, all at once, with no warning? Helen put on her fur coat. The train was slowing down; it was slowing. When they were at the station, Adele got off the train holding tight to Helen's hand; she buried her face in the sleeve of the fur coat, which was soft and silky and cold. The station was packed with people, their voices rising like smoke into the high, curved roof. Adele's mother came and stood beside her, with Andrew in her arms. Adele didn't want her mother; she wanted Helen. Helen's hand was warm inside her glove, which was deep green and matched the scarf she wore at her neck. Then Adele saw her father making his way through the crowd; she identified the exact moment when he spotted them. No, no, she said silently; go away. She didn't want anything to do with either one of her parents, or even with Andrew. She wanted Helen. War was about to break out in her head; she had such a feeling of disaster, of sadness. By the time her father reached them, Helen was gone. How had it happened? She had disappeared into the crowd; she hadn't even said goodbye. Adele had known this would happen; she had known it. She kept looking around, straining to see, but every face was the face of a stranger. She allowed herself to be led out of the station, into the night. She couldn't see the ice, or the snow on the roofs of the houses, but she knew it was there; she could sense winter, cold, cold; she was breathing it in, as if it were an entirely new atmosphere, the clean, untasted air of the moon.

Dreamland

In India, Lillian's husband shot and killed a tiger. She did not herself witness this event and found it difficult to imagine her husband, an austere and proper man, intimately involved in that uncompromising moment of blood and passion when the tiger took the shot into its living body. But it was happily conceded by everyone who had been on the hunt: The tiger belonged to Lillian's husband. Its skin was displayed on the polished floor of the house they occupied in Madras State. The tiger's skull was unexpectedly small and innocent; its eyes were gold-coloured glass, blind. Lillian sat with her feet resting on the tiger's back as she read or sewed. Secretly, she asked it to carry her away, to the hills, to the far-off mountains.

For nearly twenty years Lillian and her husband lived in India, most of the time in Madras State. They had four children, all boys. At about the time that Lillian could count on the fingers of one hand the years left until her husband's retirement from the Indian Civil Service, he invited her to his office and showed her a map spread out on his desk. The map was of Canada, a country about which Lillian knew absolutely nothing. Her husband pointed to a dot of land on the left hand side of the map.

"This is where we are going," he said.

Lillian did not understand. She placed her hand on a corner of the desk to steady herself, to keep from falling into the cold, painted waters, to keep from catching her hair and dress on the jagged edge of the ochre land mass. Her husband began to talk about annual rainfall, mean temperatures, a temperate climate, the benign influence of certain ocean currents. He spoke of the mystery, the beauty, of the northern rain forest, of which he had lately read, and in fact heard, from various sources. And the silence, he said. And the distance, the enormous, incontestable distance from India, the India of the British Raj, of which he had had more than enough.

"But we are going home," said Lillian, meaning home to England.

"We are not 'going home,'" her husband said. Then he tapped the map sharply with his finger. "We are going here. This will be our home."

He seemed to gloat: He looked ferocious, and triumphant. Lillian thought: The soul of the tiger has entered his soul. She felt afraid of her husband, not, perhaps, for the first time. As soon as she had returned to the house she went straight to a table in the sitting room where she kept writing paper and a pen. She wrote her husband's name quickly on a scrap of paper; then she burned the paper in a brass censer that hung in the sitting room and was meant to be only decorative. But she put it to use. The flames consumed her husband's name and in this way she removed him from her mind.

ᔆ

That was in India, in 1919, and now it is one year later and Lillian and her children actually inhabit the place on the map: It is where they live. They are on the west coast of an island that is itself on the extreme west coast of Canada. They live in a fishing village of perhaps two hundred people, or less. Her husband brought his family here and then he returned to India, alone, to finish up the three years until his retirement. He went back to India and left Lillian and the boys here as if this were an entirely reasonable thing to do. "You will be safer here than anywhere," he told Lillian repeatedly. "The boys will be happier here than anywhere else." This new life would make men of them, he said.

While he was with them he had a house built on a piece of land at the edge of the inlet waters, a tall house of wood with a steep roof and two rooms up, two rooms down. He had some furnishings shipped from Victoria by boat: a table and chairs, a sideboard, a bookcase, and a wood-burning stove, which he proceeded to install himself. He unpacked a shelf full of his books, including Homer's *Iliad*, Darwin's *Descent of Man*, a volume entitled *Principia Mathematica*. He spoke of the time when he would return, and how he would sit in a chair by the window, undisturbed, reading these books. He nailed the tiger skin hastily to the wall, not minding what he damaged.

During the long days of rain that ensued, the tiger glowed

like a lamp, like the Indian sun at dawn, only beginning to attain its true brilliance. In Lillian's estimation the tiger's face appeared less blind, less innocent, as if adversity were pushing it toward some new and interesting truth.

Her husband stayed for six months in all. In early December he left on the mail boat, in a storm. The mail boat had to go along the open coast, which could be rough and dangerous at any time of year, in any weather. She stood on the dock watching the boat as it plunged into the waves, and at last she called out her husband's name. The name was torn from her, a great cry for help, for assistance of some kind, and she was for a moment appalled at the sound. But the wind was fierce; no one heard her. *He* certainly didn't hear her. The mail boat was swept into the rain and fog and soon it was obscured.

There is no road out of this village. There is Lillian's house and after that there is nothing much, only a rough trail leading into the bush. At first everything she sees offends her eye: the ugly twisted pines, the straggly cedars, dead snags, blackened stumps where land has been partly cleared and then abandoned: visions of despair, of desperation. Some days she thinks the constant rain and fog will surely destroy her. And then the west wind starts up, chilling her to the bone and making her feel somehow vagrant, dispossessed. Her boys seem to exult in the wind, as they do in everything here. They climb trees, wade in the sea, throw rocks at one another, hide on her when she calls them. They are being made men of, she supposes. She stands listening, watching at the place where the trail leads off into the woods. No one lives there. It is an absence, an absence of life, of all but the most dangerous, elemental forms of life. She can see that it bears no relationship whatsoever to the milder forests of England and certainly none to the light-filled, dry, tumbling vastness of India.

No one Lillian has spoken to in the village can tell her who made this trail, or when, to what purpose. It is simply there. As a diversion, almost against her better judgement, she begins to follow the trail into the forest. Underneath the trees she sees a surprising number of plants: sword fern, salal, thimbleberry, water hemlock and a species of frail, wild lily, the name unknown to her. She begins to make a project of naming as many of these plants as she can, and to make sketches of those she cannot yet name. All that first spring and summer she does this, drawing pages and pages of wet, inky ferns, the fronds translating themselves willfully into mouths, eyes, the palms of hands; human features that delight Lillian, although she cannot decipher their meaning, or identity.

At night when her boys sleep, Lillian gets up from her bed and travels again down this trail, feeling her way in the dark. She is blind, her eyes full of a wonderful innocence. This is the night and she is in it, like a creature of the forest, a small animal. She feels, she knows, that this is a foolish practice, walking here by herself at night, but she cannot give it up, must not give it up. She feels the danger beating like her heart against her ribs, although more robust and sustaining. Easily she could lose her way, easily fall, tripping over a vine or tree root. And there truly are wild animals out here, dangerous animals. The village is rife with stories of encounters between men and bears and mountain lions. She chooses to discount these stories. Nothing in this forest is in the least interested in her. It even amuses her to imagine her husband's consternation, if he were called back from India simply because his wife had lost herself in the forest, in the night, and had been gobbled up by a bear. What does *his* discomfort matter to her, however? What does any of it matter? She is a small forest animal, padding down the trail, snuffling and whistling. Impossible to tell just where Lillian leaves off and the damp night air begins.

As well as the tiger skin there are several other objects brought all the way here from India. There is a collection of brass vessels of different sizes, the largest nearly three feet tall. Lillian likes to fill it with ferns and branches and wild flowers she gathers out in the bush. As a result, the house smells persistently, and not unpleasingly, of damp earth. Upstairs in her bedroom is a plain sandalwood box with a hinged lid in which she keeps her hairpins and combs. These are her own belongings, her possessions. She bought them herself, over the years, at market places in India. She went shopping in a rickshaw pulled by one of the servants. The rickshaw flew over the street, its wheels humming. There was a time when Lillian felt it wrong to be pulled along in this way, by another person, by a human being who might, after all, resent being used in this way. Her husband had laughed and said, "Oh, don't be ridiculous, Lillian," and so, after awhile, she thought only of the wind on her face, a sense of flight arranged for her pleasure, and now she misses it, she misses all of it. She misses India.

In the marketplace, beggars held out their hands. Her husband warned her: "You will only encourage their indolence." That was the way he looked at it. To her the beggars didn't seem indolent; they seemed rigid with intent and purposefulness. Their hands were lean and dark, sinewy and warm with the stored energy of the omnipresent sun. She gave them money, as much as she could spare. Her husband hated weakness; poverty, sickness. Once he pointed urgently to a dark shape huddled in a gutter and said, "Can you tell, is that a child or a monkey? Can you see which it is?" He had been very agitated.

She said, "Oh, a monkey," but the truth was, from where they were standing, it was impossible to be sure. Her husband was a Tax Collector; he took money from the Indian people and gave it to the ruling English. That was how it worked. It was an important position her husband held, but he was, at least in this case, a realistic man. He said the taxes were paying for some very fine meals and elegant homes. "Could India survive on her own, however?" He doubted it. "Look at Mohandas K. Gandhi, for one example," he said. "And the trouble he is causing."

An incident occurred in India. Lillian went into her dresser drawer for something, a lace collar to wear with her dress. She pulled her hand out only just in time. Nestled in her folded petticoats and clean handkerchiefs was a scorpion. One of the servants had plainly hidden it in her drawer to hurt her, to kill her possibly. Shaking with anger and fear, she told her husband, and he assembled the servants on the verandah at dusk. The sun was a red disc spinning on the rim of the earth. Her husband went up and down the line of servants, saying, "Above all else, I expect you to be open, honest, above-board. Play fair with me and I will play fair with you." He wore a white suit, a white hat; he was a tall man, dark-complexioned, with dark eyes. Later, he took Lillian aside and said that it was her job as mistress of the household to see that this kind of thing did not happen again. It was obvious to him, he said, that she did not have the respect of the servants. "Less daydreaming, Lillian," he said. "And more attention to the task at hand."

There is one more thing from India here in this new house on the inlet, and that is the brass censer in which Lillian burnt her husband's name. She cannot precisely remember packing it in her trunk before leaving India, but here it is, somewhat tarnished it's true, but still beautiful, a lovely object, hanging from a hook in the front room. One morning, in a reflective mood, she dips her finger into the bowl of the censer and brings it out coated with a fine white ash. Her husband's name. She puts her finger to her mouth to lick it clean, then stops. In the pantry she scrubs her hands clean with a bar of soap, lathering her arms to the elbows. His ashes, she thinks. How awful, what a thing to do. In her mind, for a moment, it is as if her husband has died and she has desecrated his remains and now he is speaking to her, shouting at her from an omniscient position: Do you see where your daydreaming gets you, my girl? Your indolence? You will do anything, won't you?

Toward the end of the second year, she writes to her husband: "I cannot tell what season of the year it is anymore. There is one long season, cold and wet, every day the same. You cannot imagine the monotony, or how it weighs on the spirit."

Her husband replies: "Last week I was forced to stay in a village stricken with disease. I am now dosing myself with quinine water. In addition, a rather brutal murder has occurred here, a Hindu-Muslim quarrel, I suspect. Every day the same, Lillian? Oh dear, oh dear."

A pod of killer whales swims into the inlet. The whales are in a frenzy, leaping high into the air, sending up great plumes of white spray. The entire village has turned out to watch from the shore, from the wharves. This has never happened before, everyone tells Lillian. The whales career wildly; the villagers call out, Oh! as if they were at a circus. Wind ripples the furiously churning surface of the water; clouds race past the mountains; everything is happening at once. Lillian drags her sons close, closer to the water's edge. You may never see a sight like this again, she tells them, as excited as any of the others. A rumour spreads, that this is an omen, that this strange behaviour on the part of the whales means something, good luck or bad. A man near Lillian says it has nothing to do with luck, it is the whales being whales, it is nature. Yes, Lillian says, yes indeed; nature. Then she thinks: The whales are in love. In love with the sea, the sky. It is too much for them, they cannot contain the energy of their love.

She feels sympathy for the whales; they could easily annihilate themselves for this love; they have lost all sense of danger.

She thinks also of the tiger, her tiger, alive and floating through the green and gold air of the mountain slopes, its prey below on the ground, and the tiger's paws flexing, its claws unsheathed, its eyes burning with love, for itself, and the object it so desires: the prey.

Lillian walks out into the land at night, where no one else has the courage to go, and she finds it surprisingly peaceful, dark, muted. It is like walking into a pleasant dream. Then she thinks, no, her dreams are not always pleasant; sometimes they frighten her. Sometimes she wakens with a cry and realizes that she is alone, she is alone on what seems the edge of the world; beyond the walls of her house there is only the sea and then nothing. That incomprehensible absence. She can't get back to sleep; how could she sleep, she is too wrought up. She lies awake and listens to the wind, to the rain, to the sea. On the whole she would rather not sleep; she would rather be out there in the forest, playing a sort of game with fate. If I stumble and fall, she thinks. If a mountain lion leaps from a tree, snarling, its teeth bared. Nothing will happen, she tells herself. I am all right, she says. One more step, and then one after that. The ground underfoot is slick, uncertain. And there is the smell of dank vegetation, of death, she thinks. She is brave; unmindful. She walks on.

It occurs to her now that of course it was the children's ayah who put the scorpion in her dresser drawer. The ayah didn't like Lillian; she gave her sidelong glances, full of meaning. She spoiled the children, feeding them candies and hot Indian food, stroking their hair with her plump, scented hands.

The ayah was there on the evening Lillian's husband reprimanded the servants over the issue of the scorpion. The ayah stood slightly apart from the others, as if wishing to disassociate herself from the matter and from her condition of servitude. She was not the same as the other servants, her posture seemed to say. In the warmth of the setting sun her face was rosy, swollen. Lillian's husband went up and down, lecturing. "One of you is responsible," he said, "beyond doubt." The ayah was very pretty standing there, her hands meekly clasped.

Lillian thinks how strange, how very strange, that only now, years later, on the opposite side of the world, is she able to clearly recognize in the ayah's combined attitudes of submission and apartness not innocence, but guilt.

Her husband taunted her. Before they left India, he said to her, "There is no society out there, you know. No English society, church teas, fancy dress balls, all that nonsense. You'll be on your own, out there."

"I was never all that much interested," she said, although she had enjoyed the fancy dress balls, the impromptu theatre. In any case, her husband was wrong. In the village there are men and women from England, immigrants, like Lillian, anxiously running their hands over the walls of moist air to see if it is real, this prison, this small place they have come to. Wearing gumboots, they wade through mud to play Mah Jong around kitchen tables; they sing songs together, and dance, and toast one another with glasses of sherry. At the end of all this entertainment, they stand and sing "God Save the King," their mouths alive, biting with great vigour into the words "victorious" and "glorious." The English in diaspora, Lillian thinks: It is the same everywhere. She does not join in the singing, but watches the energy of the open mouths with interest. She is amazed that the words still have meaning for these people, not only these words, but any words at all. Any spoken words. For her, words have become as vague and formless as the mist that wreathes the mountainsides. She begins to avoid social occasions; she develops a most unlikely habit of running to hide when people walk down the road to visit her. She hides in her garden, behind the trunk of a cedar tree, or she runs into the house and locks the door. Anything she or anyone else might have to say seems suddenly pointless, irrelevant. (Quite, quite irrelevant, she hears her husband's voice saying.) She is a small animal, solitary, making her way down a trail no one else dares to take.

Of course, she isn't an animal. She is Lillian, with her sketchbook and her pen and ink, getting it all down on paper, recording the shapes, the mysterious, scarcely apprehended shapes and forms that green growing plants can take. As she draws, she is fascinated to see human features behind the branches, mixed in with the vining stems and fleshy leaves, appearing magically, independent of her pen. The corner of an eye, the tip of a nose, a full, pouting lower lip.

Even the tiger is there, his black stripes boldly visible against the delicate tracery of a sword fern. The tiger makes

her smile. He is arrogant, indifferent, strutting on the paper:
Did you intend to forget me? he asks.

Lillian ventures farther down the trail than she has ever gone.
She plunges on and on through the bush. She scratches her
hand on a branch; pauses to pull her skirt free of a thorned
vine. Then she arrives at an open place, unlike anywhere else.
She has an idea, from studying maps of the area, and from
hearing people talk, that she has come to the mud-flats,
where the sea at last wears itself out and becomes engulfed
by the land. The ground is marshy, like a peat bog, and the
water is everywhere shallow and blue and motionless. Tall,
bearded grasses grow along the shore. A blue heron stands
one-legged not far from her. Everything is quiet and seems
consecrated to this singular moment. Lillian sits down on a
log and places her sketchbook open on her knee. Will she
find her way back? she wonders. Will her sons notice that
she's been gone for an unusually long time? It is July and
surprisingly hot. She is wearing a wide-brimmed hat tied
under her chin with a scarf, to shade her eyes. It is, in fact, a
hat she wore many times in India, while engaged in just such
an activity as this: sketching the indigenous flora and fauna
of the land. She draws a long curved line meant to represent
the heron's long neck, which ought to look graceful but is
instead strangely clumsy, unmanageable. She turns to a fresh
page. Behind her in the bush there is a noise, as if something,
an animal, were creeping up on her to have a better look. She
doesn't turn around.

Her husband said to her before he went back to India, "I suppose you will forget me once I am gone." He had been at the window looking at the inlet, at the small, dark islands that rise abruptly out of the water. She wanted to tell him that it was too late: She had already forgotten him, she had forgotten his name; she had written it down and let it be consumed by fire. Instead she said, "The children might forget you. Three years is a long time to a child." He replied that it was her responsibility to see that they did not forget him. Then he began unpacking his books, telling her she must encourage the boys to read these books, it was important that they read and exercise their minds. "I will write to them," he said. "A letter for each child, every month."

Of course, even after all this time the boys have not forgotten their father, although they mention him less and less as the weeks and months go by. And even after reducing it to a fine white ash, Lillian remembers her husband's name. She hasn't spoken it aloud since the day he left on the mail boat, but she does remember it. No, the irony is that it is herself she has forgotten. Her self, her physical presence, seems to have become amorphous; parts of her float through the cedar forest; parts of her catch on dead snags. Her husband said, "The great beauty of this place is that you can make anything you want out of it. No one has really discovered it yet. It is a sort of dreamland, waiting. You can make what you want out of it. That's what I want. That's exactly what I want."

He spoke with such enthusiasm; he so badly wanted his dreamland away from the rest of the world, away from India, away from the ancient populated parts of the world. But Lillian knows what her husband does not know, even yet:

That the land makes what it wants of you. The land is not clay waiting to be shaped; it is a monster already formed, with claws and a hungry mouth. A shiver runs down her spine. She can sense something behind her, although common sense tells her nothing is there. She is alone and at any moment she can get up and begin the walk back.

She draws, curving a slender grass stem deliberately across the clean white page. Her hand moves quickly, forming a lattice-work of sea grasses bending as if swept by a fierce wind; only there is no wind. Behind the grasses elusive human features appear, shy, diffident. They lack an identity, although it seems to Lillian they might at any moment assume one. She sees an ear, then the open palm of a hand. The fluttering edge of a scarf; the brim of a sun-hat much like the one she has on her head. And an eye, wide, surprised; knowledgeable.